Over the Edge

Books by Mary Connealy

From Bethany House Publishers

THE KINCAID BRIDES

Out of Control
In Too Deep
Over the Edge

TROUBLE IN TEXAS

Swept Away

Also by Mary Connealy

SOPHIE'S DAUGHTERS

Doctor in Petticoats
Wrangler in Petticoats
Sharpshooter in Petticoats

LASSOED IN TEXAS

Petticoat Ranch
Calico Canyon
Gingham Mountain

MONTANA MARRIAGES

Montana Rose
The Husband Tree
Wildflower Bride

WILD WEST WEDDINGS

Cowboy Christmas
Deep Trouble

Nosy in Nebraska (a cozy mystery collection)
Black Hills Blessing (a contemporary romance collection)

THE KINCAID *Brides* BOOK 3

OVER THE EDGE

MARY CONNEALY

BETHANY HOUSE PUBLISHERS
a division of Baker Publishing Group
Minneapolis, Minnesota

Published by Bethany House Publishers
11400 Hampshire Avenue South
Bloomington, Minnesota 55438
www.bethanyhouse.com

Bethany House Publishers is a division of
Baker Publishing Group, Grand Rapids, Michigan

Printed in the United States of America

Library of Congress Cataloging-in-Publication Data

Connealy, Mary.
Over the edge / Mary Connealy.
p. cm.—(The Kincaid brides ; bk. 3)
ISBN 978-0-7642-0913-0 (pbk.)
1. United States—History—Civil War, 1861-1865—Veterans—Fiction.
I. Title.
PS3603.O544O98 2012
813'.6—dc23 2012006419

Scripture quotations are from the King James Version of the Bible.

This is a work of fiction. Names, characters, incidents, and dialogues are products of the author's imagination and are not to be construed as real. Any resemblance to actual events or persons, living or dead, is entirely coincidental.

Cover design by Dan Pitts

Cover photography by Mike Habermann Photography, LLC

Author is represented by Natasha Kern Literary Agency

12 13 14 15 16 17 18 7 6 5 4 3 2 1

In many ways I mark my writing life by my youngest daughter, Katy. I started writing my first book when she went to kindergarten. I held my first published book in my hands the year she graduated from high school. When I look at how she's grown up I take pride in her at the same time I know it's mostly coming from inside her and I have no right to pride. All that talent and charm and intelligence are her own, gifts given to her by God that she uses so well. I love you, Katy.

I also dedicate this book to Luke Hinrichs, my editor at Bethany House. He's worked so hard and contributed so much to my books. Luke and Charlene Patterson have this great eye for weaknesses in the plot and how to make the book stronger. It's a privilege to work with both of them and all the people at Bethany House.

CHAPTER 1

OCTOBER 30, 1866

A bullet slammed through the door of the stagecoach, threading a needle to miss all four passengers.

"It's a holdup!" Callie grabbed her rifle. "Get down!"

The stage driver yelled and cracked his whip. More flying lead hit, higher on the stagecoach. The man riding shotgun got his rifle into action.

"Get on the floor!" The woman sitting across from Callie was frozen with fear. That endangered Connor and it made Callie furious.

The bullets came fast. The stage was moving slow on a long uphill slope. With the driver's shout they picked up speed. From the roof, she heard a steady volley of deafening return fire.

Reaching across, Callie grabbed the woman by the ruffled front of her pink gingham dress and dragged her off the seat. The woman shrieked but didn't put up a fight, which was smart of her. Callie would've won that fight.

Somewhat more gently, Callie picked Connor up from the seat beside her and set him on the woman's lap. Eight-month-old Connor yelped, more a shout of anger than a cry. But crying would come soon enough. Her little wild man didn't do anything quietly.

"Can you shoot?" she shouted at the young man, hoping he'd snap out of whatever panic had seized him. He shook his head frantically. "Get on the floor, then."

Callie used her whiplash voice and hoped it got the man moving. She threw herself across to the woman's seat to face backward. With her Colt in her left hand and her Winchester in her right, she shoved the curtain aside. The flare of the orange and yellow aspen lining the road blocked any sign of the gunmen.

Callie didn't bother to push the man to the floor. Let the idiot figure that out himself. She got a glimpse of the robbers riding around a curve. Bullets hailed on the coach. Callie held back, waiting for a clear shot.

Connor's yelling turned to a cry. Callie was enraged that her son was in such terrible danger when he should have been safe on her father's ranch in Texas.

The noise overhead said the driver'd slid off his high seat to use the stage as cover. She heard the man riding shotgun land flat on his belly on the roof. The driver's shouting and the gunfire slashed like a sharp knife through the cool October morning.

"Try and calm Connor down." Not much chance of that. Connor had been a whirlwind since birth. And the two caring for him were more upset than he was.

She counted four outlaws. The varmints had picked this uphill slope a few miles outside of Colorado City because the stage had slowed to a crawl.

Callie had plenty of bullets, but she was a conservative woman, and she didn't intend to fire blind and waste lead. She was mighty low on money and she needed ammunition for when she finally tracked down that worthless Seth Kincaid.

The stagecoach yawed past a curve and it put them out of the line of fire until the outlaws could round it.

The young woman was hugging Connor. The man had wedged himself onto the floor, putting his body between Connor, his wife, and the gunfire. Maybe he wasn't completely worthless.

A bullet cut through the stage door. Splinters exploded and slashed Callie's left hand. She flinched and got her hand right back on the trigger of her Colt.

Callie braced her rifle against her shoulder and took careful aim; the whole world slowed down, the noise fading into the background. She felt pulled away, out of the action. Her mind was working clearly, her nerves steady. The bleeding hand didn't hurt. As she looked at the trail behind, the colors were so vivid and her vision so sharp it was almost painful.

The pulsing hooves gave away the attackers' exact location. And the slow-moving coach gave her a chance at a steady shot.

A glance over her shoulder told her the trail would twist just ahead. Their pursuers would be swallowed up by the heavy forest lining the road. They appeared and disappeared in the thick plumes of dust.

Callie saw shining silver on the band of a flat-topped black hat. The man was a fool to wear silver if he wanted to make his living sneaking around.

Callie inhaled slowly, then exhaled halfway to relax her chest, waited for the glint of silver, and fired.

A bright splash of red marked the desperado's shirt as he fell backward and was gone. Another outlaw took his place at the front of the pack.

Connor shrieked at the loud sound of shooting so close. Callie separated herself from her mother's need to comfort, because the real comfort came from a ma who would protect him. She'd dry his tears later.

With the cool ruthlessness of a mama wolf defending her young—a mama wolf with a fire iron—Callie drew a bead and fired. Her target kept coming. Bullets shattered the door just above her head. They'd aimed at the roof mostly, but now they knew someone inside the stage was in the fight.

Hating that she'd drawn their guns and further endangered Connor, she kept on firing. From overhead she heard the same. A steady man guarded the stage. The driver kept shouting, cracking his whip. Another steady man was at the reins.

A second outlaw went down. A third pressed forward. She'd counted four, so they were close to finishing this nonsense.

They crested the hill. A few more yards and they'd pick up speed. Colorado City was at the base of this rattlesnake of a trail.

Hold them off. A few more seconds.

Callie fired. A bullet whizzed so close she felt the heat.

A sudden snap under the stagecoach lurched them to the side. They tipped, lifting Callie's side of the bench seat up, up, up. She saw the woman wrap her body around Connor and the man wrap his arms around both of them. Her son surrounded by a flesh-and-blood shield. A sickening crunch told her the stage had hit the rocky outcropping on the side of the trail. A chunk of wood bounced into the dust behind them. Part of one wheel.

The brake came on hard as the driver tried to stop them from rolling out of control. Another thud shook Callie so hard she was thrown backward on the bench seat and smacked her shoulder into the side of the stage. The stage, slow anyway because of the climb, slued sideways, tipped so Callie was nearly lying on her back, then shuddered to a halt.

Callie heard the coach's team of four horses go pounding away, broken free from their burden.

The guard overhead shouted, "Stay inside!" He fired and now the driver's gun came into action. Callie spun on the seat now tipped upward at a steep angle. She lay on her side, shoved her feet against the downhill side of the stage, and got back up to the window.

A bullet whistled past her face.

There were two left. They'd taken cover and were trying to pick the men off the roof. Callie focused her eagle-sharp eyes on the pair attacking them. The tip of one gun was visible. In the motionless stage she could now aim with real precision. She fired. A cry of pain sounded as the muzzle vanished.

Return fire hailed on them from one remaining outlaw.

A sudden shout from overhead told her one of the stage-coach men was hit. She watched for the last remaining gun and saw it just as another shot came from farther up the trail. The bullet hit the window frame. Shards of wood slashed her face.

A second bullet was just as close, and she dived low to give them less of a target.

"You're hit!"

She looked down at the young man, who was using his body as a shield to protect her son. "Just wood. The bullet missed."

"Give me the gun."

"Can you shoot? Can you hit what you aim at?"

The man's jaw went rigid, then stiffly he shook his head no.

"Then stay down there, city boy. Let us handle this."

Bullets came now from three guns. She knew three of the four men were hit but apparently not bad enough to stop them from shooting.

Another cry of pain came from overhead and the gunfire from the stage stopped. Callie swiped at the blood flowing, blocking the vision in one eye, which wrecked her aim and put her at a distinct disadvantage in a gunfight.

"Throw out your guns or we'll shoot until every man aboard is dead." The voice was chilling, ugly. Callie heard fury in it. And pain. The man wanted vengeance. The people on the stage had drawn blood, and the man yelling didn't sound like the type to let them go on their way.

"I hear a child on that stage." The voice sent a chill through her veins. "You want him to live, throw out your guns."

Connor's wailing made it hard for her to think.

Protect him, save him. God, please save my son.

Callie gripped her pistol. Soon they'd be in close-quarters fighting. It was going to come to that and when that happened it was hard to tell the winners from the losers because everyone got bloody.

No matter how young.

"Just surrender. Let them take what we have," the young man whispered.

Callie looked at him. These men might let a woman go on her way with a child, but they'd blame this city man for the shooting from inside the stage, no matter how fast he talked. He was very close to death and it was her fault, at least to the extent that it was anyone's fault but these outlaws.

"Stay down. They won't let you walk away from this." Connor's cries kept building. His blue eyes were drenched with tears.

"I'm a man of God. Many bandits won't shoot a parson."

She refused to pull her attention away from the outlaws to try and persuade the parson of the long chance he'd be taking. Instead, with her pistol in her left hand and her rifle in her right, she waited, watched, prayed. Careful not to let the muzzle of her rifle protrude from the window, she hoped to get a shot at the unwounded man. It might be enough to break off the attack.

They came in a rush.

Three men erupted from behind bushes and boulders. Callie fired at the one running fastest and he went down and rolled out of sight along the edge of the trail. The men fired back, but she kept up the assault with both rifle and pistol. The outlaws ducked behind boulders. The stage was tipped nearly sideways on the trail. Held up from being flat on its side by a boulder that poked through the door she wasn't using.

Callie got an idea. When she was praying this hard and

she got an idea, she always thanked the Lord, even if He hadn't carved it with a fiery fingertip into a slab of stone. They'd wheeled around until the trapdoor in the roof was facing downhill. With a quick twist of her body, she kicked the trapdoor on the stagecoach roof open.

"Get out of here." She turned blazing eyes on the parson. "Take your wife and my son and go. The wagon blocks their vision of the downhill side of the trail. They won't see you leaving. Run for Colorado City and get help. We're not more than a mile or two out. All downhill. I can hold them off."

"No, I won't run like a coward and leave a woman to defend me."

She respected that; she really did. She was also tempted to lay a butt stroke across his skull. "You can't shoot. I can. Get away and get help. With my shooting, we all have a chance to survive this. But with your shooting, all of us are going to die."

The parson's jaw went so tight she thought his teeth might crack.

"Go, you're wasting time. I think one of them is down and the other three are wounded, but not seriously."

A bullet slammed into the stage. Callie ducked and faced uphill again. "Go, please. With your help my son has a chance to live." Her tone had changed from issuing orders to begging.

She glanced at the parson and saw him nod.

"Hurry, you're wasting time. Cover Connor's mouth so they won't hear you." The cruelty of that made her sick, yet it was the only way the baby wouldn't bring these men down on all of them.

The parson helped his wife slip through the trapdoor, handed her Connor. Callie tore her eyes away from her son and it felt as if she tore her own flesh. Connor's cries cut off, and Callie blocked the parson's exit with her rifle. His deadly serious eyes met hers.

"When you get to Colorado City, if . . . if I don't make it, Parson, find Rafe Kincaid. He's got a ranch near Rawhide, a little mining town to the west. He's Connor's uncle and he'll look out for the boy." Callie hoped it was true.

The parson nodded, clawed his way through the trapdoor out into the crisp fall air. Callie saw him slip his arm around his wife, who carried Connor. They ran. Another bullet fired and Callie had to turn away from her child. Just like Seth had turned away from both of them. The urge to cry shocked her. She wasn't a crying kind of woman, but saying goodbye to her son, well, that was worth a few tears.

She wondered if this goodbye would be forever.

Another bullet smashed through the stage wall and made her forget everything but the fight.

Callie returned fire. The outlaws poured lead into the stage. She was forced to duck. Peeking out, she saw three men slip closer and she let loose with her rifle. They vanished again. Closer, closer every time.

She couldn't cover three men, and that meant she couldn't keep them pinned down. But she could make their advances slow. Give the parson every possible second. Make these thieving coyotes pay a high price for every step.

The gunfire stopped. The outlaws were out of sight. Waiting. She could only hope and pray they'd wait long enough. She searched the scrub pines and blazing aspens and boulders along the trail.

The men started shooting again. Callie returned fire.

The sharp smell of sulfur and blood stung her nose. Splinters sprayed her hands and bloodied them, making her grip on the trigger slippery.

The men ducked out of sight and silence reigned.

Were the stage driver and the man riding shotgun dead? If they weren't, if they'd just been wounded, maybe knocked out, maybe they'd come around and get back into the fight. Even one more gun and she'd have a chance.

The men fired, rushed forward, and dropped. Callie reloaded while the men hid. Time inched forward. She could almost hear the parson's running steps. Down toward town. Help would come.

The coach was so shredded it was little protection anymore. She'd like to shout a threat to the men, let them know help might well be on the way; maybe they'd cut and run. But then they'd know she was a woman and that might make them even more brazen.

Callie noticed the seat across from her had been blasted loose from the frame of the stage. She grabbed at it and moved the thick slab of wood into place in front of her like a shield.

All three of them popped up and dashed forward, shooting. The stage splintered. Needles of wood gouged and slit. Her buckskin jacket and leather riding skirt were decent protection, but her face had been clawed by the wood. A chunk of oak slammed into her head and knocked her backward. She fought her way back to the window. Blood flowed into her eyes and she swiped at it with her forearm. Her vision cleared for only a moment before more blood flowed.

They charged again, shooting. She saw where they went, though each time they'd slip around and emerge in some unexpected place. Then, with their guns in play, her grip shaky and her vision blurred, she couldn't take good aim.

They had about two more of these charges before they overran the stage.

Had it been long enough? There should be men in Colorado City who'd come running, especially to protect a woman, but also to fight for the stage, to fight for right. She knew the West, and yes, there was lawlessness, but there were also plenty of men who used their strength to maintain the peace.

C'mon, Parson. You've had time. A man on a fast horse could be coming soon.

She watched out the window, eyes riveted on the trail. Watching, hoping, praying for anything to aim at. Did God answer such a violent prayer?

A sudden flash of silver drew her attention. That first man she'd seen with his stupid silver hatband. He was close enough to gain the stage. She saw even with just this glimpse of him that his muscles bunched to run. Her last chance. Her son's last chance. At least his last chance to have a mother who was alive to raise him.

She aimed her rifle, swiped the blood away from her eyes, stilled her trembling hands through sheer will, and fired.

A cry from the bushes stopped everything.

The three men didn't appear for another charge. Callie watched for another shot. Time moved as slowly as if her pa's pocket watch ticked in her ear.

There was nothing.

And then the sound of hooves pounding toward her from Colorado City. They gave her such hope that again she was hit by a need to cry.

Waste of time.

She heard more running horses. This time from the outlaws. They'd been driven off.

Time to come out now. Time to go get her son.

Forcing her eyes to move, she saw her hands. There was a lot of blood. Looking down, she saw her jacket soaked in crimson. A stab of pain drew her eyes to her left arm. An ugly stake of wood at least three inches long stabbed through the leather of her fringed jacket. Blood poured from that wound.

How much blood did a woman have to spare anyway?

Her hands were rigid on her rifle and pistol. The stage was riddled with bullet holes.

Her mind told her hands to let go, to ease off the triggers before she accidentally fired again, this time into the chest of some rescuer.

The horse from Colorado City stopped and she saw a man's legs and backside as he swung down from a pretty gray. The edges of her vision darkened until it was like looking through a long, narrow tunnel.

Then the man turned.

It was Seth Kincaid.

Alive and well. He'd have been better off dead.

She could arrange that.

She still had her gun.

CHAPTER 2

Seth saw the stagecoach driver lying halfway in the bushes on the side of the trail. He'd ridden right past him. Seth wheeled around to go help.

A bullet whizzed out the window of the stage and missed him by little more than a foot. Seth drew his six-gun.

"Seth Kincaid, you get back here and let me shoot you, you low-down skunk."

A woman.

A woman who knew his name.

A woman who knew his name and wanted to kill him.

He'd never had much luck with women.

He was pretty sure he'd heard that voice before, but he couldn't place quite where.

The memory conjured up a pleasant feeling in his chest. Which sure didn't match with the threat and the gunfire.

Almost getting shot was thrilling. Grinning, he dropped to his knees and crawled forward. He saw the open trapdoor of the stage. The gunshots had come from the other side, so maybe he could disarm the woman threatening him.

And maybe not.

Maybe he'd get shot.

Finally he was having some fun.

His heart banged and he felt more alive than he had in weeks. As he crawled he tried to figure out why her voice made his spirits rise in a way that had nothing to do with the reckless fun of being in a gunfight.

Just when he was ready to poke his head up so he could get a look through the trap, riders approached from the direction of Colorado City. He ducked into the undergrowth alongside the trail in case the outlaws had circled around and were coming back. He waited until he saw the star on the man who led the way. He holstered his gun. Then stepped out, his hands in plain sight.

"I just heard the gunfire and came running, Sheriff. I'm Seth Kincaid. We've met."

"Howdy, Seth." The sheriff had sharp eyes, and with a quick look around he snapped out orders. "Four of you men stay behind and help the wounded. The rest of you follow me. The parson said the outlaws are wounded. Maybe we can round them up." The sheriff spurred his horse and about half the posse charged on past the stage.

"Kincaid?" A man riding like he'd never before sat a horse brought up the rear of the six armed men. "I'm Parson Frew. She told me to find Rafe Kincaid."

"That's my brother. We can talk later. There are two wounded men here and there's a woman in the stage." Seth raised his voice. "Are you all right, ma'am?"

"Seth Kincaid, you get over here where I can get you in my crosshairs." The woman sounded purely loco.

Seth liked her more all the time.

But since she wanted to shoot him, he didn't obey her.

"The sheriff's here now, ma'am. His'll be the first face you see." The sheriff was gone, but Seth wasn't in the mood to go into details. He just wanted the woman to quit shooting long enough to disarm her.

The parson swung off his horse and ran toward the stage.

"Have a care, Parson, she just took a shot at me." Seth followed after the man, knowing his chances of living through this scrape had just gone way up. After she plugged the parson, she'd feel bad and all the fight would go out of her. Too bad for the parson. Too bad for Seth, because all the fun was gone.

"I've brought help." The parson didn't even pause as he stuck his head into the nearly shredded door of the stage. "Dear Lord, have mercy!"

The tone brought Seth along fast. He looked in the door to see a woman coated in blood. Her face, her jacket, her hands. She looked dead. Two guns lay at her side, but her hands were lax on the triggers.

"She just spoke to me." Seth felt the wildness that always haunted him as he shoved the parson aside and ripped off what was left of the door. He reached in to the steeply canted stage, driven by a terror that made no sense—even for someone as prone to jump into danger as himself. Catching her around the waist, he dragged her out of the stage, cradled her in his arms, mindful of the nasty wooden shard high on her left arm. The bleeding was terrible. He couldn't begin to know what she looked like.

"I've got to get her to the doctor." Seth raced for his horse. In his urgency he only distantly noticed that she fit in his arms in a way that was near perfection. It was all strange. How did she know his name? Why did her voice touch something deep inside him? Why did he feel like he'd held her before?

Why had she tried to shoot him?

Although honesty forced him to admit he had that effect on a lot of people.

He looked down at her as he swung onto his horse. He could make out nothing through the bleeding.

"We're right behind you, Kincaid. These men aren't as torn up as her, but they need looking after, too." A deputy waved him down the trail. "Doctor's office is—"

"I know the way." Juggling the woman and his horse was trouble. Her blood seemed to flow faster with each bump. To cradle her more gently, Seth slapped the reins between his teeth to get both hands free, spurred his horse, and charged downhill. It struck him that he didn't know who she was. But he knew on a soul-deep level that this woman was someone important.

Goading his horse, he charged over a twisting trail at breakneck speed. He felt as if the devil himself were in hot pursuit as he ran for his life.

Except he was running for the woman's life, not his.

He heard hoofbeats from behind and glanced back. The parson was coming after him hard. The man sat on his horse like an easterner. An easterner who'd never been on a horse.

Trying to keep up with Seth would probably be the death of him. And yet the woman didn't have any time to spare. She was bleeding out even as he held her in his arms.

Seth leaned low over his horse's neck until the woman was pressed against his chest. The trail finally straightened and hit a level stretch.

Without slowing, Seth finally had time to look at the woman and saw a fast-moving trail of blood coming from her temple. Trying not to jostle her, he pulled the kerchief off his neck and pinned it to the cut by pressing her face to his shoulder.

There were more wounds, but he couldn't tend them and make good time.

God, protect her, care for her. Don't let her die, please, God.

It was the most fervent prayer Seth had prayed in years. In fact, the only prayer since he was a kid when he spent an afternoon dancing with the devil.

Seth had escaped the pointy-horned varmint that day in the belly of the cavern, but he'd been haunted ever since by the notion that he'd paid for survival with his soul. He'd left it behind, deep in the bowels of the burning belly of the earth.

He'd been looking for his soul ever since. And now this woman had inspired a prayer.

The strange idea fled as Seth galloped into Colorado City. A doctor had his office on the edge of town and Seth raced straight there.

He swung down, the woman still fitting perfectly in his arms, and rushed for the doctor's office.

"I need help." He slammed the door wide, shouting, "Fast. This woman's bad hurt!" A small entry room was empty. Before

Seth could get through the next door, it swung open and a gray-haired man took in the situation with one glance.

"Follow me into the back." He wheeled around, moving fast for an old man.

Seth still almost ran him down.

The doctor pointed at a table. "Lay her there."

Seth set her on the high, hard bed as gently as possible. He still had her temple pressed to his chest, holding the kerchief in place.

"Get me some water. There's hot water on the cookstove behind me." The doctor issued the rapid-fire order and Seth obeyed. There was no one else there, no patients, no nurse to help the doctor. Seth returned with the basin and set it beside the doctor, then rounded the table.

"Let's get her jacket off." The doctor reached for the front of her buckskin coat and stopped. "That's as good as pinned to her arm."

The doctor leaned close and pulled at the edges of the jacket to see the wound. "What happened to her?"

"She was in a stagecoach holdup. The sheriff should be right behind me bringing in two more wounded. I don't know how bad they are."

"I hate to pull that out. I'm not sure how much more blood she can stand to lose. And I don't have time to give her much tender care if more are coming."

The doctor looked at Seth, almost as if he was asking for a second opinion. Seth shrugged. "It's gotta come out sometime, Doc."

With a firm jerk of his head, the doctor said, "Let's get her coat off the other arm before I pull out that peg."

When only her wounded arm was still in the jacket, the doctor pulled the wooden shard out quickly. The woman moaned. The first sign of consciousness.

"Get her jacket off. We'll stop the bleeding in that arm first and then see what else we have to deal with." The doctor cut her dress sleeve away.

Seth and the doctor fought a short brutal fight against the pouring blood. Soon her arm was tightly bound. The doctor was quick with a needle on four slashes on her scalp. He clipped the hair away in all four spots with ruthless disregard for a woman's vanity.

"No bullet wounds." The doctor washed the woman's bloody hands. "Ugly scratches but no stitches needed here." He turned with his cloth to bathe her face. Reaching for the water, he hesitated. Seth saw how dark red the water was.

"Get me some clean water. How long was she out there bleeding?"

"I heard shooting and came running for the stage. She was still conscious when I got there, but the shooting was over."

He didn't count the shot she'd fired at him.

After all, she'd had a hard day. If she'd been just a little further from death, she'd have been thinking more clearly and she might not've pulled the trigger.

"The sheriff came along a minute after I got to the stage."

A commotion in the front of the building turned the doctor's head. He shouted, "Bring 'em on back!"

The door opened and the parson came in alone.

"I thought there were more wounded." The doctor looked from the parson to Seth.

"The sheriff isn't far behind me."

"Parson, do you know this woman?" Seth remembered what the parson had said. "What did you want with my brother?"

"She stayed behind." The parson looked overcome with guilt. "I said I'd stay, but she was good with a gun. She said if I stayed to hold off those outlaws, we'd all die. If she stayed and I ran for help, we all had a chance to live. But leaving a woman behind . . ." The parson's throat worked as if he couldn't push the words past his shame.

Seth well understood how the man felt. But he'd seen the man ride. This woman, with her buckskin coat and two guns, her voice full of challenge, she'd made the right decision.

The doctor began bathing her face. Seth watched, riveted on the slowly emerging woman. Who was she? How did he know her?

Which reminded him. "What about my brother, Parson? What did she want with him?"

A woman entered the room and drew Seth's attention. She had a baby in her arms. A fat little dumpling of a boy wearing brown overalls with a brush of dark brown hair. The boy was younger than Ethan and Audra's baby Lily.

The baby smiled straight at Seth with a devilish glint in his wild blue eyes.

"She said if she didn't survive the robbery, Rafe Kincaid was her son's uncle and he'd care for the boy."

"U-u-uncle?" Seth couldn't seem to get any more words past his throat. In fact, he barely managed that one.

"Yep, did you say Rafe Kincaid is your brother?"

Seth nodded, words still beyond him.

"Well, then, you're the boy's uncle, too." The parson smiled.

The doctor was cleaning up the woman, and Seth thought maybe, if he turned to look right now, he might recognize her.

"That's great. You can see to the boy, then." The parson lifted the baby out of his wife's arms and stepped toward Seth.

Dear Lord God in heaven, I'd better recognize this woman!

The parson extended the fat toddler toward Seth and the little guy smiled, his eyes flashed, and in the course of a few seconds Seth had a vivid, terrifying parade of memories of all the reckless things he'd done throughout his life to risk his neck. This little one seemed eager to do the same.

The parson thrust the baby into Seth's arms, and Seth had to hang on to keep from dropping the tyke. The baby giggled and kicked Seth in the belly and slapped him in the face. Except for the giggling, Seth expected much the same reception from the boy's mother.

Seth sure hoped he did recognize her.

Because it looked like she was the mother of his child.

CHAPTER 3

She was beautiful. Stunning. Skin darkly tanned. Features as beautiful as an angel. She had lush, curling dark hair. Even snarled and bloody, he was tempted to run his hands into it. His fingers almost itched to touch the silky length.

Callie. This was her. He knew the name from her letter and he knew nothing else. Especially nothing about a child.

Eyes flickered open. Dark eyes. So black he couldn't see where the center began.

Seth stifled his frustrated regret. He'd really been hoping her eyes were just as blue as the boy's.

She looked right at him, and flat on her back, barely conscious, riddled with wounds, her first reaction was to swing her fist.

It wasn't a bad shot, but she'd lost a lot of blood. Seth ducked in time.

He hoped she would cheer up before she regained her strength. Until then, he shifted around so the baby was right in her line of sight. The kid made a decent shield.

"Seth Kincaid, get your hands off Connor." She pushed at the doctor's restraining hands.

Connor. He had a son named Connor.

"Lay still now, Mrs.—" The doctor looked at her, then Seth.

She was too busy trying to attack to answer the man.

"Kincaid. She's Mrs. Kincaid." Seth knew that because of the letter. A sudden flash of memories almost weakened his knees. A shotgun blast to his back. The war. Fire. He was on fire. For a second he was drawn into the fire as if it were now.

"This is your wife?" The doctor cut off the waking nightmare.

"Uh . . . wife. Yep, sure enough." Sure wasn't the right word to use. Although he was sure. Being sure and remembering were two different things.

She muttered something that he couldn't understand, yet her tone held a threat so dire he was glad she was disarmed.

He'd bet anything that she was going to expect him to remember her.

The outer door banged open again. The sheriff came in supporting a bleeding man. Behind him, two men carried a second injured man who was beyond walking.

Seth glanced at them but he didn't take his eyes off the injured woman for long. Apparently, despite a lifetime of reckless behavior, he had some sense of self-preservation.

He leaned closer to her, finding a second or two of privacy

in the chaos that came along with the new patients. "The baby is fine. It sounds like you saved the day."

For some reason he wanted to say, "As usual." Seth would be the first to admit that much of what went on around the end of the war was real hazy in his memory. Between starvation, bullet wounds, laudanum, and the way he was haunted by memories of war and fire and nightmares, he'd lost big chunks of time.

And one great big ol' chunk was wriggling in his arms right now.

"So how are you?" Seth barely controlled a flinch at the lamebrained question aimed at the half-massacred woman. Next he'd be asking her about the weather.

"I'm not all that good, Seth Kincaid."

"W-we're . . ."

Be a man.

"We're married?" He shouldn't have made that sound like a question. He might as well admit it, though. He wasn't going to be able to lie his way through it. Not that he was a man for telling lies. But he didn't have to spout every single word of the truth every time he opened his mouth, now, did he? "And we have a baby?"

Callie made a sound Seth had never heard from a human being before. Sorta like a wildcat crossed with a wounded grizzly bear during a Civil War battle in a cyclone—in hell. Only way, way more fierce.

"I'm sorry. Real sorry. But I haven't been well, Callie." Seth said that fast, before she unleashed her claws. She lay there, coated in blood, sewn up like a ragged quilt, and here he stood telling her he wasn't well.

"That comes as no great piece of news. You've never been well, not since I've known you." Callie seemed to gather herself as she twisted on the table, swinging her feet off until she sat up. Her tanned skin had turned to ash gray.

"Here now, you lay back down." The doctor glared over his shoulder at her. He had his hands full all the way to his elbows with the two men the sheriff had brought in.

"I'm watching her, Doc." Seth shifted the baby into his left arm and steadied Callie with his right. He was glad the cast was off his ankle because he was going to need both arms and legs to hold them up.

His family.

He had a family.

Seth leaned close, mighty brave considering she might be preparing to pounce—then have his head for lunch.

"I'm sorry, really. I got your letter and I've been riding around searching. Rafe and Ethan, too. We've been looking for you. I can't even remember how I got to Colorado. So much of the end of the war is lost to me. Then a man drugged me and I ended up living in a cavern real close to my home ranch. Then both my brothers got married and I broke my leg and Rafe made me claim a homestead and build a cabin." He really needed to quit listing all his problems, considering hers.

Seth glanced at the little boy and didn't want to hear what Rafe had to say about this. Rafe was crazy for family and responsibility. Seth figured his big brother wasn't gonna be real proud.

"Did I mention I was sorry?" Seth finished weakly.

His wife's square little shoulders slumped. She frowned so

deep, for a minute Seth was afraid she might cry. He wasn't looking forward to that.

"I have a cabin built. My brothers helped me. And since we got your letters and knew you were coming, we made it big enough for a home, not just some lean-to shack." It was big enough for the baby, too, but that was just good luck.

"Get me off this table, then, and let's go home."

Smiling, Seth slipped an arm around her waist and helped her off the table. "You're not upset? You're going to forgive me and come live with me without a fuss?"

"No." Callie's smile had edges just as sharp as cougar claws, and fear curled in Seth's belly. Her letter had come from Texas. He reckoned she was as tough as the rest of her state. "I'm going to get you alone where no one can save you."

Seth didn't hide the flinch this time. There she stood with her sleeve cut off. A heavy bandage over stitches in her arm. Big old clumps of her hair shaved off with ugly black stitches showing on her scalp. Her face white from blood loss and fatigue, the rest of her red from where the blood that was supposed to be inside her had gotten out, and Seth didn't doubt for a minute he was going to have his hands full saving himself.

He looked at his grinning son. He deserved whatever havoc she wanted to wreak.

"Okay, let's go. We'll get a room for the night. You can't ride to my place until you've had some rest."

"It'll be a switch having you take care of me." Callie moved at Seth's gentle urging toward the door. "I wonder how long that'll last."

The parson blocked their way. "I don't think you're up to leaving yet, Mrs.—"

"Callie Kincaid." Callie reached her right hand out and rested it on the parson's shoulder. "You saved us, Parson. You saved all of us on that stage, and most important to me, you saved my son."

Seth hadn't said thank-you yet. Callie moved on to the parson's wife. "Thank you. I saw you running with Connor. I saw your husband using his body to shield both of you from stray bullets when you were inside the stage. I know it didn't suit either of you to leave me, but you saved us all. Me, the men riding on the stage, Connor, and yourselves. You did the right thing."

The parson's expression changed. Not to pride, like some men might've felt if a woman bragged on them like Callie had just done, but more like relief that he didn't have to feel ashamed. Seth could understand that. Running for help while a woman stayed behind would shame a man. That bit of shame faded to acceptance of the way he'd handled things. Seth was glad of it.

Callie was right. The parson and his wife had saved everyone. "Thank you both." Seth didn't shake the parson's hand because he was busy holding his son and keeping his wife from melting into a heap on the floor, though Callie probably didn't melt easy. Seth turned to the doctor. "I'm going to get a room for Callie. She's exhausted. I'll come for you if there's any trouble."

Callie didn't talk, and from what Seth knew about her—all learned in just the last few minutes—he figured she was near collapse, since she seemed like the type who would balk at being taken care of, and she didn't.

The doctor rapped out several orders. Seth nodded and

eased his family . . . odd, he had a family. Of course he'd always had a family. Rafe and Ethan. But now he had a wife and a child.

More than odd.

When they got onto the street, Seth saw his horse standing there at the hitching post. He turned around and called, "Parson."

The parson and his wife came outside.

"Can you put my horse up?" Seth jerked his head at the livery stable visible about two blocks down. "I'm going to get a room in the hotel right across the street, but I don't want to leave my family."

Family.

Almighty odd.

"I'd be glad to." The parson seemed eager to help. Probably still felt poorly about leaving a woman in the middle of a gunfight while he ran for help. Seth didn't have time to reassure him.

"And we'll see about getting anything she left on the stage."

"Your wife is my size," the parson's wife said with a smile. "If we can't find her things and a change of clothes, I'll send over a clean dress out of my own satchel."

That struck Seth as a really good idea. "Thanks, ma'am. We appreciate it." He was as good as carrying Callie by the time they got across the street.

The hotel manager took one look at Callie's bloody, partly shaved head and gave them a room on the ground floor. Seth appreciated not having to carry her upstairs.

"Can you send us some food and some warm water? She needs to wash up." Seth looked at Callie. She was standing, except his hand was bracing her up.

"Right away, sir. We'll be glad to help you in any way we can." The manager led the way to a door, unlocked it, went in and set the key down and hurried out.

Seth eased Callie onto the bed. She groaned and then lay still. He hoped she was asleep; otherwise they would need the doctor again.

A slap in the ear turned him around to look at his son.

Odd didn't begin to describe it, but he'd be hanged if he didn't like it.

"Hi." Seth jerked in surprise. "Uh . . . Callie?"

She lifted her eyelids as if they weighed a pound apiece. "What?"

"What's his name again?"

There was too long a silence. Finally she said, "His name . . . your son's name . . . is Connor. And you're lucky I'm too weak to kill you, Seth Kincaid." Her eyes went shut again.

Seth decided not to ask any more questions. "Hi, Connor."

The boy gave him a reckless grin that scared Seth just because he thought he understood it completely. Seth Kincaid had sown the wind. Now, with his son's help, he was going to reap the whirlwind.

A scary thought, but life would never be dull. Seth hated dull. He smiled. "You and me, little man, are going to have us some fun. You're really gonna like my cavern."

CHAPTER 4

Callie's eyes flickered open, and in the dim light she saw a roof over her head. A roof that wasn't carried along on wheels.

She'd been a long time traveling.

Connor!

She swung her legs over the edge of the bed—or rather tried to—and it all came back to her like a closed fist.

The pain was a big ol' reminder.

Then a face popped up right over her head, which she'd never managed to get raised. The look in his eyes, like blue lightning, excited, a little crazy. She'd found her husband.

"You've got a lot of nerve being alive, Seth Kincaid." Talking hurt. "Get out of this bed." She'd have shoved him out, but even thinking of it hurt.

"Shh, you'll wake Connor." Seth's smile eased into concern and he moved closer. "How bad does it hurt?"

"Like a wolf pack had half of me for supper and now they're finishing me up for breakfast."

The room was in darkness, except for a low-burning lantern. Seth looked sleepy. Which meant he'd been right here beside her for long enough to fall asleep. It was a wonder she hadn't been jerked awake by his nightmares.

"The doctor sent me some medicine for the pain." Seth held up a bottle clearly marked laudanum.

"Get it away from me." Callie wrinkled her nose and noticed the pain. From wrinkling her nose? She wondered just how battered she was. "You used to have terrible nightmares when you took that stuff. Did I get shot?"

"Nope. The splinters from the stage cut you up something fierce, though. Doc had to sew you up here and there. And you have dozens of scratches that aren't bad enough for a needle and thread. You've got blood in your hair and, well, everywhere honestly. You look awful."

Callie remembered that her husband had always been unfailingly honest. She wasn't all that thankful for the trait right now. She tried to lift her hand to examine her injuries, and it hurt like blue blazes.

"There's food if you can stand to eat it."

"I feel on the verge of casting up what little is in my belly, so I won't try eating. Maybe a drink of water, though." Callie tried to sit up and it wasn't working.

Seth looked nervous, but he slid his arm under her shoulders, and with a gentleness she remembered from before, he eased her into a sitting position and moved some pillows around so she could lean back. Everything hurt, every breath, every thought.

Seth lifted a glass of water to her lips. The sip stuck in her throat and had to fight its way down.

"Wait." She managed to lift one arm and push him away. He stopped without her having to wrestle him. He was paying really close attention, which was sweet.

How dare he be sweet?

Then the water went down and it was like it opened her throat and thirst came roaring to life. "More, please."

Seth eased the water back to her lips and gave her a tiny swallow, then another. She could drink now. She was desperate.

Then as suddenly as she'd been desperately thirsty, she was afraid she'd be sick.

Turning her mouth, Seth was quick to notice that no water was spilled.

"I think I . . . I might be . . . be sick."

Seth set the glass aside and had a damp cloth ready. Icy cold. In the chilled October night, even in a poorly heated hotel room, the cool cloth felt good.

"Let me press it against your neck." He shifted her body and it hurt a bit less than it had at first. The cold cloth at the base of her skull eased her nausea.

"I taught you that."

"You did? I don't remember learning it. It's just something I know." His hands were so strong.

He had a way of focusing on her so completely that she felt like the only woman on earth. She remembered how he'd paid attention to her. But then her memory wasn't in question, was it?

Their eyes met as her stomach settled. Aching muscles relaxed as she began to hope she'd avoid humiliating herself by needing to empty her stomach.

Not to mention how much it would hurt to vomit. The very thought was agonizing.

And speaking of agonizing thoughts . . . "Seth, why did you leave? What happened?"

His eyes, so vulnerable she'd been done in by them from the first, looked sad. "I'm sorry, Callie. I don't even know what happened. I—when did I leave, was it?—I don't remember there being a baby." He shook his head as if denying he'd done such a thing.

"You don't even remember there being a wife. Connor wasn't . . .well, I wasn't up to traveling for a while; that's why it took me so long to come after you."

"He's beautiful. I have a son." He leaned close and kissed her.

No warning.

She was sure she'd have refused his kiss if she'd had a chance. The kiss deepened. It hurt, but it was so wonderful to be with him again. Which didn't match with the burning desire to fill his belly full of lead.

She lifted her arms to pull him closer, and her left one wouldn't move. But her right one, though sore, moved just fine.

"I remember this." Seth spoke against her lips.

The words brought tears to her eyes, the gentle kiss clashing with the realization that he'd forgotten all about her.

She turned her head aside. "How could you forget me, Seth?"

Resting his forehead against her temple, Seth didn't try

another kiss. But she remembered it well, the fire that blazed between them. Only her pain and his guilt kept that from happening right now because she'd missed him so terribly.

After long, sweet moments with Seth holding her so gently, Callie pulled back. "How is Connor?"

"He's sleeping right beside us on the floor."

"Did he eat? I didn't have any way to feed him except . . ." Callie fell silent. Then she raised her head to look right in Seth's eyes. "I don't even feel like I know you anymore."

"You kissed me like you know me real well."

Callie raised a hand to rest on his cheek and pushed him away, not far away but enough that she could think.

"We're married, Seth. Nothing changes that."

"And I've got a cabin we can move into tomorrow."

Silence stretched between them. "You don't know me. You don't remember your commitment to me, and you can't say you love me. I'm not your wife until you remember me, Seth."

Seth opened his mouth, no doubt to say something crazy. Callie touched his lips with one finger to stop him.

"I came out here mostly because I was afraid you were dead. I wrote that letter to you on the long chance you might get it, but mainly I wanted to contact Rafe and Ethan. I thought it was fair that they knew they had a nephew and that they claimed him. There was trouble back in Texas and my pa died and I had nowhere else to go. You said you had a ranch out here and I wanted to give Connor whatever birthright goes with the Kincaid name. So I deliberately sent that letter and set out before your brothers could tell me to stay away. So I'm here and I've found my abandoning husband, and just like before, you seem drawn to me and eager to kiss me."

"I'm both." Seth sounded fervent.

"I believe you, but it's not enough. You were both of those things before and you ran off as soon as you felt well enough, or maybe your nightmares drove you into the night, or maybe you're just crazy. Whatever the truth is, you did it."

"I'm sorry."

"And I'm not going to resume the whole of being married until I know I can trust you. I'm not going to be abandoned again, with another baby on the way. You shouldn't be here in this bed with me. So yes, I'll come to your cabin, but you, Seth Kincaid, are going to have to prove to me that you have a firm grip on your sanity."

"How do I do that?" He showed no signs of leaving the bed. His broad shoulders were bare and she could see his terrible scars.

She fought the compassion he always awakened in her. "It's the kind of challenge that'll probably drive you crazy."

"How will we be able to tell?" Seth sighed. "Go back to sleep. As soon as you're feeling better, we'll head for home." He adjusted the pillows and eased her onto her back.

It wasn't a satisfying end to this first real conversation she'd had with her husband in a long time. But there was no help for that. She shouldn't even go to sleep and leave her son in the care of a lunatic. But she was too battered to stay awake, and if her husband ran off again, she'd at least be able to find his hopefully sane older brothers.

Seth pulled her into his arms so gently it hurt her heart and that, combined with the beating she'd taken yesterday, helped her keep her mouth shut.

As she fell asleep, she noticed he hadn't moved away at

all. In fact, he was closer than ever. He was warm and strong and gentle and so wounded she didn't have the will to kick his backside out of her bed.

And didn't that just describe their whole relationship.

Seth felt the licking flames. Fire crawled along the rock, following the line of spilled kerosene.

It leaped at him, a living thing. His sleeve caught fire.

He jerked awake. His heart pounded but the pain hadn't come. And the screaming. Something had broken in just as the dreams started. Nightmares, not dreams. Not even close to dreams.

He lay awake, alert as a western man—and a soldier—learns to be. But he couldn't quite identify the noise he'd heard. It didn't strike him as dangerous.

Then he felt a tickle on his chin, and in the dark room, dimly lit by the moonlight, he saw dark curls and realized his arms held something.

Someone.

There was a woman in his arms. His heart flipped from fear to excitement, but it raced just as fast and slammed in his chest as his hold on her tightened.

Who was she? Where was he? She fit in his arms so perfectly he felt like he'd come home in a way he'd never been before. Or maybe he was still dreaming.

But his dreams were never like this.

The sound again. What was it? Some little squeak.

He wanted to revel in the feel of this woman, but the sound invaded his thoughts again and a tickle spooked him.

He looked down toward his arm—the right one—the one not wrapped around a woman—and met the eyes of a child.

Connor.

Everything snapped into place.

Seth remembered crawling into bed after Callie had fallen asleep, glad he couldn't ask permission. They were twined in each other's arms. But on the very edge of the bed where Connor could easily reach. He hadn't gone to his wife; she had come to him.

And clearly, Connor had crawled out of the blankets Seth had lain on the floor and pulled himself up to stand by the bed. Connor squeaked and his little fingers clawed at Seth's bare arm. He bounced on his chubby little legs and smiled so big that Seth's heart hurt from the sweetness of the moment. A chubby baby. A beautiful woman. He hadn't done much in his life to deserve this.

"Papapapapapapa." The boy was getting loud.

Seth realized he had about ten seconds to quiet Connor down before he woke the boy's exhausted, battered mother. With the deepest imaginable regret, he eased Callie aside. She didn't even twitch. The woman was worn clear out.

"Papapapapapa." Connor held on to the edge of the bed and bounced faster, grinning and occasionally clawing at Seth some more.

Seth slipped out of bed, dressed quickly and hoisted the boy into his arms.

The soggy boy.

With no idea how to proceed and Connor's "papapapapa" getting louder with every passing second, Seth slipped out of the room, barefoot.

Soggy baby in hand.

At least he could quiet the boy down—or not—far from Callie.

Glad of an excuse to stop sleeping before the nightmares came, he took Connor out to the lobby. Seth found a night clerk with his head down on the desk in the hotel entry. Seth's footstep on a creaky board roused the young man.

"Howdy." Seth didn't know how to proceed.

Connor bounced in his arms. "Papapapapapa." He waved at the night clerk. Maybe the baby was saying bye-bye.

"Your son woke you up, huh?" The night clerk smiled at Connor. Seth had a feeling the cute little wiggler would get that reaction from everyone he ever met.

"Yep, and his mother had a hard day yesterday. I'd like for her to sleep."

"How about I get him some milk from the kitchen?"

Seth heaved a sigh of relief. "How do you know what babies need? I sure don't. His ma just brought him out here yesterday."

"Your wife is the one who held off those outlaws that tried to rob the stage, isn't she?"

Seth reckoned he had himself a famous wife. "That she is."

"My uncle was riding shotgun on that stage. Your wife saved his life."

"In that case"—Seth wasn't sure just how to ask, but something had to be done—"do you know what to do about a soggy diaper?"

The night clerk smiled. "I'm the oldest of five brothers. I reckon I've changed my share of diapers." The boy jerked his head at a satchel by the door to the outside. "That's your wife's bag. I'll see if she's got diapers in there; otherwise we can swipe a towel out of the kitchen."

"Now, don't go to swiping things, son. It ain't right and your boss'll fire you. I don't want that." Though Seth did badly want a dry diaper for Connor.

The boy laughed. "The boss is my pa. He's mighty grateful that his brother is going to be all right. He'll be glad to donate a towel or two."

"Can you check the satchel? Or do you want the boy?"

"You've already got a big old wet spot on your shirt. How about I leave you to hold him, since you're already wet, and I do the searching?"

"Sounds fine."

Connor yelled, "Papapapapa!"

"Hey, he can call you papa. He looks real young to be talking. He's a smart boy."

That hadn't occurred to Seth that the boy was making sense. It just sounded like baby jabbering. Maggie could say a few words, including calling Ethan papa. And she was the only baby Seth had ever been around, except for Ethan's younger baby Lily, and she wasn't to talking age yet.

It warmed Seth's heart. "Say papa."

Connor bounced and yelled, and Seth and the night clerk laughed. It was a mighty fun game. Until they tried to change Connor's diaper. Then they had a chase on their hands. The boy could squirm and roll and crawl fast as greased lightning.

Seth and Connor had another nighttime adventure about three hours later and another half-grown boy was manning the desk. This one knew his way around a diaper, too.

By the time morning came, Seth had gotten to know his little son pretty well. He could crawl so fast, Seth didn't dare take his eyes off of him. He laughed and screamed with equal volume and he didn't like wearing a diaper. It had taken both Seth and the clerk to wrestle him into one.

Seth arranged to have the parson's wife come early, and when she arrived, he left her with Callie, who hadn't stirred since that one middle-of-the-night talk they'd had.

The parson's wife had brought a few things along and she set to work washing and mending the clothes Callie had gotten so tattered yesterday.

CHAPTER 5

Because Connor seemed inclined toward rowdiness, Seth took his son with him to buy supplies.

"You back, Kincaid?" Russ Stewart at the general store took Seth's order.

"Yeah, but I'm probably done with my trips to Colorado City. I met my wife on the stage yesterday." Connor bounced in Seth's arms and Seth couldn't hold back a smile at the husky toddler.

"The one that got robbed?"

"Yep."

"Heard a woman held off four armed bandits."

"That's my wife." Seth grew a little taller with pride. He patted Connor on the back. If Connor had a good dose of his ma in him, he was gonna grow up to be about the best son a man ever had. Of course before they could concentrate on raising their son, Seth had to figure out a way to get Callie to stop trying to kill him.

"I knew the stagecoach driver real well. He's got a lot of friends in this town and the man riding shotgun's got family here, a wife and young'uns. I'm obliged to your wife."

"I'm mighty glad she's here. I've been riding out to meet the stage for a while, waiting for her."

"Your boy is the spittin' image of you." Russ tipped his head at Connor. "I'll bet you're glad he finally got here."

"I am at that." Glad to know he existed was more like it. "And my wife, too. I've got a big order there, Russ. I didn't figure I needed to fill it when it looked like I'd be back a few more times. But now I'll stock up for winter. It's a long trip from here to our ranch, and I'm hoping to leave before noon."

Seth hesitated as he thought of how battered Callie was. "I might be waiting a day so my wife can rest up. Can you just get the order together? I'll come by with my string of horses when we're ready to leave."

"Sounds good. A Rocky Mountain winter can slow a man down. Best to lay up supplies."

Seth left only to come face-to-face with the parson. "Thanks for sending your wife over."

The sidewalk was busy enough that they stepped off it to stand beside horses at the hitching post. Wagons drove past. Horseback riders plodded along the dusty streets. A cold wind whipped past them, and Seth drew the collar of his buckskin jacket up to protect his ears and wrapped his son inside his coat. The boy was dressed warmly, thanks to the hotel owner's knowing wife.

"Your wife is a tough woman, Mr. Kincaid."

"That she is, Parson Frew. That she is." Seth smiled to think just how tough.

"I don't know if, in the middle of all that went on yesterday, I thanked her." The parson looked down at his boots as if it was hard for him to go on; then his head lifted and his eyes blazed. "I'm trying not to be ashamed of abandoning her. But whatever my actions, it doesn't change the fact that she saved me, my wife, the men on that stage, and your boy here and herself. She's a woman to be proud of."

The letter Seth had gotten came from Texas, and he had a sudden flash of memory. Callie had grown up on the frontier. "They grow 'em tough in Texas."

How had she ended up caring for a Union soldier in Georgia? Seth knew Andersonville was in Georgia, but maybe he'd met her somewhere else. He sure wished he remembered a little more about how he'd come to be a husband and father.

A smile spread on the parson's face. "My wife, the most kindhearted, peace-loving and God-fearing woman I've ever known, asked me if I'd buy her a gun. She's determined to help settle the West."

Seth laughed. "You'll have your hands full with her whether you say yes or no. Good luck to you, Parson."

"I felt God call me to this place, Kincaid." A somber expression replaced the parson's smile. "But now I'm not so sure. I hate knowing that my wife especially could be in danger. I knew it was a wild land, but until the first man opens fire on you . . . well, I didn't really understand just how dangerous.

I'm not sure we'll make it out here. I'm not a tough man with a gun, and my wife certainly isn't a ball of fire like yours."

"My brothers are both married. I wouldn't say either of their wives are what you'd call tough."

"There aren't that many women out this way. I'm surprised to hear of a family with three women."

A man strode by heading for the general store. The parson stepped sideways to let him pass.

"My brother Ethan married the widow of a man named Wendell Gilliland. Rafe got himself yoked to Gilliland's daughter."

The man stumbled and Seth's hand shot out to keep him from falling.

"Thanks." He gave Seth a look so sharp it earned Seth's attention.

"Glad to help."

With a nod, the man turned to the parson. "My wife and I enjoyed meeting you last night, Parson. We're looking forward to you serving our town."

The parson shook the man's hand. "I remember you from last night, Henry. I was glad to see a good crowd."

"Are you looking for a church, too?" Henry turned to Seth.

Seth didn't want to give the man any information. "Doubt it. We live a long way out."

"Well, I'll get on. We'll see you around, Parson." Henry moved on toward the general store but not quite so quickly as he'd moved before.

Because being on edge was a good way to stay alive, Seth made note of the man. There was nothing out of the ordinary about him. Black hair and eyes, with white at the temples.

A mouth that, just for a second, curled into cruelty. He was dressed like any other western man, in brown broadcloth shirt and pants. Still, Seth would recognize him later.

He waited until the man went on inside, then turned back to the parson. "So that one man, Gilliland, brought two of the women with him. My wife just rode out here, and I . . . Seth couldn't make himself admit he'd run off from his wife. He hugged Connor with regret. Connor thanked him by slobbering on his shirt. "Callie and Connor have joined me now that I've got my cabin built."

And now that they've tracked me down.

The parson clapped Seth on the back. "Good luck in your new life. I understand a Colorado winter in these mountains is a fearsome thing."

Seth smiled. "I grew up with it. But I reckon Callie is in for a surprise. I'd better get back to her. You have my thanks right back for getting help for my wife and protecting my son. I've been riding out to meet the stage real regular. Callie's letters weren't clear on when she'd get here."

"God bless you, Seth. Look me up if you're ever in Colorado City again."

The man who'd gone into the store stepped out with a bag of flour over his shoulder.

Seth wondered why a man bothered to walk all the way to the general store to buy just one thing. Of course if a body lived close, it was probably common enough.

With no interest in furthering his acquaintance with someone from Colorado City he'd never see again, Seth said to the parson, "I'll head on back to my wife now and send yours home."

Seth shifted his gaze to look the newcomer in the eye. Unarmed, dressed like a farmer, his eyes too sharp for an honest man. In one hard look, Seth hoped this man, whatever his business was with the parson, got the clear message that Seth Kincaid wasn't to be taken lightly.

Seth jerked the brim of his hat, took in the lack of a gun, even noting the man wore no coat where one could be hidden, then turned and walked away. He had an itch between his shoulder blades, but common sense told Seth a stranger without a gun wasn't about to shoot him in the back in the middle of a busy street.

He walked to the hotel, hoping his wife was up to heading out. Seth was eager to get shut of this town.

Jasper slammed the door and it drew Trixie's full attention.

Bea, her name was Bea now. He'd thought he was getting used to calling her that, but right now it gnawed on his temper.

"What is it, Jasper?" She'd quit doing whatever she'd done to keep her hair a vivid red. It was now a mousy dull red streaked with gray. She still had a good figure, but it was concealed in modest gingham instead of being showcased in revealing silk. She'd left her garish face paint behind. And she was still a beautiful, appealing woman.

Jasper hadn't been able to give up his name, so they'd compromised. He was Henry Jasper Duff, married to Beatrice, called Bea. He introduced himself as Henry Duff, but Bea at least still called him Jasper. If she hadn't agreed to do that, Jasper felt as if he'd cease to exist.

And he was a farmer. Not even a prosperous one. They

lived on the edge of town with a few rocky patches planted to a garden or kept as grazing for their three cows. But Bea had rat-holed enough money to let them have everything they wanted, as long as they didn't want too much.

Jasper wanted a lot.

"I ran into one of those Kincaid brothers and heard him talking about the Gillilands. It burns bad that they've got all my money while we live in this shack."

Bea set aside her embroidery hoop and rose, smoothing her skirt. Bea wasn't a stupid woman.

"We talked about this." There was no innocent confusion that would have given Jasper a chance to calm down. "You're free to chase after that money for the rest of your life. Break whatever laws suit you and hurt anyone, man, woman or child, who gets in your way. Staying here has always been your choice. Except—"

"I know!" Jasper cut her off before she could give him the ultimatum again. "If I go, don't come back."

And Trixie—he shook his head—Bea. His wife had all the money.

"I know we live a good life. We're happy." Jasper was currently bitterly unhappy. "We gather eggs. We milk a cow."

"I milk a cow. I gather eggs." Bea gave him the soft look that reminded him of how hard she was. She chose to be decent. She chose to be honest. She'd turned her back on the saloon she owned and the women who worked abovestairs, just as Jasper had turned his back on his opium trade and a dozen other criminal enterprises he ran in Houston when Wendell Gilliland had stolen his money and left him owing the wrong people.

Jasper's fingers itched to find his derringer and load it. Carry it in his sleeve like he used to. Demand respect like he used to.

"I'm just—" Jasper cut himself off. "It was just running into him like that. I could have grabbed him and shaken him until he told me where my money is."

Except he couldn't because one look told Jasper that Kincaid was a tough man and Jasper had been unarmed and defenseless—weak. "It burns to be a nobody in this one-horse town when I used to run a good share of the crime in Houston."

Jasper raised his eyes to glare at his wife, his living, breathing, bossy wife.

"Are you trying to tell me you think that's something to boast about? Running crime in Houston? Because it's something to be ashamed of, Jasper, and you know it. You heard what the parson said."

That reined Jasper in a bit. He had no business taking his temper out on her. "We've got a decent life here. I don't want to go back to what I was before."

Well, maybe just for a short time, until he got his money.

"Then give up on that money. It's blood money, Jasper. It's only yours in the most sinful sense of the word. Losing that money is going to save your life and if you'll let it, your soul."

He was married to a preachin' woman for a fact. He took a few steps and it brought him all the way across the room. He'd owned a beautiful mansion in Houston. He wore silk shirts and smoked fine cigars. Now he lived in a house the size of his bedroom back home. He wore broadcloth that itched every time he moved. With a derisive laugh he admitted he didn't want to smoke anyway.

There was a flash of fear in her eyes as he approached and it shamed him. "I'm not going to hurt you. Don't even think it, Bea."

He reached out and rested two hands on her strong shoulders. He drew her close, then closer. "I know you're right. A man just has a bad moment now and again." He kissed her and she was the only fine and silky thing he needed.

She was as generous as always.

Seth got to the room just as Connor fell asleep in his arms. He found Callie up and wearing a clean white dress, her dark hair washed and braided in a way that covered most of the damage done by the doctor's clippers. She was so darkly tanned it was hard to judge if she was weakened by blood loss or fatigue, but how could she not be?

Callie set a fork down on an empty plate as Seth came in.

"How is she, Mrs. Frew?" Seth had a hard time taking his eyes off his pretty wife. Callie was looking right back, but Seth thought he saw something other than admiration in her gaze.

"Better. The bath and clean clothes helped. A good meal and a good night's sleep, too. I'll go along now." Mrs. Frew gathered up the dishes from the small table where Callie sat.

They said their goodbyes and thank-yous. Seth laid Connor down on the folded blankets, where the boy had spent the night. Then he sat on the bed. Callie was on a chair pulled up to a bedside table.

"How are you?" They were only a few inches apart.

"I'm steady. Not full strength but I'll survive. The doctor came while you were out. He thought I needed to rest a few days because of the blood I lost, but I'm ready to get out of this town."

"We can head out, then. It's a long ride home, and if you wear out along the trail, we can camp for the night. Ethan's house is closer than mine, so if you last long enough we can stop there. I've got supplies at the general store and horses to carry things home. Some of the trails are too narrow and too hard a pull for a wagon."

"Did you have a good time carrying my son around town?" She had enough strength to shoot arrows at him with her eyes.

"He's a fine boy, Callie. I'm sorry I—"

"I've heard 'I'm sorry' enough," Callie cut him off. "Let's get on for home."

Seth hesitated. There was something about the fire in her black eyes that drew him like a moth. "You're hurt. Can I say I'm sorry about that?"

She shrugged. "Saying you're sorry doesn't change anything."

"I know. And wishing I'd gotten there sooner so I could help you doesn't do a bit of good. But I'd have spared you the danger you were in if I could." He lifted a hand and drew it along a scratch on her cheek. "The town is buzzing about the woman who stood off a band of outlaws. The stage driver and the man riding shotgun are well known and well liked. They're both going to live because of you."

"I'm glad. They were tough men. They put off the moment when I'd be fighting on my own. And the driver got us closer to town than he might have. That gave the parson a chance to get away and to protect his wife and Connor. We all worked mighty hard to survive that holdup yesterday. It wasn't all my doin'."

They were so close, it was easy to lean forward and steal a kiss. He pulled back and she followed after his lips for a second.

She caught herself. "There won't be any of that."

But he'd seen it. Her words didn't match the way she moved. But he also knew he couldn't use the powerful draw between them to tame her. It would be cheating.

"Sorry is just a word, Callie. You'll believe me when I prove it. I reckon I deserve every bit of your distrust. I aim to spend as much time as it takes to earn it back."

"It's not that I don't believe you." Callie's eyes had a hopeless look as she drew a gentle finger down his cheek. "I'm sure you mean it when you say you're sorry. And maybe you even care about me to the extent you can remember. It's just that until I'm sure you won't run off again, I don't dare to trust you. Being left alone in Georgia was a heartbreaking thing. I went home to my pa, and he took care of me through Connor's birth."

For some reason that lifted Seth's heart mightily. "So he wasn't born before I left?"

Callie frowned. "Can't you even remember that?"

"Had you told me he was on the way?"

There was an extended silence. Finally she said, "No. I didn't know about him yet. We'd only been married a short time. I knew you were still sick. I knew you were haunted by the war and weak from your wounds. I never should have married you when—"

He kissed her until he was sure she would quit blaming herself in any way. "I can't remember what sent me running for home, and I don't know enough about being sick in the head to understand why I've forgotten someone as sweet as you."

And as handy with a gun.

"It was bound to be a hard business getting here, and I don't remember much of it. I was turned aside for a time. But, Callie, what you stir up in me is fierce. I suspect we'll have our hands full keeping ourselves from . . . from having . . . well . . . any of that."

He watched her until he was sure she understood just what that was. "The truth is, I'm not sure I'm going to be much help avoiding that. But we'll get through this and that. I promise you we'll be fine."

"Are you still having your nightmares?"

Seth straightened, surprised. "I don't remember having a nightmare last night."

"You never woke me up with one, anyway."

"I was up with Connor twice, so maybe that interrupted my sleep before the nightmares could take hold." Seth smiled.

"Connor woke up and I slept through it?" Callie twisted to look behind her to reassure herself the boy was alive and well. Seth saw her wince with pain.

"Yesterday was a real hard day for you, honey. I reckon you'd've woken up if I hadn't heard him before he so much as whimpered. I fed him down in the hotel dining room."

"In the middle of the night?"

"Yep. And changed his diaper twice. The night clerk helped me. Having a son wake me up in the night might be the best thing that ever happened to me."

"Connor normally sleeps soundly all night. I'm sure he's stirred up from the traveling."

"And the gunfight."

"Yeah, that too." Callie turned back to Seth. "Latta told

me she and the parson didn't send you out to the stage to help me. How'd you come to be on that trail?"

"I've been searching for you for over a month. I had a broken leg when your letter came. I couldn't start hunting for you right away, but Rafe and Ethan rode out as much as they could. But we didn't know which trail you'd take. Since I've been fit, I've been combing the trails. I've probably ridden this trail a dozen times to meet the stage and see if you'd come. I'd go home for a few days and help Rafe and Ethan with my house for a while, then ride out again."

The corner of Callie's mouth turned up in a sad kind of smile. Seth thought of a thousand questions he needed to ask her, yet there wasn't time for any of that now. "Are you sure you're ready to ride?"

Callie nodded. "Let's go home."

CHAPTER 6

Callie kept moving just because it had been bred in the bone from her growing up in Texas. Every breath, every step hurt, and yet none of that stopped her.

Seth was a good cowboy; she'd give him that. It set wrong with her, but she stayed inside while he went off to saddle the horses, load the supplies, and talk to the sheriff one more time before they left town.

Most of Callie's things had been delivered to the hotel, though Callie wanted her rifle and six-gun back. She left tracking them down to Seth while she sat in the hotel dining room. Seth had even arranged for a young boy to chase after Connor.

When Seth pushed through the swinging doors of the

restaurant, Callie knew it was time to go. She gritted her teeth to keep from groaning as she stood.

Seth scooped Connor into his arms and Connor bounced and, if Callie wasn't mistaken, said, "Papa."

Of course, Connor called her papa, too. And he called his feet papa, and his milk. Still, it bothered her a little, especially since the little imp didn't ever say mama.

Seth carried Connor and rested a hand on the small of her back. She wanted to hit his hand away, except she needed the support. His touch was warm and it seemed to ease her aching muscles. Or maybe she was just too stubborn to topple over with her abandoning husband as a witness.

They were leaving the dining room when the hotel clerk rushed up to meet them. "You saved my brother's life yesterday, Mrs. Kincaid. There's no charge for the room or for anything else. You have my thanks."

"You're welcome." Callie nodded and it really hurt.

"Can you help me with this?" Seth shook out a strange-looking leather contraption.

"You got the carrier my wife sent over?" The clerk reached for it. "Good."

Seth handed it over. "Help me get the boy situated."

Callie watched curiously as the clerk slipped Connor's chubby legs into the leather; then Seth let go of her, turned around, and put Connor on like a coat.

"You're wearing Connor?"

With a smile, Seth put his hand back on her and she realized she'd missed his touch. It made her mad to admit it.

"I've got two little nieces, and their mom wears the baby like a papoose when she needs her hands free. I mentioned it to the clerk this morning and he said his wife had something she could fix up for us. All their children are old enough to ride on their own." Seth urged her forward, which she appreciated, not wanting to stand—not even to accept gratitude—a minute longer than was necessary.

"You've got two nieces? You never mentioned your brothers being married."

"We've got a lot to talk about, Callie. We'll get to all of it."

They stepped out on the street, and the stage driver was approaching, his head bandaged and one arm in a sling. "I'm glad I got here before you left, Mrs. Kincaid."

Callie wasn't all that glad. She did her best to smile.

The stage driver handed her a small cloth bag. "Our company has a standing one-hundred-dollar reward for anyone who heads off a robbery. And the sheriff went after those men yesterday and caught all four of them. Three of them have a price on their heads. It adds up to a five-hundred-dollar reward. The marshal will put the money in the bank here when it comes."

Seth nodded at the bag. "We'll take this with us."

The driver nodded. "Much obliged, ma'am. My shotgun would've come, but he's still at the doctor's office. Although he took a hard hit, he's going to make it, thanks to you." The driver tipped his hat, and Seth urged her toward a beautiful little black mustang. One of five horses standing in front of the hotel hitching post. Three of them were loaded down with supplies.

Seth reached for her waist, and while it set wrong to be helped onto a horse, Callie didn't think she'd make it on her own. Before he could lift, someone else could be heard treading the sidewalk toward them. The newcomer was on them before Callie could mount up and get shut of this friendly town.

Callie stifled a sigh, turned to be thanked again and looked at a half-grown boy who had Seth's exact coloring. In fact, he looked enough like Seth to be his brother. Right down to a pair of wild blue eyes.

Seth felt like he was looking at Connor at about age ten. Maybe, though, this was just someone else who wanted to congratulate Callie for being a steady hand with her gun and the resemblance was nothing but a coincidence.

"You're Seth Kincaid, right?" The boy had his fists clenched like he was getting ready to take a swing.

The youngster wasn't here to thank Callie for nuthin'.

"That's right," Seth replied.

"I've been hunting you." The kid looked killing mad.

Seth sort of wished he'd gotten Callie's six-gun into her hands. He might need the help. Although a shootout with a ten-year-old was just plain embarrassing.

He'd tucked the gun in his saddlebag rather than hand it over for fear she might take a notion to use it on him. "Well, you've found me. What can I do for you?"

Lots of people had blue eyes. Seth tried to pull himself back from the crazy conclusions he'd jumped to.

"I understand you're my brother," the boy said.

Seth went right back to jumping. "Uh . . . no . . . I'm not."

Yes, he was. Seth knew it even as he denied it. Those were his eyes. Eyes he shared with only one other person on earth. His pa. Oh wait, two people. His son had his eyes. Now there was a third.

"I've got a letter here, in my ma's hand, saying my pa—"

"Your pa?" Seth interrupted.

"Yes, my pa. Gavin Kincaid."

Seth had known that was coming.

"My ma told me, if I needed help to go find my brothers, Rafe, Ethan, and Seth Kincaid. She said you own a ranch near Rawhide, and a fourth of it's mine."

A dozen questions came to mind as Seth stared at the boy—who was way too old, considering Seth's pa had been a married man until Seth reached the ripe old age of twelve.

The question that got out of Seth's mouth first was, "How old are you?"

"I don't have to answer any of your questions." The boy bulled up. But it didn't matter. Unless this child was no more than eight years old, he wasn't near young enough.

"I'm twenty-one." Schooling had never been Seth's strength, but he could add and subtract. "My ma, Gavin Kincaid's wife, died when I was twelve. If you're not at least twelve years younger than I am"—and that didn't even need to be said out loud since the kid was obviously older than that—"then we've got us a real big problem."

"You're telling me your ma was still alive until you were . . ." A dull red stole up the boy's cheeks. Seth felt the shame.

Seth had a wife he couldn't remember. He got kicked in the back by the son he'd never heard of before yesterday. There were a lot of people who'd accused him over the years of being crazy. Pretty much everyone he'd ever met, in fact.

As he stood there in that cool breeze of an October in Colorado, Seth wondered if he hadn't oughta just forget all about being crazy. Sanity was proving to be stranger than any fevered notions his head could cook up.

A tug on his sleeve drew his addled mind back from the wild ride it was on. He turned away from his new brother and looked at Callie. He braced himself for his forgotten wife to tell him they had five children instead of one. And for the whole herd of blue-eyed sons and daughters to come charging out of the alley.

Instead of hooking a bunch more children on his back, she thrust the bag holding her reward money at Seth and said, "We're gonna need to buy more horses."

CHAPTER 7

Like every other time when she'd had dealings with her husband, right from the moment she'd found him feverish in an army hospital in Georgia, Callie had to do all the thinking.

And considering her blood loss from yesterday, thinking was quite a chore. But she could see clear as the sunrise that Seth wasn't up to it.

"When did you eat last?" she asked the boy.

He looked half starved, as most growing boys always did. But he was gaunt and his cheeks were hollow.

The boy got a stubborn look in his eyes, and for a second Callie thought his pride might force him to refuse an offer of food. "I reckon it's been a while."

Callie nodded. "Seth," she said, shoving the money bag

in his hands, "go buy two more horses. And the general store oughta have some—" Callie stopped as she thought of all they needed to clothe and feed a young boy for the winter. She really didn't have the strength, but Seth probably didn't have the sense. Then the parson came walking down the street, whistling. A man this cheerful was clashing badly with the general mood of the Kincaid family. Fortunately he had his wife with him, and she seemed to be possessed of a practical nature.

"Just buy two more horses."

"What do we need two horses for?" Seth's brow furrowed.

"We're gonna need another pack animal."

"For what?" he asked, looking thoroughly confused.

"Just do it. And get saddles and leather for one of them, too. If you spend all that money, tell the bank to cover the bills out of what comes in from the price on those outlaws' heads." There went her reward money. "Then take the pack animal to the general store, load it with the things the parson and his wife are going to pick out for us, then come back to the hotel." Callie turned to the newly discovered Kincaid brother. She sure hoped they weren't all as crazy as Seth. Life was vexing enough.

"Go on into the hotel," she told the boy. "Tell the clerk you want a meal, just as big as you want to make it. I'm Callie Kincaid. Tell them I'll be in to pay directly. He can come out here and ask me if he needs to."

She reached into Seth's money pouch and got the price of dinner. She was just too tired to shop for all they needed. The boy must've been hungry, because he went straight inside.

Not ten seconds later the clerk stuck his head out the door. "This boy with you?"

"Yep," Callie answered. Not waiting for Seth. "Go ahead and let him eat."

"My pleasure, Mrs. Kincaid. On the house."

"No, it's not. I pay my bills." She gave the man a look she'd learned from standing down men during the war in Texas, and as she had to fight her way across the West to find her husband.

It worked this time, too. The clerk nodded and ducked back inside just as the parson and his wife walked up.

Callie gave them direct, clear instructions and told them to ask the clerk at the general store to get the money out of a nonexistent bank account. She was supposed to be a town hero, so she'd use up her goodwill and get out of town fast. The parson and his wife headed for the store.

"Callie, honey, why are you buying all that stuff?"

"You don't have a brain in your head, do you, Seth Kincaid?"

Seth shrugged.

"Buy the horses, gather up what the parson's ordering for us, then come back and pick us up. We should be ready to head home by the time you've gotten everything done that needs doing."

Seth turned toward the stable. Connor grinned and waved bye-bye to her.

"Stop!"

Seth turned back and Connor giggled. "Leave my son. If you disappear again and this time take Connor with you, so help me, Seth, I will hunt you down and shoot you dead."

Callie needed to sit down and there was no sense denying it. Not that she was going to admit it out loud, but neither could she deny it to herself.

"I'm not going anywhere, Callie. You and Connor are stuck with me." Seth handed over the baby.

If only she could trust that.

Of course, he'd been acting crazy when she'd married him, but she'd seen so much potential for sanity. It was a hard lesson she'd learned about looking on the bright side of things. She wouldn't make the mistake of being optimistic again.

Seth headed for the stable.

Now all she needed to do was feed an angry, starving boy, hope she'd bought supplies enough for winter, and ride miles across rugged mountains to get home. And she had to do it without collapsing.

When she made it to the dining room without falling in a heap, she thought things were looking up.

Seth's brother . . . Callie shook her head. Whoever he was, he was already eating.

"I'm Callie Kincaid." She sank heavily into a chair across the table from her pint-sized brother-in-law and settled Connor on her knee. "I've never heard the name Gavin Kincaid before, but it looks like he's my father-in-law. I'm married to Seth. Tell me your name."

He kept chewing. His plate was about half emptied already, but there were plenty of mashed potatoes and tender-looking roast beef left. The dining room had been generous in their servings.

"Your name." She jabbed her finger at the boy. He gave her a dark look and filled his mouth with potatoes. She had a startling impulse to give the boy's ear a good yank to twist some words loose. She decided to chalk it up to her generally poor condition and forgive herself, since she hadn't gone ahead and attacked him, now, had she?

A young boy came in from the kitchen carefully balancing a heavy white pottery cup brimming with steaming coffee. The boy smiled and flashed the deepest dimples Callie had ever seen and distracted her from her violent daydream. "My pa says the coffee is free and not to argue with him."

She knew for sure the man had sent this little one out because he was so irresistibly cute. How was she supposed to refuse coffee from him? "Thank you and tell your pa thank you, too. I appreciate it."

The boy giggled and set down the savory brew without spilling a drop. "Can I hold the baby? I've got two little brothers, so I know my way around young'uns. I can play with him down on the floor while you visit."

"Thanks, I appreciate it." She really did. Connor was gaining a pound a minute in her shaky arms.

The boy took Connor and retreated to the far corner of the room, which was good. She could ask her questions a little harder than if there'd been a witness at hand. She didn't think she knew Seth's little brother well enough to do any ear twisting, though she didn't completely abandon the idea.

"I just joined the Kincaid family yesterday—in fact, I haven't all the way joined it yet." That got his attention. "Seth, the brother you met outside, is my husband. We married back East after the war, and he . . ." She hesitated, not sure just how honest to be. Well, she could always fill in details later. "He came back to Colorado and got a house built while I stayed with my pa in Texas to birth our baby."

Not a single lie in that little speech. Unless there wasn't really a house. Seth might've imagined that.

"So I don't know the Kincaids much at all. Seth is the youngest of three brothers. He talked about his family some, of course." She hadn't known what was true and what was a product of his feverish nightmares. Seth had a talent for ranting. "There is an older brother, Rafe, and a middle brother, Ethan. Now, what's your name?"

She'd wrestled her share of longhorns, backed a hungry cougar off a newborn calf, and she'd shot a rattlesnake or two. She wasn't one bit scared of this young'un.

The child didn't answer, but he was eating like a half-starved wolf, so she didn't think his silence was all about angry pride. She added, "I have no particular loyalty to the Kincaids, except for my husband and son." Her son more than her husband, but she didn't admit that. "Since we look to be joining the family at the same time, maybe we could be friends. It'd be two against three."

"I'm not joining the family." The boy finally spoke, and it was more a snarl than words. "I'm here for my share of the ranch. I aim to sell it and move on. When my ma died, I found a letter that said Pa had a ranch near Rawhide and I was to go there if I was in need. Papa liked the gold fields, and he did some trapping. He took off about three years ago and never came back. Ma told me he died. He'd've never left us otherwise."

Callie had heard from Seth that his ma was dead, and she knew how old he was at the time. She could add and subtract good enough to know that Gavin Kincaid had a distinct lack of honor in his dealing with both of his families.

"Things were mighty tight without Pa," the boy went on. "But we ran his traplines, and Ma taught me to hunt as well as her. She had a good garden and we got by. After Ma died, I found a letter. It was about Pa's other sons."

Callie thought she knew how this pinched the boy's pride, and she couldn't fault him for his hard feelings.

"What your pa owned needs to be divided between his children. It sounds fair to me." Callie's pa had owned a ranch, and she knew how bitterly upset she was that she hadn't been strong enough to hold it after he died. Seth and his brothers might well feel the same about this youngster coming in to demand they sell one-fourth.

"I'm Heath Kincaid." The boy nodded his head. "I won't be around long enough to bother anyone."

Callie didn't have to know much about the Kincaids to have a real good idea that this was going to bother everyone.

Anyhow, the boy was all bluster. He looked like he knew how to live off the land as well as any frontier child, but he wasn't up to doing it all the time.

He didn't need money; he needed a home. She had a cabin, or so Seth said. And she had a ranch, or so Seth said.

If there was a cabin, there was enough room for one more. If there wasn't, this youngster could sit around a campfire and tend Connor while she helped Seth build one.

"We'll be setting out for the Kincaid spread as soon as Seth gets back. Do you have anything we need to pick up? Clothes?"

The boy jerked his chin. "There are a few things. I stowed 'em under the back steps of the hotel. I'd asked after Gavin Kincaid, and there was a man who knew Seth was kin and he was staying here."

"We'll pick your things up, then. It's a long ride to the Kincaid place, so we may be sleeping on the trail tonight."

Heath had obviously been a long time traveling on precious little food and with few warm clothes. Considering what she'd heard about a Colorado winter, Callie couldn't help but think the boy had found his family at about the last possible minute.

As she tried to figure out what to say next, Seth strode into the dining room, spurs clinking, boots clomping.

"Done?" she asked him.

"We're ready."

Callie swallowed the last gulp of her coffee, gathered her strength and stood, doing her best not to wobble. "Seth, I'd like you to meet your brother Heath. He's done eating. Get Connor." She wasn't all that sure she could pick him up. Oh, she could. She'd grown up in Texas. She could do whatever had to be done. But right now she was glad not to push herself to the limit. "Let's go home."

While Bea settled in beside him, Jasper stared at the ceiling. He could feel the call to comfort. Silk. A fine house. Power.

On the other side, the love of a good woman, respect from honorable men, God.

But it was his money.

When he heard Bea's breathing even out, he slipped out of bed to walk into the next room, one of only four in this not-so-fine little shack.

He stared out the window.

It was his money.

Kincaid was staying in the hotel on the north side of town.

Jasper could walk there in a few minutes. He could get his hands on Seth Kincaid and find out everything he needed to know and be back before Bea woke up.

The money was bound to be at the Kincaid property if both Gilliland women were married into it, but Seth would give up the money to protect his wife and that little boy he was carrying around.

Jasper had no doubts about his ability to convince a man to divulge all his secrets. He lifted a box off the mantel and opened it.

His derringer.

It was his money.

He looked at the door to his bedroom and slowly, silently, lifted the derringer out of the box.

CHAPTER 8

"We've got a couple of hours before dark, Rafe." Julia Kincaid reached for her husband's hand, ignoring his groan of impatience.

A chill wind buffeted them where they stood by the barn door. It blew a strand of her red hair across her eyes, and she swept it aside and tucked it behind her ear. She wouldn't need her woolen bonnet in the cavern, so she had left it behind when she'd spotted Rafe riding in from checking the herd. She'd dashed out to catch him while he was still wearing his coat.

"The chores are done and the dinner is simmering and will be for another two hours. There are no killers in the cavern."

"That we know of." Rafe arched a brow at her, and she weaved her fingers between his and tugged.

"I've been really patient, Rafe. You know I have." And she'd loved helping to build her home. Rafe was the carpenter, but he'd talked with her about all the decisions, and she'd even helped with some of the finer woodwork. Mainly handing him things. "But we're already getting steady snowfall. When winter comes we'll have our hands full surviving in here without adding exploring."

She hoped to explore all winter, but she had to get him started first. And she'd found bad weather could be the goad behind getting almost anything done.

"I should ride out next time." Rafe closed both hands gently over her chilly fingers. "Seth needs time at his place to get settled."

"It's been wonderful building here and helping at Seth's." She had gotten so she appreciated Seth, too. He was full of stories about her cavern and she'd taken extensive notes. She'd written some more articles and sent them off and she'd started her book. She knew a lot, but she hadn't begun to learn everything. They were close enough to town that she got Rafe to take her in to check the mail quite often for a reply about her articles.

Seth went back and forth between the three cabins. Hers and Rafe's. Ethan and Audra's. His own—which was still a bit raw, but he could live in it.

"I wonder where his wife's gotten to." Rafe tightened his hold on her hand and lifted until he kissed her fingers.

"I hate thinking about her out in the wilderness somewhere." It distracted Julia from the gnawing need to explore that cavern. "Maybe hurt or lost. She should have been here by now."

Rafe was silent, and it drew Julia out of her worry and her impatience. "What are you thinking?"

"I shouldn't have let Seth go."

He wanted to take care of his little brother. She should have known. "He's gone before."

"Yes, but never for this long. Every time I worry that he might not . . ."

Into the silence, Julia said, "He might not come back."

Their eyes met and Rafe nodded. "He still doesn't think straight all the time."

"He's been pretty good. Mostly." They'd ridden over to his cabin early one morning and found him sleeping in his barn, cuddled up next to his horse. It was bitterly cold, and he'd said his horse was warmer than his cabin with his fireplace roaring. It might've been true, though it was just plain strange behavior.

"What about the nightmares?"

Julia hated to think of Seth alone fighting those dreams. He had one nearly every night when he stayed with them, and it stood to reason he had them at his place, too. "He might always have them, Rafe."

"It seems like he shouldn't be staying alone in his cabin until he can shake those ugly dreams about burning up."

"But you said he had to stay, to prove up on his homestead." Julia decided that since her husband was worrying about his brother, she'd just drag him toward the cave and hope he was distracted enough to not think up one of his endless excuses.

"He's been gone too long this time." Rafe's feet were moving.

Julia remained silent, not sure if this was cooperation . . . and not wanting to remind him if it wasn't.

"You were away more than a week once when Seth was still laid up with his broken leg. Ethan was gone almost that long. And two other times you left for three days."

"There's a trail from Rawhide to Denver, but it's a sidewinder, and not well marked. There's another one that angles west that some mule skinners use, and if she was determined to ride to Rawhide, she'd be coming on a freight wagon unless she's riding horseback. And probably she'd be on the most likely one to Colorado City. She could take a train to Denver, then a stagecoach to Colorado City, then find a wagon coming from there to Rawhide. But if she got to Colorado City and asked after the Kincaids, there are plenty of folks there who know us. They'd send her straight to Ethan's house."

"Seth's only been gone a week. It's too early to start worrying."

"It's never too early to start worrying about my little brother." Rafe quit walking and spun Julia around to face him. "And I've noticed you're walking toward the cavern."

She smiled.

He kissed her. When he was done, she was almost as distracted as Rafe.

"Let's go." He surprised her by walking on toward the cave entrance. "I've put it off long enough, and you've been a mighty nice wife not to nag at me."

Which Julia was pretty sure wasn't true. She'd been nagging real steadily. So it might mean Rafe wasn't listening to her at all when she talked about the cavern, which was annoying.

Rafe paused to look up at the sun. "The day's gettin' on. I don't think we can get to that room Seth was leading us to, but we can go to the one you're always talking about, with the fish on the wall."

"Really, Rafe?" She was so surprised she threw her arms around him.

"Yes, I've been dragging my heels because I just plain flat out don't like that cavern."

"You've been busy, too."

"I have for a fact. But I could have taken a few hours to go in there. I promised you. Today I start keeping that promise."

Julia had lanterns just inside the cave. She had rope and a stack of torches and paper and pencils to take notes. When the day finally came that Rafe would go down with her, she didn't want to give him time to change his mind.

Rafe had matches on hand as always. Julia did, too. They'd learned the hard way to plan ahead so they never got stuck in the dark. They set out and turned to go down the steeply sloped tunnel toward the hole Seth had fallen through so many years before.

"Can you believe this?" Rafe asked.

"Believe what?" Julia got a little shiver up her spine when her voice echoed.

"We've been in here, what? Five whole minutes? And no one has shot at us. No one has kidnapped you. No one has even jumped out of the dark tunnel to surprise us. It just don't seem natural."

Julia couldn't deny that the tunnel had given them a lot of trouble.

The tunnel was a tight one, and Rafe walked with his head bowed and his shoulders hunched to pass through.

They emerged into a big room. "Where's this fish?"

She pointed at the first one, high on the stone wall.

He walked to the fossil. "And the layers in these rocks. What do you think caused that?"

"Something else to study and write about." Which she found thrilling. "I think the fossil is some kind of shark."

The fossil was at eye level. She ran her hand over the clearly outlined jawbones. "I've studied fish fossils. The bone structure and the shape of the teeth are similar to a shark's. Look at the curved jaw and the triangular teeth. I can't be sure without more study, but if it's a shark, then what's he doing so far from the ocean? How did it get in here? How did any fish get in this deep? If it's a shark, that's interesting in itself. But any fish is very interesting."

"In one piece, too. No one was eating this fish for dinner." Rafe turned from the fossil and smiled at her. Gracious in admitting he'd been wrong. If she hadn't already been deeply in love with her husband, she'd have fallen right then.

"It had to swim up there." Her voice rose with the excitement and echoed back at her. "This cavern had to be full of water, up this high. How could that have happened?"

"Noah's flood. This is what's got you so excited. To write about floodwaters so high that they must have covered the whole earth."

"I believe God led me here, to this place, to the cavern, to write about that fossil."

"I can't look at that fish up there and not take you seriously."

Which was somewhat insulting—that he hadn't taken her seriously without proof, but Julia didn't let it bother her.

"And named after the discoverers?"

A light laugh echoed in the chamber. "I'm not going to insist they name it a Julia-fish-osaurus."

"I am." Rafe leaned down and kissed her soundly on the lips. "This is your discovery. I'll help you however you need me to, to get your papers written, to explore more, to get more things mailed off. I wonder if Seth or Ethan can draw worth a lick."

"I could try and chisel the fossil out of the wall, but where it is here is as important as what it is. Let me show you something." Julia pulled out a sheet of paper and went to the fish fossil and laid it over the fish's head. With her pencil she began drawing back and forth covering the paper, rubbing the skeleton's shape into it.

When she finished, Rafe looked closely at her rubbing, and the attention he was paying warmed her heart.

"Are there more fish fossils?"

Nodding, Julia said, "There is so much more, Rafe. I could write about the wonders of this one cave room for a year. I've already started a book. Can you see how exploring down here could last me a lifetime?"

"I can indeed. Now show me the rest." He switched his lantern to his left hand and reached out his right to her. She took it and pulled him between the stalagmites and fossils, talking as they went.

Julia smiled. "Thank you."

She tugged on his hand until he turned to face her. She stretched onto her toes to kiss him. His strong hand sliding around her waist drove out the shivers and the dark imaginings. "I love you, Rafe Kincaid. Thank you for understanding about this cavern."

"I think the cavern is finally safe. We'll be careful in unexplored caverns, in case the floors might be thin, but the rest of it is finally safe. No half-blind tracker thinking he can force some secret about treasure from you."

"A secret treasure I know nothing about." Julia wondered what fortune her father had taken and where he'd hidden it.

"No wandering, confused brother to scare us all to death."

"Well, except he's still confused and he's wandering right now."

"But not in the cavern," Rafe pointed out.

"No outlaws to threaten Audra." The outlaws had mentioned a boss, but Julia didn't remind Rafe of that.

"Now all we need is to get someone who can draw." Rafe's brow furrowed.

"We'll worry about that later. Let's go home. It's suppertime."

They walked out together, and Julia caught herself grinning to realize that the cavern was in fact safe now.

"Jasper, wake up." "Jasper, wake up."

The jab in Jasper's ribs sent him grabbing for the knife. It wasn't there, so he attacked and had things under control before he was fully awake.

And looked down to see his wife glaring at him—with his hands wrapped around her throat.

He shook his head to clear it of the lingering nightmares and let her go.

"You want to go after your money, then go. I can tell it's making you crazy."

"What happened? I thought you . . . someone . . . was stabbing me."

"You were dreaming. You were yelling about your treasure.

I tried to wake you up and you attacked me. I mean it, Jasper. Go if you've a mind to. I'm not going to sleep at night afraid my husband might use me to punch out his frustrations."

"I punched you?" Jasper's stomach lurched.

"No," she said grudgingly, as if she wanted him to feel guilty.

Jasper sat up on the edge of the bed. The dream swirled in and out of his thoughts. He'd been hunting. Searching everywhere. His money. It was driving him mad. He'd put the derringer back in the box last night. He'd done the right thing. Then in his dream he'd gone to the hotel to have it out with Kincaid.

Jasper had nothing to do but let the frustrated anger build.

"I thought I was over it." He buried his head in his hands. "When I saw Kincaid in town . . . it's been . . . been eating at me. All that money. The work of a lifetime. I'm going after it, Trix."

"What would a fortune do for you? A bigger house? Silk shirts? We don't dare draw attention to ourselves, not now that we know there are wanted posters out on you back in Houston. Living quietly is our best chance to be happy."

"I wouldn't hurt anyone, Bea. I'd sneak around. I lived by my wits in the Louisiana bayou country after my father kicked me out. I know how to slip around unseen and how to follow a trail."

"You haven't done any of that since you were a boy."

"I was good. I can do this, Bea. I can listen, get the lay of the land. Figure out where that money is, grab it, and come back. No one will be the wiser."

"I told you once, Jasper, you leave to go after that money, don't bother coming back." She turned away as if to go to sleep.

"You're my wife." He grabbed her shoulder and slammed her onto her back. Her hands came up to block her face and he saw fear.

Jasper thought of how he'd left her to a terrible life for years, when he should have married her. "I'm not going to hit you, Bea. How can you think that for a second?"

She lowered her hands. "You've never been like that. It was just a reflex. Plenty have, you know. In my old life a lot of men had plenty of evil in their hearts."

Jasper pulled her close. She didn't fight him.

"Bea, why don't you come with me?"

"No. I told you, I'm not going to live like that anymore. I want a decent life."

"Then come with me and keep me on the straight and narrow. I am not going to hurt anyone. I promise you that." Jasper suspected he was lying, but honestly, if Bea came along . . . "You can help me, darlin'. You can stop me if I stray."

"You can stop yourself."

Jasper kissed her long and deep. "Please. For better or for worse, you promised."

"For richer or for poorer, you promised that."

"Sure, but why not try and be richer if we can?" Jasper kissed her again and felt her love for him. He used that. "You can save me. You can be the judge of what we do."

"Jesus needs to save you, Jasper. That's not a job for a wife. You need to choose it for yourself."

"I do choose it." And Jasper thought maybe he did. "I want to live an honorable life."

It was true. He wanted that. But there was nothing wrong with an honorable life with some money.

"Come with me, Bea. Be my partner in this. We'll scout around, not hurt anyone. And I'll . . ." Jasper had a really good idea and it was the clincher that would lure her along. He wanted her at his side mainly because he wanted to come home to her. And if she threw in, then she wasn't cutting him out of his life. "I'll give a nice donation to the new church. A real nice donation. I don't want to live a life of luxury in a mansion. I promise you I'm going to go straight. I don't want to attract undue attention by having money I can't explain. But that money is mine. I'll do good with it, but I can't do it if I don't have it."

Bea was a smart woman. Too smart. Too used to lies. Untrusting as all get out. But she loved him and he knew it. She wanted to be with him.

"You'll really give some to the church?"

"I will. And you can help me decide how much. We won't make a huge donation right at first because that might raise suspicions. But we'll give enough to make fixing up the church easy. And we'll give steady for the rest of our lives."

There was a long silence and Jasper fought back the urge to kiss her again, to tempt her.

"All right. I'll come."

Jasper smiled and lowered his head.

Bea slapped a hand on his chest. "But we will do things my way. And when I say we go home, we go. You have to promise me that, Jasper."

"I'll swear it on a Bible if you say so, Bea. We'll try and get that money back and whether we succeed or fail, we'll do it honorably. I promise." A chill blew down Jasper's spine as if a window had been left open. What happened to a man who swore an oath on a Bible when he knew he might not keep his promise? God was supposed to be forgiving. Jasper decided then and there he'd be testing that when this was over. And maybe, just maybe Jasper could keep that oath. The only thing he knew for sure was swearing it wouldn't stop him from doing things however he saw fit.

He'd find his money, get this hunger for it settled, then make his peace with God.

When he returned with his money, he'd come as a man of faith and settle gracefully into the life Trixie wanted so bad.

CHAPTER 9

There was a sort of ring around Callie.

Seth could almost see the donut. Callie was the donut hole and then there was the donut, a ring around her he couldn't enter. But he was right outside the donut, leading the little band of traveling Kincaids when the trail was narrow. Riding alongside Callie when the trail was wide, ready to jump in if she collapsed.

Every time he got a little too close—say into the eatin' part of the donut—she'd snarl at him. He didn't mind that so much, kinda fun, but he could see being mad tired her out.

He said, "A donut would taste good about now."

"What?" Callie asked from behind him.

He turned and smiled. "Nothing."

She muttered, but he didn't want to know what she was saying so he didn't ask.

They set a steady pace. Him mostly in the lead, carrying Connor on his back. Callie in the donut hole. Heath bringing up the rear. Heath was young, but he was a steady hand. Gavin Kincaid had a knack, it seemed, for forcing his children to grow up young.

They didn't travel as fast as Seth would've gone, but then Seth rarely rode his horse without risking his neck. Riding was way more fun if there was a little danger. He had a baby on his back so maybe it was time to be a little more careful.

He blanched and looked over his shoulder at Connor. He could just see the top of the little guy's head, covered with a cap. "When you're old enough to ride, you'd better not risk your neck."

"What?" Callie's voice pulled his eyes on past Connor to see her watching him.

"Nothing." He smiled and turned back, facing forward.

She muttered again.

He didn't ask.

The trail wound around the base of a mountain or two, sometimes they'd climb awhile, then descend, and sometimes they'd switch back and forth as they went up and down. Heavy woods on both sides of the trail, some with branches that reached out to grab a person. Boulders higher than a horse to wind around. If the trail was wide enough, he'd drop back to ride beside Callie, not right beside her. She was the donut hole, after all. But close.

The wind picked up and snow began sifting down. It fell light for this time of the year. In October they'd had some snow almost every day, but they hadn't gotten any of the heavy snowfalls of winter yet. But it was time. Seth saw the darkened clouds and he felt the weight of the oncoming weather. He loved riding in a blizzard. It'd be hard on Callie and Connor, though.

A glance at her showed a jaw clenched to bite down on pain. She stared down at her pommel and didn't notice him looking. And Callie struck him as a noticing kind of woman.

The trail widened again and Seth dropped back to Callie's flank—well, her horse's flank—well, her flank, too. Shaking his head, Seth didn't think it was a good idea to focus much on Callie's flank. "Heath."

Callie jerked her chin up, and Seth knew she'd been dozing in the saddle.

The boy came alongside Seth. He sat a horse well, held the reins like he'd done his share of it, kept the packhorses in line. Heath had watchful eyes like anyone who'd lived in a hard land. The ones who didn't watch were all dead.

Seth dropped back farther, leaving Callie out of listening range—taking into consideration that she probably had razor-sharp hearing. She did everything else with unusual skill.

Speaking low, Seth said, "Callie's about all in. Keep an eye on her. If she looks like she's falling, give a shout."

Heath gave Seth a look that had no ounce of good nature in it, but the boy understood.

"I'd thought about sleeping out tonight." A stiff gust of wind cut down Seth's neck as if goading him to hurry. "But with this weather, we might see a blizzard by morning. I want to get to my brother's cabin."

"I can keep going as long as you can," Heath said with a frown.

"Don't worry, we'll figure this out. You've got a claim on what Pa left."

The kid huffed at that.

Seth didn't blame the boy, although it sure wasn't any of Seth's fault. "We'll push on late." Then he added with a whisper, "If my wife doesn't fall off her horse."

Seth had to fight back a smile to think of the damage Callie would do if she heard him say such an insulting thing.

Heath jerked his chin in a gesture Seth was starting to recognize. The boy wasn't one for unnecessary chatter.

Seth kicked his horse and caught up with Callie just as the trail narrowed. He was glad of an excuse to not have to talk to her because he was afraid his worry would show. As he passed, her hand shot out and grabbed his horse's reins. Then she shifted her grip to his arm.

"Something wrong, honey?"

A fire-breathing dragon was riding on horseback.

"I haven't fallen off my horse since I was six months old," Callie said. Her fingernails sank so deep into his arm, he was afraid he'd have claw marks cut into his skin—and he was wearing a buckskin jacket. "And I didn't fall off the horse then. I just hadn't gotten to ride until that age."

Razor-sharp ears for a fact.

"If it wasn't for the blood loss, I'd have never suggested such a thing. I apologize." Seth ran those two words through his mind a few times: I apologize. He needed to get comfortable with them because he had a feeling he was going to spend the rest of his life saying them with some frequency. "Now if you'll take your pretty little claws out of my skin, I'll lead the way."

She snarled at him. Claws and maybe fangs. She was a regular little wildcat. Marrying her had to be the sanest thing he'd ever done.

"This trail divides ahead and I can either lead or spend the ride hollering at you when you pick wrong." Seth grinned at her. He knew he shouldn't. She wasn't all that fond of him. But he liked her more every minute. He'd've never been content with a woman who didn't terrify him at least a little. That wouldn't have been any fun at all.

"We need to take a break. Connor needs a dry diaper by now."

"The night clerk showed me the way of diaper changing." Seth sure wished she'd be impressed. He'd slept beside her long enough last night that he wanted her to like him something fierce. "You want me to do it?"

"No. Not this time. We need a break, anyway." She let go.

Seth chafed at the delay, but he yelled, "Hold." Then he swung off his horse, and by the time he'd fetched the satchel tied on the back of Callie's horse, Heath was leading their horses into the woods and tying them to a low branch that had protected a bit of windswept grass from being buried in snow. The horses fell to cropping grass with a sharp crunch. The wind gusts were picking up speed and the snow was coming faster.

Callie made short work of the diaper change to keep the little boy from being exposed to the cold more than a second longer than necessary. Then she produced bread and jerky for the youngster, who ate it like he was starving.

Which he probably was.

Seth was ashamed of himself for not noticing. Callie took a few steps away and put a tree between herself and the menfolk.

Seth didn't like it. He walked over to see what she was up to and his little wildcat snarled again.

He didn't run. He'd never given much thought to how babies ate, but it stood to reason.

"Get out of here." Callie shifted a blanket around so she was covered from neck to knee.

"How are you feeling?" He wanted to stay. He'd never seen anything as natural and loving as the way Callie cuddled Connor to her breast.

"I'm feeling like I about got skinned by four armed gunmen yesterday. I'm feeling like I'm short about half the blood I oughta have. I'm feeling like if you don't get out of here, I'll show you how I feel instead of telling you. Go on now." She'd said the last in a kinder voice.

"Connor's a lucky little boy to have you for a ma. I'm going to try and make him glad he's got me for a pa, Callie. I'll do my best to be a good husband, too."

Her lips turned down and she looked away, to stare down at the completely swaddled baby. "All we can do is see what happens, Seth. I don't trust you. That's what it all amounts to. It's not that I don't want to trust you. I've just got too much sense."

Seth had to admit that spoke well of her.

"Now go stay with that hungry boy. And give him more jerky before he decides to eat the horses."

They were back on the trail in a few minutes with Connor strapped on Seth's back again. He got ahead of Callie, but still not real far ahead. The donut thing was still working on him. The gray clouds kept getting darker, blotting out the sun. The wind swirled and seemed to come from all directions.

Snow began to build up on the trail in spots. Mostly it scudded along, the trail swept clean by the wind. But a sheltered spot every now and again had a healthy coating of snow. Between the heavy woods and the mountains, the sun was only a midday thing along this trail and they'd barely gotten started by midday. Even when the sun wasn't covered by clouds, it dipped behind the mountain early. What little light the sun cast through this storm barely kept the world dark gray instead of black.

Seth pulled Connor around in front of him to tuck the blankets over his head. The baby swatted at Seth, and when Seth pulled the blanket up, the baby gave a deep-throated chuckle. Seth covered the boy again. The little flailing hands broke loose of the blanket and Seth lifted it. The boy's wild blue eyes met Seth's and they both laughed.

Seth played at that for a long time, enjoying his child more than he'd ever imagined. Finally Connor tired of the game and his eyes grew heavy. Seth pulled him close until Connor's chubby cheek rested against Seth's chest, pressed right against his heart. It hurt in a way so sweet and good, Seth couldn't understand what he was feeling. But he didn't tuck the sleeping boy away in the blankets and into the pack for a long while.

Finally Seth gently wrapped the baby, making sure all his toes and fingers were protected from the growing cold, and put him back in the pack.

When the trail widened, Seth dropped back beside Callie and called to his newly discovered brother, "You come up closer."

He waited until Heath rode within easy earshot.

"It's suppertime now, but we've got about three more hours to ride. Longer if the going gets rough." A blizzard definitely qualified as rough going. The snow kept coming. Wind whipped through the trees, whistling and taunting, cutting through their clothes. "It's getting colder by the minute."

"It ain't so bad." Heath said it like he was calling Seth a weakling.

Since he wasn't one, it didn't bother him overly.

"We have to make it to Ethan's to beat this weather. It'll be the middle of the night when we get there. We've still got a long, cold ride ahead of us. We could look for shelter and sleep on the trail. With a big fire it'd be all right. What should we do?"

Heath and Callie looked between themselves and him.

"Connor's gone to sleep." Callie reached over and adjusted the blankets around Connor. "We need to bundle him up tighter, then I say we push on."

Seth wasn't surprised that his wife voted for whatever was hardest, especially since she was the one who was closest to collapsing.

She added, "Pass out some more jerky. And I've got apples in my saddlebag and some biscuits." Callie looked at Heath and their gaze held. Seth felt left out by that look.

Heath jerked his chin. "I'm fine."

Callie said, "Seth, hand out the supper. We can eat while we ride. Let me have a few minutes to change Connor and then he'll have his supper on horseback, too."

It was the work of a minute to feed his family and get Connor's diaper dried. They moved on down the trail, and after a bit Seth judged Callie to be done feeding the baby, so

Seth reclaimed the tyke. Before long he had Connor wrapped tight and sleeping on his back again.

A bitter cold hour passed. When a wider spot presented itself, Seth rode alongside Callie. Heath was right behind them.

He hoped to be at Ethan's by midnight, but as the night got colder and darker, the sky unbroken by stars or moonlight, the wind began to howl. It called out to something wild in Seth, and he wanted to turn into the heavy forest and go toward that sound.

"It's like wolves. I want to howl back."

"What?" Callie said, turning in the saddle.

Seth shrugged, unable to explain. "Nothing."

Shaking her head, she kicked her horse and got ahead of him. He fought against whatever called him into the woods, choosing instead to keep up with his wife. But he was stirred up inside, anxious and excited. He looked into the woods and it took him back to another place, a roaring place. Pain in his back. Pain everywhere. Heat burning his whole body. Falling. Fire.

He saw the dance of flames in the forest and knew he could get warm. He'd lead his family there. Care for them in the wild. His hands tightened on the reins to head for the fire. Then instead of warmth, it was flaring up. Dancing right in his face. Racing for him like a river of fire. His sleeve leaped into flames. Rafe! Where was Rafe? He needed Ethan. He needed help.

A limb slapped him in the face and the fire vanished. Shaken, he looked around. How long had he been gone? He looked right into Heath's eyes, and the boy was watching him.

"You need something?" Heath asked.

"No." Seth wondered what had prompted the question. Had he made some sound? Glancing toward Callie, he noticed she hadn't looked at him, so he probably hadn't said anything out loud. He stared into the woods again, wondering what was real and what wasn't.

Then a particularly sharp slash of wind cleared his thoughts. He thought of a fire, but this time at Ethan's house, in front of the hearth. A warm bed and sleeping next to Callie again. That tamed the wild in him—or maybe it was better to admit that it woke up a whole different kind of wild. And it made him want to stay right near her.

The hour grew late and the cold became crushing. When they had maybe an hour left to go, he was riding alongside Callie and a sudden move drew his attention.

He had just enough time to catch her when she slid off her saddle.

He hauled her into his arms and held her tight. Tying her horse onto his pommel, Seth noticed Callie's breathing was regular. She was just sleeping—he hoped. But it was a deeper sleep than he liked.

"She all right?" Heath's voice drew Seth around. For a long moment his eyes met Heath's. Seth felt a strong connection to this youngster who looked so much like him.

Brothers.

Seth wasn't a very good brother; he knew that. He'd scared Ethan and Rafe half to death. He'd as good as killed his ma. Maybe he'd even been the reason his father had lived two lives.

"Were you a better son to him than I was?" he asked Heath.

With a shrug, Heath said, "Not good enough to keep him from always going back to you."

A humorless laugh escaped Seth's lips. "And I wasn't good enough to keep him from going back to you, neither.

"I keep checking Connor. I don't want him wrapped so tight he smothers, but I have to keep his whole body covered too, even his face. Now that I'm holding Callie, I'll have trouble doing that. If he'd get a hand out of the blankets, I wouldn't be able to see he'd done it until he was frostbit. Would you be able to carry him?"

"Sure, I can carry him." Heath did a fair job of lifting the boy out of the pack. His hands trembled from the cold.

"I'll take him back if you need me to."

"I can do it." Now Heath wanted to fight him for the job.

"Thanks. Stay close. We don't want to get separated in this storm." Seth turned forward and rode on into the howling night, his wife sleeping in his arms. His son asleep, cuddled by his uncle. His whole surprise family riding along together.

He couldn't wait to tell Ethan all about it.

CHAPTER 10

The wind drove pellets of slashing ice at Seth. He pulled up his kerchief to protect his face and checked Callie every few minutes to make sure she was covered.

The horses trudged through snow a foot deep in places, two feet in others. When they reached a stretch blown clean, the going became faster but the wind meaner. Seth kept his eyes on the trail ahead, afraid he'd miss the turnoff to the ranch. He ignored the howling wolves calling to him, the occasional flickers of fire deep in the woods telling him the wild was dangerous and reckless and he should come and join the fun.

Shaking off the notion, he kept his focus on the task at hand. Yet nothing looked right; the snow and wind blinded him and obscured everything.

He twisted in the saddle and saw Heath barely visible in the growing blizzard.

"Stay close!"

Callie didn't stir when he shouted. Not good.

The trail widened. He slowed until Heath, cradling Connor in his arms, drew up and rode alongside Seth. Heath looked mighty steady for one so young.

Seth looked at Heath. "We need to pick up speed. I'm worried about Callie. She's been deep asleep for too long."

Heath's blue eyes flashed with determination.

"I know the horses are tired, but we have to push on." A sudden swirl of wind opened up his visibility and he saw a fork in the trail. Seth pointed. "We go that way. It's not far now, mostly downhill."

He kicked his tired horse, and the dapple gray mare perked up her head as if she recognized that they were nearing home. The slope was treacherous with drifted snow, though it helped to be headed downward. He trusted his horse now more than his own eyes. Let the wind talk to him. It didn't matter so long as he let his horse take him home.

Seth wasn't sure how much later it was when the little mountain mustang began trotting. Finally, through the blowing snow, Seth could make out Ethan's ranch house ahead.

The horse began heading toward the barn, but Seth tightened his hold on the reins and guided the animal straight to the front-porch steps. Everything was dark—house, barn, bunkhouse. But Ethan would be there and he'd help. He'd get everyone settled and the howling would go away.

"Let's get inside." Seth swung down off his horse. "Get the baby up here."

Heath dismounted with uneven movements, and Seth saw how stiff and cold the boy was. He hated demanding so much but didn't have the strength to do more than goad them on.

The horses stood motionless, their heads hanging. Seth had to see to them as soon as he got everyone else inside. He reached the steps and tripped, nearly dropping Callie. The bottom step was buried in snow and he'd misjudged it.

Heath's hand shot out and steadied him.

"Thanks," Seth said. Now that he was home, he realized just how exhausted he was. He climbed three steps that felt like ten and pounded on the door with the side of his fist.

"Ethan!" Seth shouted, and Callie didn't even stir. No one stayed asleep when someone was shouting in her ear. The ride had been too much for her.

Seth tried the door, knowing Ethan would throw the heavy bar at night. He pounded harder, hoping the noise carried over the shrieking wind.

The door jerked open so suddenly he stumbled forward. Ethan, in pants and an unbuttoned shirt, a rifle in hand, took one look and said, "Get in here!" He caught Seth's arm and dragged him inside.

"No, take her. I've got to see to the horses."

"Shut up," Ethan snapped, then looked past him to Heath. "You, too. Get inside."

Ethan's ranch hand, Steele, came out of the pelting snow, armed, his eyes sharp. He saw Seth. "I've got the horses." Quickly he gathered them and left for the barn.

"There's a baby." Seth jerked his head at Heath.

Ethan shook his head, swung the door shut against the

brutal weather, then turned to take care of Heath and his burden. Seth headed straight for the fireplace with Callie.

Dropping to his knees, Seth lowered Callie to the floor near the glowing embers of the fire. He almost dived for the woodbox beside the hearth.

Ethan blocked him. "I'll build up the fire. Get her unwrapped."

"I'll get something hot for them to drink." Audra's voice gave Seth a desperate kind of comfort.

Seth looked up at his sister-in-law. "Food too, if you've got it."

She nodded and hurried to the kitchen.

Ethan took the bundle from Heath's arms and unwrapped Connor, who yelped. "You took a baby out in this storm?"

"Wasn't storming when we set out," Seth said. Thankfully Connor sounded strong and healthy. With a huge sigh of relief, Seth turned to Callie. He removed her coat. She had her hat tugged low and he had a time pulling it loose. Her dark hair spilled, the ends of it frozen, clicking on the floor.

"She's been too cold for too long. She shouldn't be asleep."

Audra dropped to her knees beside Seth. "Get her closer to the fire. Is the baby all right? Ethan, do you need help with him?"

Seth looked at Connor. The boy waved his arms and slapped at Ethan, wide awake and cheerful. Ethan tested the little boy's fingers and toes for a chill while the tyke was whacking him and grinning.

There was talking, rapid and loud as Ethan and Audra asked questions. Heath must have answered them and it was all about getting warm, none of the more interesting information

Seth had to share. For now he could only concentrate on tending to his wife.

"Get her boots off, Seth. We need to get her feet warm." Audra jumped up and vanished. Seth saw Ethan, with Connor on his hip, helping get Heath's coat off. "Callie thought of coats, food too. She saved us." Seth got one of her boots off and nearly fell over backward. His fingers were numb and his thinking might've been a little numb, as well.

"This is Callie?" Ethan asked. "Your wife?"

Seth nodded as he dragged her other boot free and tossed it aside. He noticed Steele shoulder his way past everybody with an armload of wood. He stoked the fire, then went to the kitchen.

Callie had good color in her toenails. "Her feet aren't frozen. She's just exhausted from all the blood she lost yesterday." Seth hoped it was just exhaustion.

"Blood she lost? What in the world happened?" Audra was back with her arms full of blankets. Ethan grabbed a few of them, while Audra knelt and spread one over Callie.

"She saved a stage from being robbed. Fought off four gunmen, mostly by herself."

"She was shot?" Audra caught Seth's arm, and he shook her off to tuck the blanket snuggly around Callie. It was then he noticed her face, which was ashen.

"No, but she got cut up. Splinters from the stage almost sliced her to ribbons."

Kneeling closer to Callie, Audra reached a hand out and touched a deep scratch that seemed to glow red on Callie's forehead. With a gasp Audra found one of the sets of stitches. She looked up at Heath. She must've checked him for injuries and been satisfied because she said, "I've got soup heating up. Are you hungry?"

The young'un nodded.

"I'll bring it in by the fire." Audra jumped up and left the room.

Ethan came around by Callie's head and crouched down, Connor in his arms. Seth was at her feet. The brothers' eyes met across the length of her still body. "Sounds like she just needs rest and coddling and plenty of good food," Ethan said. "Maybe we should let her sleep until she wakes up instead of trying to feed her."

Seth felt some of the terror subside as his big brother made decisions. Ethan was no hand at giving orders like Rafe, but he ran this ranch well. He was a steady man.

It finally settled in his mind that they'd made it. He'd escaped the howling of the blizzard wolves that called to him. And the flickering of the taunting fire he knew was nothing but a mirage. He'd fought it and made it to the warmth of the ranch. To controlled fire. He was lured by fire and he hated it. But this was Colorado in October.

A man had to make his peace with fire.

Callie's feet were well wrapped. Her breathing was steady. Her hair was melting.

Seth sagged sideways and rested his back against the warm stone hearth.

"So tell me who you brought with you, Seth." Ethan looked down at Connor first, then over to Heath. It struck Seth that if Heath qualified as a wise man and Audra and Ethan as shepherds, they were about one burro and a couple of sheep away from being a Nativity scene.

Connor chuckled. But Seth knew for a fact the kid could cry up a storm, no silent night for this little one.

Heath sat down close to the fire on the far side of the hearth opposite Seth. He stretched out his hands toward the warmth.

"Meet your brother, Ethan," Seth said.

"What?" Ethan looked at the baby.

"Not him." Seth realized he had a lot of explaining to do. "Heath. Turns out our pa had another family tucked away."

"What?" Ethan said again, his tone switching to anger.

Heath looked up, anger in his eyes. "You're the family he had tucked away, not us."

"Tucked away?" Ethan's eyes cut to Seth.

Heath shook his head and then turned back to face the fire.

"I'll explain later," Seth said, feeling the weight of his exhaustion.

Ethan lifted Connor to eye level. "And who is this little guy?"

Seth chuckled then. "Well, truth is, I kinda had a family tucked away, too."

The heat of the fire, the hard ride home in the bitter cold, the effort it took to resist the temptation of the wild wind, the stress of having a family he couldn't remember—all of it caught up with Seth, and he sagged back and let the long, long day end.

CHAPTER 11

Callie shoved her eyes open by pure force. She stared right into the wild blue eyes of the man she'd been hunting for a year. Of course it hadn't all been spent hunting. She'd taken some time off to give birth and raise her son to a few months of age and bury her pa.

"Where'd I put my gun?" It sounded like growling, and that probably described her attitude pretty well.

Seth reached down and rested his hand on her forehead. "Mornin', honey."

Callie felt around and found no fire iron, so she decided to leave payback for later. "Where are we?"

"We're at my brother Ethan's house."

The last couple of days came rushing back to her.

The shootout. Bleeding—she'd done a lot of bleeding. A whole lot. Raising a hand, she thought to check the stitches in her scalp. The tiny movement made her left arm hurt so bad she had to bite back a howl of pain. She quit any unnecessary moving.

Her runaway husband was still there, and still just as annoying. And blast the man, he was as good-looking as ever. Better in fact. Clean-shaven now, unlike after the war. And he'd been skin and bones then. He was still too thin, yet it wasn't as scary. His hair was cut short instead of being long and shaggy as a buffalo. She'd never really seen how sharp his cheekbones were, or how full his lips, or how square his jaw. That had all been masked by his beard and his raving.

"And there was a surprise brother?" Callie was finding it hard to concentrate over the pain.

"I'd never seen him before yesterday."

"So they weren't just a surprise to me, then?"

"A mighty big surprise to us both."

Which reminded Callie that her husband had forgotten her. So the man had a mighty surprising day all around.

"Are you sure? You forgot me. Maybe you forgot your little brother, too."

"Nope." Then Seth hesitated and looked over her shoulder. "We'd never seen hide nor hair of him before yesterday, had we?"

"No, that boy was a surprise to all of us." Another, less annoying face appeared over her husband-the-abandoner's shoulder. A pretty blond woman who looked like a stiff wind would blow her away.

Turning back to Callie, Seth said, "I was sure of that before

I asked. It's just that these days I've sort of started doubting all the things I'm sure about."

"Howdy, Callie." Audra peeked around Seth's shoulder. "I'm Audra. Ethan's wife. Which means we're sisters. You've been asleep since Seth brought you here late last night."

Audra, who looked younger than Callie, said, "Step aside and let me see her, Seth."

"Audra, give me a minute to—ow!" Seth jumped and turned to the woman. "Why'd you pinch me?"

Audra the Dandelion Fluff Woman gave Seth a look that made him stand up from where he sat on the bed and step back. Then, sounding as sweet as sugar, she said, "Go on. Let the poor woman have a minute to wake up."

Seth stepped around so he hovered behind Audra.

Then Callie sat bolt upright. "Connor!" The movement clawed pain through every joint and muscle. Her head gave a sickening throb. Her stomach swirled, and for a second Callie fought against emptying her stomach. Her stomach was empty, which helped her control her collywobbles. "Where's my son?"

"He's fine," Audra said. "He's sitting at the breakfast table with Ethan and my two little ones."

Agony didn't stop Callie from swinging her legs toward the edge of the bed. "I have to see for myself that he's all right."

"You have to stay in bed. You've got a fever." The dandelion rested surprisingly strong hands on her shoulders.

Or maybe Audra wasn't surprisingly strong. Maybe, instead, Callie was surprisingly weak. "I need to go to Connor."

The heat of her skin hit her as soon as Audra said the word *fever*. Callie struggled against Audra.

"Help me, Seth. We need to keep her here."

Seth rushed around to the other side of the bed, and there was no resisting his strength. His hands replaced Audra's, and Callie found herself flat on her back. Seth sat on the bed beside her, frowning, watching every breath she took. A pillow that must be goose down felt good on her throbbing head.

"No, please. My son." With every word Callie's voice lost power. Wrenching against Seth's hold sent pain through her shoulder until it could have been on fire. The only clear thought in Callie's head was to get to Connor. To assure him she was still there to care for him. The death of Callie's parents rushed into her thoughts as if drawn there by her fever. It had hurt so badly. She could not do that to her son. "I'm all he's got. I have to go to him. He'll be so afraid."

"Audra, go get him. Please." Seth didn't let go.

Tears burned salt into Callie's eyes. She couldn't stay in bed when Connor might be terrified, confused.

Audra stood. "I'll be right back with Connor."

"I'm from Texas," Callie said as Audra disappeared out the door.

"You mean you're tough enough to get out of this bed?" Seth asked.

"I mean I'm tough enough to do anything I have to do."

"I like having a tough wife. It's gonna be fun being married to you."

Callie narrowed her eyes at her polecat husband. Her good-looking polecat who was grinning at her like he didn't have a brain in his head.

And she'd married him, so what did that say about her?

"Audra, where are you with Connor?" He raised his voice, not afraid to call for help when he needed it.

"Connor tipped a plate of food onto himself." Audra's voice wafted up the stairs. "Ethan has him in the sink, giving him a bath. I'll be a few minutes."

Seth was going to have to face his wife all on his own. He lifted one hand from Callie's left shoulder. He'd been careful to avoid bumping the deep puncture wound on that arm, but even the least little touch had to hurt.

She showed no signs of getting up or attacking. In fact, he was sorely afraid she might hit him with something even worse—salt water. Tears threatened to roll down out of her eyes, and he couldn't stand it.

Seth rested the hand not busy restraining her on Callie's cheek. The woman was battered for a fact, and Seth knew a fever was a mighty serious thing.

After all, hadn't a fever just killed Audra's husband a few months back?

He brushed her hair back off her forehead and the silk of it tickled a memory Seth couldn't quite bring into focus. He had touched her hair before, though, he knew it. Of course they'd had a son together. He reckoned there'd been a chance to touch her hair mixed up in that somewhere.

God, please protect and heal my wife.

The prayer startled Seth into straightening from where he leaned close to his pretty wife.

It wasn't a prayer exactly. Instead it was almost a . . . a still, small voice inside him. It seemed to come from the same place he'd heard the cavern call to him and the storm last night and the wolves. It was almost like God gave him the prayer, rather than Seth giving one to God. It was a wonderful, powerful feeling. On the other hand, Seth wasn't sure having more voices inside him was a good thing. But if one of those voices was God, maybe it was all right. Maybe he'd better listen.

He tried to search for that voice again, tried to pray on his own, and he stumbled over it and turned back to Callie before he could look for his soul and instead find emptiness. Or maybe find so many fears they amounted to madness.

"You had a fever when I first met you." Callie spoke quietly. Neither crying nor attacking. Seth decided he needed to pray more and longer and harder—if he could just remember how.

"Is that why I don't remember things?"

Callie shrugged and her shoulder lifting under his hand was a wonder to him. He had a wife. A beautiful wife.

"Why do I have a fever?"

A sick wife.

"Are my wounds infected? Is that what's causing the fever, Seth?" She was losing that killer tone to her voice.

Much as he didn't want his wife to be killing mad at him, he thought it was a bad sign.

Seth inspected the deepest cut on her forehead. "It looks a little red, but probably just from being sore. I don't think it's infected. The puncture wound on your arm is the worst injury." She had a hundred small scrapes that added up to a lot of pain and blood loss, but nothing fatal.

"My arm feels terrible." Her arm rose about an inch before she quit moving. She had on a long-sleeved flannel nightgown.

"It's the worst of your injuries." Seth, pursuing only medical interests, unbuttoned the gown. Callie didn't seem to notice, which was probably best for Seth, survival-wise.

The row of little white buttons on the soft white flannel distracted him for a few seconds and he sort of lost focus on his purpose and unfastened a few more of them than was strictly necessary. He caught himself and returned to doctoring. "It's got a bandage tied around it to protect the stitches."

Easing the wide neck of her nightgown aside, baring her unbelievably smooth, lovely shoulder, he squelched a few non-doctoring thoughts and reached for the bandage high on her arm. As gently as possible he untied the knotted strip of cloth.

"Stitches?" Callie frowned. "I've never had stitches before."

"Me neither." Seth hated the thought.

"Yes, you have. I helped pull the threads out."

Seth looked up and saw how flushed she was. Annoyed at him for forgetting something else important. And so sick. Her eyes had a watery, glazed look. He leaned forward and kissed the red apple of her cheek slowly, gently, alarmed at the waves of heat coming off of her.

God, help her. Heal her. Make me smart enough to know what to do.

The prayer came again from that hollow place inside him. He took a second to think that maybe, just maybe, God was inside him somewhere. Looking for his soul.

Seth hoped fervently God could locate it.

Pulling the bandage aside gently in case it was stuck to her arm, he uncovered the puncture wound. It was red and angry looking. The six stitches looked painful with the swollen skin acting like it wanted to bust the threads apart.

"Did I get shot?" Cassie studied the ugly wound without mentioning that Seth had partially disrobed her. Yep, she was sick all right.

Seth remembered very clearly that he'd told her the answer to her question already. He'd have pointed that out if he wasn't bent on sweet-talking her into being his wife in all ways.

"No, you didn't get shot. But the stagecoach was real shot up. There was a piece of wood, a big splinter that stabbed you here. The doctor put in some stitches."

"Seth, it's so ugly." Callie looked away from her wound and stared at him, her black eyes brimming with tears. "I'm so ugly."

Her lower lip trembled. Seth thought she looked ridiculously young. "You're the prettiest thing I've ever seen, honey."

He ran his hand into her hair, mindful of the stitched-up places on her scalp. She looked like she'd lost a fight with a whole barn full of wildcats, and she was still so beautiful he could hardly draw a breath.

The fever had made her hair hot. He left off touching her, though it wasn't easy, and reached for the basin of cool water Audra had on the bedside table. Wringing the cloth out thoroughly, he folded it and rested it on her forehead.

A sigh of relief escaped her lips and her eyes drifted closed. Seth wished she'd sleep some more. The healing power of sleep.

He thought of his nightmare. Sleep had been a torment for him most of his life.

"Here's Connor." Audra came in, and Callie's eyes snapped open and went to the chunky little guy.

Callie reached out her arms toward him, and a tiny gasp of pain, quickly suppressed, escaped her lips. "Let me have him."

Seth doubted very much Callie could hold the husky boy, but with all her Texas gumption she'd never admit anything was too much for her. He went to Audra, whisked Connor out of her hands, and carried him around the bed to sit beside Callie, keeping Connor's weight yet within reaching distance.

With a trembling hand Callie reached for Connor.

"Papapapa!" Connor dove at Callie. Seth almost lost him, but managed to keep the boy from pouncing on his wounded ma.

Seth moved so Connor was sitting right beside Callie. Her arm went around the baby's waist. "Hi, little guy. I'm sorry I'm not taking care of you today."

Connor laughed and slapped Callie on the belly a few times before Seth could stop him.

"You can see he's fine, Callie. Let him go back to playing with Maggie." Audra came around the bed to fetch him. "She threw a fit when I took him away."

With a few more touches as if to be sure he was there, touches too feeble to go with his fiery little wife, Callie nodded and Audra scooped Connor up.

"I'm going to get some broth for you." Audra settled Connor on her hip like an old hand at mothering, which she was.

"And some water, please."

"We've got some here beside the basin." Seth wanted to kick himself for not thinking of it before Callie had to ask. "I'll help you get a drink."

"You need to rest." Audra headed for the door. She looked back just as she stepped into the hall. "We're going to take very good care of you, Callie. You'll be up and about in no time."

Audra was gone, and Callie looked after her son as if it might be the last time she saw him. Considering Callie's fearlessness, it about scared Seth into an early grave.

"We need to make sure you drink plenty of water." He slid

an arm behind Callie's shoulders and raised her with aching slowness just enough for her to drink.

She took several sips and then stopped. "Enough. I'm afraid I'll be sick."

Seth lowered her back to the bed. Her eyes seemed to lose focus; her lids fell closed as if they weighed ten pounds apiece and her body went limp.

It was the most frightening thing Seth had ever seen, and that included watching his own flesh burn.

"Audra!"

Seth wasn't sure how he sounded, but it must've been bad because footsteps pounded up the stairs. Audra was running by the time she got in the room. She looked at Callie, then at Seth.

"She passed out. I think she's hotter than she was, too."

That might just seem so because Seth had gone stone-cold with terror. He thought of his cave and wanted it desperately. Things made sense down there. The empty part of himself wasn't so noticeable in the pitch-dark.

He didn't have to face hard things. When life got to bothering him, Seth had always run to ground in that cave. He knew that place better than anyone. That gave him power.

Then he saw himself knowing all the holes he could sneak into and never be found. For the first time ever, that struck him as being cowardly. It was like a rabbit hole. A mighty big rabbit hole. And he was mighty small thinking like a scared rabbit and hiding from trouble when he had a wife and child to care for.

"We have to get her fever down." Audra came to Seth's side of the bed. "You have to go, Seth. I'm going to give her a cool bath, and it's not fitting that you should be here."

"I'm her husband! I can be here." Seth knew even as he said it that Callie wouldn't like it one bit if he helped undress her. Only being so feverish that she couldn't tell what was going on had kept her from objecting when he'd checked her arm.

"Go, Seth. Please. You don't even remember her. It's not fitting that you should help me bathe her." A crash came from downstairs, followed by childish laughter and a dismayed shout from Ethan that echoed up the stairs.

"Go save Ethan. I promise I'll call if I need help."

Hesitating, Seth looked at his deathly still wife.

"Close the door on your way out, Seth."

Seth felt like he was tearing flesh when he turned away from Callie. Worried sick, he went to the door. Looking back he saw Audra wringing out the cloth Seth had used on Callie's forehead. His wife was in good hands. But he couldn't help but feel like he was turning his back on her for the second time. And that felt unforgivable.

CHAPTER 12

Seth walked down the stairs feeling as if he was leaving his wife on the battlefield. He stepped into the kitchen, and it was full of people Seth hadn't even known existed a few months ago. That included everyone but Ethan. Connor, Ethan's girls, and Heath.

Seth looked at Ethan and thought maybe Ethan was reading his mind. Life was changing too fast.

"How is she?" Ethan had his baby Lily in his arms. Maggie was toddling around the kitchen. Ethan sat at the head of the table, close to the back door. There was a lean-to over it so they could open the door without letting the wind howl in. Seth heard the blizzard, still raging. He thought of how sick Callie was, and he was tempted to answer the voices he heard howling.

He and Ethan had gone out and checked the cattle before the sun rose and did what chores they could, along with Steele and the other hands. But today was a day to stay inside as much as possible.

Heath sat on the floor in front of the big iron stove. He held out his arms to block Maggie when the little girl staggered toward the burning heat, which explained what Heath was doing down there.

Connor was standing up, clinging to a chair leg, bouncing his fat little legs as if he was just wild to chase after Maggie. He turned when Seth came in, squealed and smiled. Took a step toward Seth and sat down hard. His little bottom lip came out and his eyes got wide.

Seth scooped up his son and sat down on the floor. The lively little boy in his arms distracted him at least a little bit from how sick Callie was.

"She's got a fever. High fever." Seth looked at Connor. Connor grinned a wild grin and Seth felt his heart breaking. It wasn't a bad feeling. More like maybe Seth's heart was hard and this was cracking the shell around it and letting him bleed feelings that weren't rooted in nightmares and dark caverns and fire.

"Ma had a high fever when she died," Heath said.

Seth decided he'd concentrate on his new family to keep himself from charging up those stairs and demanding Audra let him help take care of Callie.

"I'm sorry things aren't like you hoped they'd be, Heath," Seth said. "We don't have much money, and if we did sell the ranch, it wouldn't bring you enough to live on for very long. All we can do is have you make your home with us, and let us take care of you."

Connor stood up between Seth's legs and reached for Heath so suddenly that Seth almost let him fall. The boy was plumb slippery.

"I can take care of myself." Heath leaned back, his arms folded defiantly.

"I can see you're a knowing boy. But you can't really want to be cast out of this house, even with cash money in your pockets. Not during a blizzard. You've got to stay for a while. We may get a few more nice days and even a thaw or two, but winter is coming fast and this is no time to be riding around the countryside."

Connor reached for Heath as if he'd known him all his life. Seth eased the baby down onto his hands and knees and let him crawl away.

Heath's eyes shifted to the door, rattled now and then by a gust of wind—even with the lean-to. As tight as Rafe had built it, snow still got in under the door, and the floor was cold away from the stove.

"Do you have any other family?" Ethan asked. "Grandparents? When the weather clears, we could help you go to them if you wanted. Did your ma have any brothers or sisters?"

"Never heard of none. Ma talked about a little brother who died young. He was buried in a little graveyard near our house along with her parents. We lived in the house she grew up in." Heath rested his head back against the cabin wall in a way that looked defeated. "And she was afeared she was dying. She'd have told me if there was anywhere to go. Matter of fact, she did tell me. That's what the letter was for, to let me know what needed to be done."

Heath pulled Connor onto his lap and let the boy bounce.

"From what she said, I don't think Pa told her about you, but she figured it out somehow."

"Maybe he talked in his sleep or left some kind of papers lying around."

"Don't reckon Pa knew how to read or write. Leastways not overly."

Seth tried to get Connor to look at him and realized he was a little bit jealous of the boy wanting Heath. But why not? Connor had known Seth only a few hours longer. "Ma taught Rafe a little reading, and Rafe taught me and Ethan. Ma'd lost interest in it by the time we were old enough. It was handy in the war and I got a mite better at it."

"Ma taught me to read and cipher," Heath said, paying attention only to Connor. "She didn't really say much, just that she'd left a letter."

Seth didn't blame the boy for being hostile, considering all the surprises his life had handed him lately. "How did your ma die?"

"She had a fever and it got so high she had to take to her bed." Suddenly Heath looked as if he might break down and cry.

Knowing tears would embarrass him, Seth spoke to head that off. "It might've been an infected wound."

Connor picked that moment to squeal and jump toward the hot stove. Heath caught the boy in time. Seth was glad to see Heath wasn't going to let his dislike of the Kincaid brothers stop him from being kind to a child.

"I didn't see any wound." Heath turned Connor to face the room. "She never complained of anything like that. But she had a bellyache. She was holding her belly low on the left side. Hurtin' bad."

"I've heard of stomach ailments that can kill a person." Seth tried to remember all the reasons men had died during the war. Usually it was all too obvious what had killed them, but sometimes they died for no reason he could ever figure out.

"She told me there was a letter in a box in her room, and to go get it. It was written in her own hand that Pa had grown sons. Just a note saying you lived around Rawhide. No names, nuthin' else. She said Pa had some land over this way and a share of it oughta be mine."

Seth looked at Ethan. This house and this property was most clearly their father's. If anyone had to give up a big chunk of what they owned, it would be Ethan.

"We'll figure out how to divide things up." The little baby in Ethan's arms let out a yelp and he rose from the table to bounce Lily, but the tyke wasn't interested in being cheered up. As he walked and bounced, Ethan added, "We've got all winter to sort it out."

Lily's fussing grew into full-out crying.

"Seth?" Audra's voice came from upstairs.

Seth was running for the stairs so fast he couldn't remember standing up, scared to death, considering she'd just barred him from the room. "What is it?"

"Can you sit with Callie and keep cool cloths pressed to her forehead while I tend Lily?"

A whoosh of air escaped Seth's chest. "Yep, sure I can. You scared me to death."

Audra rested a hand on Seth's shoulder. "I don't see any infected wounds, at least nothing like what Wendell had. We just need to keep her fever down. If she wakes up for even a moment, try and get her to take a drink of water."

"Connor!" Callie twisted in her sleep.

Seth surged from his chair by her bedside. All day she remained in either unnaturally still sleep or she'd cry out, shout Connor's name, then toss and turn.

"Get Connor out. Go!" She was refighting the battle with outlaws at the stagecoach. "Where's my rifle!"

Seth, careful of her cuts and bruises, took hold of her shoulders. The feverish heat of her skin terrified him.

"Callie, wake up, honey." Words weren't enough. Seth shook her gently but relentlessly until finally her eyes flickered open. He knew the torment of nightmares, and it made him sick to think they had Callie in their grasp.

"Take a drink of water." He slid an arm under her shoulder and lifted her, an inch at a time, knowing every move hurt, until she was sitting up enough he could lift the tin cup to her lips.

"Where's Connor?" She always asked the same thing first.

"Connor is fine, honey." He coaxed her into taking a drink.

She reached up her hand and rested her open palm on his face. "Why did you leave me?"

"I was sick, honey. Out of my head. I'd have never left you if I'd been thinking right." He knew that had to be the truth. Holding her as he was now, he couldn't imagine letting her go. He got another swallow of water down her throat and for a few seconds she seemed to realize what she was doing and took a long gulp.

She turned her head from the cup, and Seth eased it away so it wouldn't spill.

"My pa was so mad."

Seth leaned close to catch her muttered words. "What about your pa?"

"He said I'd picked a husband who abandoned me. Said I was stupid."

"I'm sorry I made things bad between you and your pa."

"He hated me for that. For having no husband and a baby on the way. He accused me of lying about being married. Accused me of being . . . being . . . with a man . . . without being married. But I had the marriage license."

"He didn't hate you, Callie. Your pa loved you." Seth said the words because he hoped they gave her comfort, but he knew not all fathers loved their children. Knew it firsthand.

"Luke ran off. Pa poked at him until Luke couldn't stand it, for fighting for the North. Then Pa got shot. I had to run. I let them take my land, steal my ranch! Pa would've hated me for that, too."

"You couldn't fight for a ranch when you had a baby to take care of, Callie. You did the right thing."

"And you weren't there. You should have been there. My pa would still be alive if he'd had a strong man to fight at his side. We'd still have our ranch. Luke might've even stayed because you could have eased things between him and Pa."

Not wanting to hear any more of her delirious honesty, Seth lifted the cup again and got her to take another drink.

She turned her head aside and he was far from satisfied with the amount she drank, but it was something at least.

He realized then that since she was mostly out of her head, this might be a good time to learn a few things about her without making her killing mad. "How old are you, Callie?"

"I'm twenty . . . in just a few months."

Seth had figured her for older. If she was nineteen and they had a son nearing a year old, then . . . "How old were you when we got married?"

"A man ought to know his wife's age, Seth. He oughta remember things like that."

Seth decided to change the subject. "How old is Connor?"

"Connor needs me." Callie's eyes closed, and Seth let her lapse back into a restless, feverish sleep.

The day went on much the same and the night, too. Over and over, Seth wrung out a cloth and bathed her forehead with cool water, constantly fighting the fever that seemed to rage out of control. He checked her wounds, terrified he'd find red streaks stretching away from them.

When Audra insisted, Seth left and allowed his sister-in-law to handle personal things for Callie. Seth went back to his wife's side as soon as Audra would allow it.

Seth stayed at Callie's side almost constantly through three long days and nights. Though he got a little water down her throat, she gagged on broth.

She lost weight, shrunk away before his eyes. Seth found she'd calm down when he got close enough that her grappling hands could latch on to him. And it was no hardship to slide under the covers with her and hold her while she fought for her life.

Finally, in the early morning hours of the fourth day, Seth woke up to find Callie soaked with sweat and sleeping peacefully.

As the sun rose, Seth saw through the small window that the blizzard had blown itself out. He didn't dare move and risk waking her, so he lay there and reveled in the feel of his wife.

He heard the house stir and still he stayed with Callie, afraid the least motion would awaken her. Rest seemed like the best medicine right now.

With Callie at peace, Seth, his head aching with exhaustion, fell asleep and the next time he awoke, the day was bright and the hour was nearer midday than morning.

As Audra swung the door open, Seth realized the turning knob had broken into his sleep. Audra came in the room with Connor in her arms. "You're awake," she said.

Seth saw Audra looking down at Callie. He turned to see Callie's black eyes wide open and clear. "Hi, honey. You feeling better?"

The instant she figured out they were lying together, Callie's brow furrowed. "Get out of this bed, Seth Kincaid."

"Hand him here." Seth ignored his feisty wife and reached out for the boy. Connor flashed his wild grin and tried to throw himself out of Audra's arms.

"Your son doesn't have a cautious bone in his body." Audra clucked her tongue as she gave Connor to Seth. "Why am I not surprised?"

Seth managed a brief smile before letting Connor sit on his chest, facing his mother.

"I'll be right back with something for you to eat, Callie." Audra slipped out of the room.

"Papapapa." Connor reached down and gave Callie a sound slap on the chest.

It distracted Callie from throwing Seth out of bed. And Seth was too busy keeping the chunky little tyke from damaging his ma to get up.

Or at least that was the excuse he made to himself as he enjoyed the glory of his healing wife and his smiling son.

CHAPTER 13

"How long have I been in bed?" Callie wanted to punch Seth for being in the bed with her. She was determined that nothing would pass between them yet. She'd made that clear as glass. And yet here he was for the second time.

Or, depending on how long she'd been out of her head, maybe it was the tenth time.

"We got to Ethan's four days ago, late at night. You've never really been awake since. Or at least not for long. The trip was too hard for you, honey."

Her husband made it sound like she was soft. That made him an insensitive clod.

"I'm feeling better." Better enough to slam a fist right in his gut. More of the ordeal came back to her. "And did I single-handedly save your son, the parson and his wife and the two men on top of the stagecoach, which led to the arrest of four wanted desperados?"

"I don't know if single-handedly is fair." Seth let Connor bounce up and down on his chest. "The driver and the man riding shotgun helped a lot."

"And I earned a fortune in reward money, which I immediately had to spend on your surprise brother." Callie started wishing she couldn't remember anything.

"Heath is your brother now, too. It was right handy you having all that money. There'll be more reward money coming, but I had to promise a good chunk of it to the general store to outfit Heath and buy extra supplies for the winter."

"So in the four days since I've found my husband, I've been nearly killed, made and spent a fortune, survived a long ride through the mountains into the teeth of a blizzard, all with a baby strapped on my back? Is that right?" Callie was yelling toward the end, so she clamped her mouth shut.

"I carried Connor from Colorado City. And I carried you part of the way. Are you feeling all right, Cal? You sound a little like you're still not quite right in the head, honey."

Audra entered the room with a steaming bowl of . . . something wonderful. Maybe beef stew. Callie's stomach clenched and she hoped she could keep something down. "But the rest of us did fine," Seth-the-Clod went on. "Connor came through with no trouble."

There was no good reason for her husband to lie there saying she was the weakest one of them. Let him fight off a band of outlaws for a while and see if he didn't get worn clean out.

Audra must have sensed that Callie was gathering her strength to pound Seth.

"Get up." Audra plunked her hands on her hips and glared at Seth. Who obeyed her. Callie memorized the exact stance and glare. She'd use it often.

Seth grumbled a bit, but he got out of bed, mostly dressed.

Praise the good Lord God in heaven.

"Callie needs a few minutes to wake up." Audra made shoo motions with her hands as if Seth were a flock of crows raiding the corn patch. "Take Connor and go eat, then help Ethan get the children fed. When Callie and I are done with her breakfast, I'll holler and you can bring Connor back up."

Seth glanced past Audra to look at Callie, as if he'd stand up to the little tyrant if Callie asked him to.

"Go." Callie wouldn't have minded kicking him to underscore the message. "Take care of your son for a change. Try and remember who I am while you're down there."

Callie saw Seth back out of the room, holding Connor like an old hand at baby wrangling. Audra swung the door shut in his face.

Audra sat on the side of the bed and picked up the bowl. "Hi, Callie. I'm Audra. I'm married to Seth's brother Ethan."

"No, wait. Stand back up. I don't need to lie here and be spoon-fed."

"You might be wrong about that." Audra gave her a kind but doubtful smile. "You've had a hard week."

Nodding, Callie said, "I might be wrong. But let me try, please."

After too long a look, as if Audra would do what she thought best regardless of how Callie felt—an annoying way to behave—Audra replaced the bowl on the little table and stood.

"Let's see how you do."

Callie tossed back the covers and her arm almost screamed aloud in protest. It would have to do the screaming because she wasn't about to let her mouth make a sound.

Forcing her legs sideways, Audra helped ease them around and lowered her feet. Callie was sitting up on the edge of the bed for about three seconds before the edges of her vision turned dark. Audra sat beside her and slid an arm around her shoulders.

"You've gone dead white. If you try and stand right now, I'm sure you'll fall on your face. But if you just sit up awhile, give it a few minutes, the light-headedness might pass. If it doesn't, you're going to have to stay in bed awhile longer."

As a rule, Callie didn't take orders from anyone. But somehow, letting such a pint-sized woman boss her around didn't seem like too much to accept.

The dark quit getting worse. Callie waited, hoping her vision would clear. As long as she wasn't doing anything, she asked, "Seth really doesn't remember me?"

"Seth doesn't remember much of anything since the end of the war."

"He was really sick. I mean, I'm not surprised he doesn't remember when we first met." She was surprised. Stunned. The big idiot. "I was helping tend the patients who came out of Andersonville. My brother was held prisoner there, and Pa and I headed east to fetch him home. Then we got there and Luke needed doctoring for a long time. I was helping with him and there was so much need. Once Luke was able to travel home, I wanted to stay behind and help." She'd met Seth by then and he'd already touched her heart. But she hadn't told her pa that.

"One of the doctors was from Texas, and Pa trusted him to watch out for me and get me home. Pa took my brother and I stayed. Seth was so sick. He was wounded. The wounds—they hadn't even removed the buckshot from his back. It was infected. He was one of hundreds who needed help. I just, we just . . ."

Callie turned to Audra. "I can't believe he forgot he was married."

"Your letter came here, along with the one to Rafe and Ethan. I'm sorry." Audra slid a supporting arm across Callie's shoulders, as much emotional support as physical. "It came as a complete surprise to him. And you never mentioned a son."

"He was out of his head a lot at first. Sick and tormented by nightmares."

"He still has them." Audra met Callie's eyes and the truth of those terrible dreams was there.

"Seth had talked about his brothers, so I knew where they lived."

"And he just left you?"

"I thought the nightmares drove him out into the night. I thought he'd come back. When he didn't, I thought he must be dead or maybe sick enough he'd ended up back in a hospital. I stayed back East, hoping, hunting for him. Then I realized Connor was on the way and I had to get back to Texas. I went home to find out my brother had taken off, left Pa and the ranch. I was already getting big with Connor, and Pa didn't even know I'd gotten married. It wasn't so easy with a baby to go hunting for my husband. Then Connor was born, and the rancher next to us wanted to grab more range. My pa died and I wasn't strong enough to hold the ranch."

Callie swallowed hard, not wanting to talk about that. "With my home lost to me, I set out to find Seth's brothers, hoping maybe Seth was alive and they'd know where he was. And if I found Seth out here, alive and well, I decided I'd kill him."

Callie looked at Audra sharply, expecting horror. In truth, Callie probably wouldn't actually kill Seth, but she might well make the man wish for death before she was done. That idea held a strong appeal.

"I've done some work on your clothes."

Callie looked down and realized she was wearing her own soft, white flannel nightgown.

"I found what must be your satchel and a riding skirt and blouse. There were some faded bloodstains, but I could see that someone put time into washing and mending them for you."

"The parson's wife, though maybe the hotel owner might have helped. He and his whole family were uncommonly kind to me."

"Has your head cleared?"

Callie nodded. "Yes, I'm steady now."

"Do you feel up to trying to stand?"

Callie smiled at Audra, and the smile alone set a few muscles to protesting. "It'll hurt like blue blazes, but it's just aches and pains. I'm not bad hurt."

"A hundred small injuries take a toll on a woman." Audra stood, a head shorter than Callie. She might look like dandelion fluff, but then a dandelion was a tough little flower. "Let's get you to your feet."

Callie found each move to be easier than the one before, which didn't mean they weren't all torment. It was slowgoing, but Audra remained patient and soon had her dressed and sitting in front of the soup. Callie took the first bite and her stomach threatened to rebel.

"I think I'll leave eating until later." Callie fought to keep from casting up the contents of her belly.

Resting one surprisingly strong hand on Callie's shoulder, Audra said, "Just give it a second to settle. Take slow, steady breaths."

It took a minute, but Callie won the battle with sickness and risked another bite. "It tastes good, but I've got the collywobbles."

"No great surprise after all you've been through. Just try eating only the broth."

The second bite set more easily and her appetite roared to life. She ate the soup while Audra combed and braided her hair.

"You've got stitches on your scalp in four places. Seth said the doctor wants them to stay in for a week. Then we can cut them out."

The soup was heavy with meat and vegetables, and every bite warmed her stomach and seemed to ease the shaking out of her bones. "Seven days for the stitches." Callie glanced back at Audra. "Aren't we close to that already?"

Gently but firmly turning Callie's head so she faced forward, Audra said, "They'll be gone before you know it. The doctor cut the hair away around the injuries."

"I reckon I look like I've been rode hard and put up wet."

"I've pulled your hair back so the wounds are covered. Your hair is beautiful, so long and thick. It covers the clipped spots. You look fine."

"I hope you don't have a mirror in this house."

"No, I don't."

"Good, then I can't call you a liar." As suddenly as she'd been starving, Callie's stomach felt stretched to the limit.

Audra gave a short, quiet laugh as she fussed with Callie's hair. "You're healing well. No infection."

Callie had to force down the last of the soup. "I reckon I'm ready to see Connor now."

And her husband, but she didn't mention him. She figured the lunatic would come along with the child.

CHAPTER 14

"Seth's got a son?" Rafe heard himself screech and clamped his mouth shut. He prided himself on being in control, and that included his voice.

"Yep. Eth was afraid you'd ride out looking for Seth's wife again, so he sent me over to stop you and tell you about the . . . the, well, your family has done some mighty fast growing in a short time, I reckon."

"And a brother who is how old?" Rafe felt his temper building. His pa was lucky to be dead and beyond Rafe's reach. "How could Pa—?"

Steele cut him off. "I didn't get no details, Rafe. I said he looked about ten or eleven. Don't start in. I don't know nuthin' 'cept Eth says you probably had oughta come."

Rafe turned to Julia, who was already banking the fire on the cookstove.

"We've been looking for Callie for so long I'd almost given up ever finding her." Julia took her apron off and pulled her coat on.

His wife's activities helped Rafe get past the shock and get moving.

"And Seth doesn't remember the baby?" Julia asked.

"Like I said, ma'am, I don't know nuthin'." Steele tugged on his gloves and hat as if they were in danger of blowing off in a windstorm. Not that easy, considering they were standing inside Rafe's cabin. Steele wasn't a talkative man on the best of days.

They left through the tunnel on the east side of their mountain meadow and rode in the snow toward Julia's old cabin.

"Can you believe it snowed so hard?" Julia said. The horses waded through ankle-deep snow on occasion, but the sun was strong and the snow was mostly blown off the heavily wooded trail. "Some of it is already melting."

Rafe hadn't been around women much, but since he'd gotten married to one of the little critters, he'd noticed they seemed to have to say out loud every thought in their head. Including stuff everybody already knew. It'd snowed. Today it was real nice. It was called weather. What was there to talk about?

"Yep, it's a real nice day." He'd also learned a woman didn't like men ignoring them or telling them they were wasting their breath when they said out loud something anyone with one working eyeball could see. "Weather can be like that in the Rocky Mountains. Winter comes early, but there can be nice days too, even after the snow starts flying."

Steele gave Rafe a look that clearly told him his ears were weary from all the talk.

Rafe didn't smile. He knew if Steele had a chance to marry a woman as beautiful and smart and sweet and warm as Julia, he'd have talked up a storm to keep her happy.

"So, Steele," Julia said, "did the boy say . . ."

Steele was a few steps ahead and he picked up speed and didn't answer. He did a good job of acting like he hadn't heard.

Rafe eased closer to his wife. "So what do you think might be going on?" It was a question he used on Julia many times to keep her talking so he wouldn't have to talk back. It gave him spare time to think about important stuff like the ranch.

They rode up to Julia's ramshackle cabin about the time Julia quit making things up that could've happened. A corner of the roof had collapsed under the weight of the snow.

"I wonder if this place will stand through the winter if we repair it." He doubted it.

Julia swung down off her horse and stepped close enough to Rafe that he saw her shudder.

"We could have been stuck in that cabin." She turned. Her long red braid came around until it hung down one shoulder. Her green eyes were shining right at him. "I'm so glad I married you."

Yep, Rafe'd be glad to talk until his lungs went bone dry to earn a look like that from his wife. And she always liked to know what he was planning, for some reason. "I'm going to need a line shack out here. You won't mind if I rip down your cabin, will you?"

Julia scowled at the miserable little building. "Tear it into a thousand pieces if you want."

"I'd like to get to it before winter closes down on us."

"You're running out of time."

"Yep." Rafe looked at Steele, who had released the horses into a sturdy corral. "We can get busy with the line shack as soon as we figure out who that boy is and how he got his family mixed up with ours."

"I can send some men over anytime you're ready."

They climbed across the fast-moving creek that separated the abandoned Gilliland cabin from the dangerous opening into the cavern Julia loved so much. Down into a steep gully, across the stream and back up, everything now slippery with snow and ice. They never used this cavern entrance anymore, not since they'd found the easier entrance near Rafe's ranchland.

They mounted the horses Steele had corralled and rode hard for Ethan's place, which kept the chattering to a minimum. When they got home, Steele took the horses as Julia beat Rafe to the house. The woman was crazy to see Seth's baby.

Which set Rafe to hoping he didn't have to wait too long to have a little one of his own. Ethan had two and now Seth had one. As the oldest brother, he wasn't holding up his end of things.

He decided he'd commit himself even more to hurrying along that day. When he stepped inside Ethan's very crowded house, he had a smile on his face.

"Hey, big brother." Seth smiled at Rafe from the kitchen table. He held up Connor, who had wolfed down a flapjack and a whole egg. "Meet my son."

"And meet your brother," Ethan added, looking grim. Seth was more used to Ethan grinning.

Rafe turned to study the stranger at the table.

Seth saw the stunned expression on his brother's face. "I told Steele to tell you about him."

"He did. I just thought . . ."

Ethan stood from the table, holding Lily, now three months old. "Julia, have a seat. I'll get you a cup of coffee."

Julia snatched Connor out of Seth's arms. Seth took a second to make sure his son was happy with the new arrangement. His boy was uncommon fond of his pa.

Connor didn't even give Seth a backward glance.

Seth rose and stood beside Ethan. When Seth turned to look at the table, he realized he stood shoulder to shoulder with his brothers, looking at the madness their lives had become.

"This is Heath." Seth nodded at the boy, who looked so much like a Kincaid there was just no way to deny that he was their brother.

Heath had gone through his share of flapjacks. Earlier, Audra had had her hands full keeping the food coming until she'd abandoned the room to take care of Callie.

"You forgot you had a son?" Heath asked with abundant hostility.

Seth felt his smile melt away, along with what little pride he had. "Well, no, not really. I didn't know he was on the way when I left. Callie says I didn't know."

"And you ran off and left her? Like Pa ran off and left you?" Heath seemed to have a burr under his saddle. Seth couldn't say he blamed the boy.

"I never really thought Pa ran off and left us." Seth could see now that it was true. "He was just gone a lot."

"He was gone a lot from us, too." Heath cut through a stack of pancakes like he was attacking something . . . or someone.

"He's a fine boy, Seth." Rafe studied Connor and his wild blue eyes for a minute, then looked back at the table. "You're a Kincaid."

Defiance flashed in Health's eye as if he was waiting to be thrown out.

"That means you've got a home here. This is the Kincaid Ranch, so you've got a share in it."

"I don't want a ranch." Heath's eyes went hard, the shining blue of them flashed, and Seth wondered if the boy ever had nightmares. Heath was close to the age Rafe had been when Seth had the accident in the cavern. And Rafe had been a man from that day on. But Heath's eyes were of a type with Seth and Pa. He felt like the boy was a true brother already.

"I want my share sold, then I'll be on my way."

A troublemaking brother. Which made him even more like Seth.

"Not a chance," Rafe said. "We can't sell the ranch. It ain't worth much and no one would buy it. I bought a huge stretch just a couple of months ago for a few pennies an acre. Its only value is to make a home for us. The part that belonged to Pa isn't that big, anyway. I added to it with money I made selling beef to gold miners in the rush of '59. But that's my land. Seth and Ethan have added to it with homestead claims besides what I bought and it'll take five years to prove up on that land. It's a good stretch now, but the part you've got a claim on is mostly woodlands. I could buy you out, but you wouldn't get far on a quarter of its worth, and no one else wants it."

"You wanted it." Heath scowled.

"Yeah, but Kincaids don't have a lick of sense," Seth said.

There was a long silence, then Rafe said, "How old are you, Heath?"

"Eleven."

"So our pa was married to your ma about a year before our ma died, is that right?" Rafe's voice brought every noise in the room to a halt. Even Connor, who was jabbering at Julia, fell silent and gave Rafe a wild-eyed look.

"That's the way it sounds. I found papers amongst our ma's things that said Pa owned land near Rawhide. I came to get it. It's my inheritance."

"Your ma knew Gavin Kincaid had another family?" Rafe frowned deep. "She knew when she married him that he already had a wife?"

Heath slammed his chair back to the wall and lunged to his feet. "You say a word against my ma and I'll beat you until you can't open your mouth."

Heath couldn't win, but Seth could see clear as day the boy meant every word.

Seth found himself wishing he could go down into the cavern. It was quiet down there. He could hear himself think. He looked at the door to the outside and wondered if anyone would miss him. He wouldn't be gone long. A day or two.

"Julia! I didn't hear you come in. Come and meet Callie!" Audra came down the stairs, guiding Seth's wife. He had a wife.

Maybe he needed more than two days. A week maybe, just until his brain settled around being a married man with a child.

Then he saw how white Callie's knuckles were as she gripped the railing. He hurried to her side just as she got all the way downstairs.

"You doing okay, honey?" He wished he could remember her. She was really pretty.

Callie glared at him.

Kinda scary, though.

Callie was diverted from that betraying coyote Seth Kincaid by the sight of Connor sitting on a redheaded woman's lap.

Callie darted toward her baby. Well, she darted for one step. Then the pain slowed her right down.

Connor saw her and gave a friendly shriek. His arms and legs started pumping in the air as if he could fly to her if he just tried hard enough.

She limped her way across the room.

The redhead stood up and said, "Hi, I'm Julia Kincaid. I guess we're sisters now. Take my chair."

Callie had to sit down on the chair or collapse on the floor, so she took the stupid chair, though it rankled to be in need of so much help. Then the redhead set Connor on her lap. Callie slid an arm around Connor's fat tummy and her aching heart eased to feel the weight of him.

Seth started introducing everyone.

"We've got a lot to do," Rafe said, cutting Seth off, "before we can sit down and get to know each other."

Ethan's eyes narrowed in a way that made Callie wonder how well the brothers got along.

"Got orders for us, big brother?" Ethan asked in a drawl.

"Yes, that snow yesterday was a warning. We need to get the ranch weathertight. We still have a couple herds that need to be moved to winter grassland. I need to get a line shack built, and we're gonna have to get Heath settled somewhere. We may have to build on to one of the cabins."

"Have I ever told you my big brother is really bossy?" Seth said to Callie.

"I don't remember you mentioning it. But I figured it out without a word from you."

"Don't build on to any cabin for me. I'm not staying." Heath showed no interest in obeying Rafe, which, Seth had to admit, made him like the boy a little more.

Rafe glared at Heath. "Sure you are."

"You can't tell someone how to live, where to live, and what to do with their own money." Callie stood, took a step toward Rafe, and squared off in front of him.

"Sure I can. When I'm right and he's wrong." Rafe didn't give Callie a pat on the head, but his words came way too close.

"How about, instead of acting like a tyrant, you have a conversation with the brother your worthless father abandoned and cheated."

"Hey!" That came from everyone in the room who was more than two years old, except Julia and Audra. Callie thought she had some allies there.

"My pa was a lot better to us than he was to these guys," Heath snarled.

"Callie, you never met Pa. You don't need to go and say—" Seth's words got drowned out by his brothers, who had a thing or two to add.

Heath came around the table as if he wanted a fight. Callie

could accommodate the little grouch in the normal course of things, but the last couple of days had taken their toll.

Seth stepped in front of Heath. "Don't you lay a hand on my wife."

"You think I'd hit a woman? That's the kind of coward you think I am?" Heath shoved Seth, and small as he was, he managed to make Seth back up.

The shouting continued. Callie stayed in the middle of it until she was hopeful no one was going to let fly with a fist. Then she turned to look at Audra and Julia. Audra watched the chaos and wrung her hands.

"Troublemaker." Julia gave Callie a look so dry it oughta'd been served with a glass of water.

With a jerk of her shoulder, Callie patted Connor's little bottom and went to stand by Julia. "You're not the first to say so. But I call 'em the way I see 'em."

"They're not ready to admit that yet." Julia scooped the little toddler girl out of her chair. "This is Maggie. She's my niece and my sister and . . ." Julia paused and frowned at the little girl with the wisps of white blond hair, who bounced happily in her arms. "She might be my cousin too, or maybe my sister-in-law. I know there was something else, but sometimes I lose track."

"Close family, huh?"

"He might've died here but he loved us." Heath stuck his chin forward as if daring someone to take a swing.

"You have no idea." Sounding tired, Audra slipped between the warring Kincaids, took the baby out of Ethan's arms—as well as taking her out of the middle of the fight—and came back to stand shoulder to shoulder with her sisters-in-law.

"What do you think we ought to do about them?" Julia asked.

"How old were you when I was born exactly?" Heath demanded of Seth. "Your pa must've been real unhappy about you to take off like he done."

"Why, you little worthless pup!" Seth stepped forward. Ethan caught his arm.

With a shrug Callie watched the war dance before her. "You got a bucket of cold water?"

Julia snickered.

"I'm not having that mess on my kitchen floor." Audra swayed gently with the baby while she considered the situation.

"So why'd Seth leave you anyway?" Julia asked Callie. "What's the matter with him, do you think?"

Nosy woman. "He was real sick." Callie studied Seth. "He's acting pretty sane right now, though. It makes sense he'd be worked up about this mess."

Callie looked down at Connor, who was watching his father behave badly. He didn't seem upset by it; the little one was fascinated. Probably taking notes on how to be a wild man. She'd had enough. "Sorry for the racket, baby boy."

She patted his plump little diaper, then lifted two fingers to her lips and blasted an ear-piercing whistle.

Everyone turned to glare at her.

Dead silence reigned.

It was a skill of which she was mighty proud.

"Since I started this, I'll end it." Callie earned herself the simmering temper of four Kincaids. "You can all pretend like your pa loved you best if you want. But the truth is, he betrayed every one of you. And now you can stand here and fight about nonsense, or you can enjoy getting to know your family."

Heath snorted.

"Now, there's no sense talking about getting money," Callie went on. "Near as I can piece together, there isn't any. This ranch and everything on it was built more by the Kincaid brothers than their pa. Did your father leave you with a lovely home and lots of money?" Callie arched a brow as she looked at Heath. "Because if he did, then it's fair for you to go gather up all those riches and share it with the Kincaids here."

More silence.

Heath finally said, "Pa didn't leave us nuthin'. He rode off one spring to sell his furs. He never came back."

"That must've been the year he died." Rafe shoved his hands into the back pockets of his pants. "He rode in here, sick with a fever. He died. He died . . ." Suddenly Rafe frowned and looked at the newcomers. "He told me to take care of his son and his wife. I thought he was out of his head.

"He meant you." Rafe's voice echoed with regret and his shoulders slumped. "He wanted me to find you. I couldn't make sense out of it. His wife—our ma—was long dead. I thought he was just raving or dreaming of a woman's gentle hand. I'm . . . I'm sorry. I think he even meant the fur money to go to you. He said something about selling it, using it to care for his wife. I hadn't seen him for almost a year. I know now that all that time he was gone, he was with you, that even before Ma died he was with you. But after, he barely even lived here. He stopped in from time to time."

"He wasn't with us that much, either." Heath crossed his arms, almost as if he wanted to hold back the words he had to say. "He'd leave for weeks at a time. Ma, well, Ma had grown up in the mountains. She could provide for us better with a skinning knife and a Winchester than most people can with a general store and a herd of cattle."

"Did she cry?" Seth asked.

Callie never was much of a crier. From Seth's tone, she suspected he wouldn't think fondly of her if she took up the habit.

"Never saw her shed a tear," Heath said.

"So, since there's no money to be had here," Callie said to Heath, "it looks like you're gonna have to take your inheritance out in land and a roof over your head." She then turned to Seth. "And since Heath's new to the family and so am I, I want him. I want help getting you through your nightmares. It wears on a body after a while."

Ethan patted Seth on the back. "So true."

Callie gave Connor a big hug. "How many bedrooms does your cabin have?"

Seth sighed long and hard. "Not enough."

Heath looked at Callie. "So when do we have this house-building party?"

"Right after the breakfast dishes are washed," Rafe said. "And then I've got a line shack I want to put up before the snow flies."

"Too late for that. The snow's already started." Seth looked out the window. "But we won't let a little blizzard stop us. Let's hit the trail."

CHAPTER 15

Seth hadn't gotten a minute alone with his wife since . . . he paused. Had he ever gotten a minute alone with her? At least when she was fully conscious?

And since Seth couldn't remember being married, it really was never. Which was maddening when he considered he'd not only married her, he'd undeniably made a baby with her.

He'd really like to remember that part.

They'd been two days building on to his house.

He saw his chance to actually speak to his wife alone when Callie stepped outside with a basin of wash water.

"Let's get packed up." Rafe was being his usual tyrannical self. "We leave at first light for the line shack." Issuing orders to Seth, Ethan, and Heath. Even though they were all men. By the amount of work he did, Seth even counted Heath . . . mostly. Men with functioning brains, Seth even counted himself . . . mostly.

Seth exchanged a look with Ethan, who had his usual phony grin on his face. He was probably daydreaming, ignoring Rafe. A quick glance at Heath told Seth the kid had already learned the skill of pretending to listen to Rafe while his mind was elsewhere.

When Rafe turned around to pick up an axe, Seth jabbed an elbow into Ethan's arm and jerked his head in Callie's direction.

Ethan looked at Callie, quirked a genuine smile, and waved Seth toward her. Rafe kept talking.

Seth slipped away just as Callie rounded the side of the house, out of sight of General Rafe. Seth came up behind her as she tossed the water out of the basin. Seth snagged her wrist. Startled, she squeaked and dropped the shallow metal pan.

He laid his hand over her mouth and whispered, "Quiet. Rafe'll hear you and come drag me back to work."

She nodded. She'd been issued a few too many orders in the last couple of days, it seemed. Seth left the basin behind when he pulled her away. He was careful to keep the house between him and the next orders.

He whispered the question that burned the worst. "Why'd you have to ask Heath to stay with us?"

He loved being this close to her. He couldn't get over how pretty she was with her snapping black eyes and the brilliant shining black of her hair. Even her temper drew him. He got the impression that when she was mad, she might be a wild woman. Almost as wild as him. The little thrill of fear was exciting enough that he considered prodding her to make her show him the full extent of her wildness.

He'd seen flashes of temper but not when she was at full strength. Which she almost was now.

"Heath needs a home. We need the help."

"We don't even have any of the herd on my land yet. The house is done. I've got two horses and a milk cow and a flock of chickens. What help do we need?"

"There's plenty to do."

"It's because of my nightmares. Seems like that's a good reason to not have him around."

Callie looked at him long and hard, as if she was searching his eyes, hoping to see inside his head. "How are you feeling? Did you have bad dreams last night?"

He studied right back. The smaller scrapes and scratches had faded, but she still had a mean-looking slice on her temple and, though they didn't show, the stitches on her scalp. Her color was better. Now that she wasn't as pale as milk, her skin was a warm tan.

"I never woke up. So I must—wait." A memory flashed through his head. He dug around trying to focus on it. "I . . . I dreamed about you last night."

"Really?" Her gaze sharpened. "Your nightmares were about me?"

"Yes, I mean, no—it wasn't a nightmare. Maybe it wasn't a dream. Maybe it was a memory."

"You mean a memory of before I showed up here?" She sounded young when she asked that. She mostly acted all grown up and then some.

"I think . . . we met when I was in the hospital. In my dream I was lying in a hospital. But it wasn't a hospital exactly."

"It was a big old house, a plantation the Union Army took over to care for the sick."

"I dreamed that I woke up in a room, lit by lanterns. You were there, bending over me, with a cloth on my head." Seth reached for her hand and drew it to his face. "You said you cared for me."

It struck Seth that "you cared for me" could be taken two ways. The way a nurse cared for her patient or the way a wife cared about her husband.

"You were so sick. Feverish. The buckshot in your back was infected. You couldn't have been in Andersonville very long or you'd've died."

Unable to resist, Seth drew her along, past an ancient oak tree with a massive trunk, out of sight of the cabin. They were swallowed up by trees still bearing the last of their bright fall colors. The snow had melted in most places and their feet crunched and crackled in the fallen leaves. He was surprised she came along.

"You were like an angel leaning over me. I hurt so bad and you stayed. You were there every time I woke up." He felt his brow furrow as he tried to remember. Their eyes met. Seth's breath hitched.

"I helped care for all the patients, not just you." A gust of wind stirred the trees and some of the last leaves still clinging overhead rained down like an orange and red blizzard. The pines stirred and their scent wrapped around Seth, giving him the solid feeling of home. It wouldn't be much longer until winter would settle on their heads. And he'd be holed up with Callie for long months with weather that drove a man to stay inside, close to the fire, close to his woman to stay warm in the night.

"There was something between us from the first, wasn't there?" Seth touched her black-as-midnight hair and couldn't believe anything was as soft and silky. "It had to be strong for me to feel this connection now."

"I don't know what was between us. I thought there was something, but if you forgot me so easily—"

Seth kissed her quiet. "I'm sorry."

She didn't slug him, so he kissed her again, longer this time. Deeper. "I don't know how I could ever forget someone as beautiful as you." He buried his hand in her hair. He had to remember this, the silky weight, the lush curls.

Callie pressed against his shoulders, gently but relentlessly. "Stop, Seth. We aren't going to . . . to be together as man and wife until I know I can trust you to stay."

"I'm not going anywhere. I'm home. Before, something must have been driving me home. But I'm fine now."

"I'm sure you didn't plan on abandoning me before."

Seth slid an arm around her waist and eased her forward. She shook her head but let him draw her. He spoke soft enough to soothe a skittish filly. "How long did we know each other before we got married?"

Callie jerked one shoulder. Seth was learning she did that when there was something she didn't want to say.

"How long?" His arm tightened on her waist as if he could squeeze an answer out of her.

"Not long enough, I reckon."

"Callie, how long?" He shook her gently.

"A few weeks." She looked confused and sad and enticed.

"A few? How many? Five? Ten?" Seth had another flash of them standing side by side in . . . it seemed like the same room he'd dreamed of last night. A parson was there. While he was still in the hospital?

She clamped her teeth shut, looking for all the world like a woman who wasn't going to let a word slip past her lips.

He let his hand slide up her backbone. He remembered something else. He could get around her, earn her cooperation with closeness, touch, as if she craved it. "Tell me."

"Two! Two weeks!" she snapped. Shoving at him, she fought her way out of his arms.

"Two weeks? And I was sick the whole time?" She probably should have had better sense than to marry him, but he didn't think it was wise to say that out loud.

"I probably should have had better sense than to marry you. We needed to open up a bed for someone else. You were past the worst of it, but you weren't well enough to just turn out on your own. You needed somewhere to go, someone to take care of you. You were having nightmares in the hospital." Her jaw clenched, but she forced the words past. "We'd shared a kiss or two and the connection was so strong. You said you wanted to be with me, marry me. I believed all your pretty words, when it was just the fever talking. Once you remember me—if that ever happens—you won't even want to be married. If it wasn't for Connor, I'd have just let you go. Pretended like nothing ever happened."

What if she had? What if she'd burned their marriage license, kept quiet about it? Lied. Married someone else. It made him mad enough to punch someone. Before she could speak any more nonsense, he shut her up by dragging her against himself and kissing her.

When her arms crept up to circle his neck, a soaring happiness swept over him. If it had only been a few weeks, and he'd been sick, then he hadn't forgotten all that much.

And if he'd kissed her a single time, of course he'd married her. "It was like this between us from the start, wasn't it?" He kissed her before she could deny it. "That's why we got married so fast."

She turned her head aside far too late to be persuasive. "I let myself get carried away."

Seth still couldn't remember the actual carrying away, but he hoped to remind himself of it real soon.

"And how long did we . . . uh, carry away before I took off?"

"I took you to my rooming house. You were still so weak, plagued by nightmares. You stayed only a few days and vanished."

"I'm so sorry."

"I searched for you. I knew you weren't well enough to be on your own."

He'd made it home, though, crossing most of the country. He'd been well enough for that. Of course he couldn't remember that, either.

"I stayed awhile longer. There was plenty of work still to do at the hospital. I kept thinking you'd come back. I spent every spare minute searching for you. I was afraid you'd gotten worse and maybe you were back in a hospital somewhere. There were so many injured men, we took over several houses. Finally I went home to my pa's ranch in Texas. I didn't know what else to do. You'd said Rawhide, Colorado. Told me your brothers' names. But I couldn't set out across the country alone, or at least I didn't think I could then. I changed my mind when Pa died. I didn't even know if you'd be there." She grabbed the collar of his shirt. "I thought you died."

"And then you found out there was a baby on the way." He pulled her long black curls forward so they danced around her shoulders. She'd had a braid when she came out, but he'd freed her of it.

"I was well gone with the child by the time I'd traveled home. I knew I was tired and sick, but I blamed that on rough stagecoaches and long days. I didn't even tell my pa I was married at first. I wasn't even sure if it was legal to marry a man who was out of his head."

It twisted in Seth's gut to think a less honorable woman might've forgotten the vows she took, counted it a stupid mistake. But she couldn't do that, even if she was so inclined because . . . "Connor made it real legal, didn't he?"

A sudden burst of wind gusted leaves down on them and rattled the branches.

With a jerk of her chin she said, "My pa had a housekeeper. She told me I was increasing."

Seth didn't know much about women, so he didn't ask how a woman could tell such a thing. He feared it was an extremely female thing and he didn't want to know. Except . . .

"Seth, get back here!" Rafe interrupted in time to stop him from asking her. It was the first time in a while he'd been grateful for his bossy big brother.

Of course it also meant their chance to talk privately was over. But it had served a purpose. "I do remember you, Callie."

"Just barely."

"I know when I hold you, what I feel isn't new. And I know the connection between us is strong. It survived my run for home and the time that separated us." And his time living down in the cavern. Short miles from home but hiding instead of going the rest of the way. No, he hadn't been well.

"We've got a lot of work to do before supper." Rafe sounded bossy, but there was a thread of worry under it. Seth knew he'd given his big brother cause to worry many times.

"Looks like we'll have to continue this talk later." Seth grabbed another kiss and then slid his arm around her and guided her back toward the cabin.

"Seth, where are you? Are you all right?" Rafe would be coming into the trees in another few steps.

"I'm coming. I'm fine, Rafe. I'm just talking to my wife for a few minutes." A few precious minutes. He wondered when in the world he'd ever get more of them.

"We've always been able to create a spark between us, Seth. But we need more than that to make a marriage. While my father was alive—"

"How'd your father die?"

"There was . . . trouble and he was killed."

"What kind of trouble?"

"There were renegades after the war. Grabbing up land. Pa controlled a lot of acres, but he didn't own them, just the water holes. Pa didn't back down and he ended up dead. And I couldn't hold the land. So I cut and ran. I took all the money I could scrabble together and left the rest of it to the vultures and came west looking for you, or at least your family."

"I'm sorry you lost your pa, Callie. He's gotta been a good man if he raised you up so tough."

"I'm not tough. I told you I couldn't hold our ranch."

"I was thinking of the stagecoach shootout. That's pretty tough."

With a shrug Callie said, "I've got nowhere else to go, Seth, so I'm staying. But I'm not going to be with you as a wife would be, not for a while."

"Isn't a wife supposed to obey her husband?" Seth swallowed hard on that wonderful thought. Then he had one even better. "And meet his needs?"

Oh, yeah, he had himself some needs.

"Read that Bible passage about obeying again, Kincaid." All Callie's warmth dried up and blew away like autumn leaves. "The husband makes more promises than the wife, and you haven't kept a single one of them. When you do, maybe I'll give some thought to obeying you. And as for meeting your needs, that won't happen until I'm sure you're a man to count on. You've got a ways to go to prove that to me."

She jerked out of his arms and stalked toward the house. She had on a black riding skirt that moved like magic when she walked, and Seth remembered that he'd always been a little wild. A little reckless, and not a very patient man.

A sudden slap on the back drew his eyes away from his fast-retreating wife.

Rafe.

"Having trouble concentrating, little brother?" Rafe smiled. A happily married man. Seth was starting to understand just what that meant.

"Nope, not one bit." He concentrated on Callie until he ached all over. She walked over to the basin and bent to pick it up, and he didn't waste one single second looking at his brother.

"I mean on work."

"Supper's ready," Julia called from inside the house just as Callie swung the door open to enter.

"Let's go in." Seth did his best not to run for the cabin. He noticed Rafe moved right alongside him. Ethan came around the cabin at a fast pace, heading for a warm meal cooked by the strong, gentle hands of a woman.

All Seth had to do was figure out a way to get his wife to trust him, and all three of the Kincaid men would be well and truly and happily married.

It was time to finish things with the Kincaid men.

In recent years, Jasper had lived one step away from all the crime done in his name, with a nice sheen of respectability. But he hadn't started there. He'd clawed his way to the top, and he had all the skills he'd been using hired guns for. He'd lived off the land, too, after his pa had thrown him out. True, it was land in the swamps of Louisiana, but Jasper knew how to rough it. He knew how to move quietly and not leave a trail. He knew how to watch someone and pick his moment.

It was time to brush the dust off all those skills.

The trail to the money led straight through Gilliland's wife and daughter. And now Jasper had seen a new Kincaid woman. She'd shot it out in a stagecoach holdup, so she was tough. But she was a woman, and she'd had the stagecoach driver and the man riding shotgun fighting at her side, so Jasper didn't take that too seriously.

And what he'd heard about her husband told Jasper that Seth Kincaid was the weak link. A crazy man, some said. If anyone would tell Jasper where that money was, it would be Seth Kincaid. And his new wife might just be the way to get to Seth.

Jasper had Bea's promise that she'd come along, to keep Jasper on the straight and narrow path. He woke her up, and while she dressed, he saddled their horses. As he worked in their small barn, he fumed over everything belonging to Bea. The house, the land, the stupid chickens, the clothes on Jasper's back. All paid for by her.

A man had no pride if he had no money, and Jasper had a fortune waiting for him. He planned to finish with the Kincaids, get his money, and then he'd live the life Bea wanted. Later, he'd prove up on the promises he'd made before God.

Right now, though, Jasper had a fortune to find. And to do that, he needed to find Seth Kincaid.

CHAPTER 16

"We've got to get that shack up." Rafe stood up from the breakfast table. The lantern was still burning. They'd roused early. "I want the women to stay here. We can't take a bunch of babies to the building site."

His wife had her own ideas. "There's a south wind blowing this morning, Rafe. That always brings in warm weather. We'll ride along with you, and if we need to get the young ones inside, the women can ride over to our cabin. It's not far. Besides, I'd like to see what you've got planned for where our old cabin stands."

While Rafe and Julia bickered, Seth noticed Callie pulling a coat on and wrapping a blanket around Connor. It looked like she was going.

He sidled over to her, moving slowly, not wanting to draw Rafe's attention. "Why are you going? You can't chop down trees with a baby on your back."

Callie hoisted Connor in her arms. She seemed to be back at full strength now. "First of all, Kincaid, don't ever tell me what I can't do. I can do anything I put my mind to."

"So you want to chop down trees?" Seth figured he'd have his hands full stopping her.

"No, I said first of all. If I wanted to, I'd do it. Second, I'm not letting you out of my sight until I'm sure I can trust you." Her black eyes flashed. Her hair hung in a thick braid over her shoulder. She was so dark, she almost looked like an Indian. Maybe some Apache blood flowed in her veins. Seth wondered how he could ask that. He had a feeling he ought to know.

After flipping a few questions around in his head, he finally decided he was safe asking, "What was your name before we got married?"

The anger in her eyes made his gut twist in fear. Through clenched teeth she said, "Stone. My father and mother were born in America, but my grandparents were all from Italy. Their name was Pietra, which means stone. They changed it to embrace their new country. Is that what you want to know? Why don't you just ask me questions straight out?"

Seth winced. "Because you're kinda scary."

Callie rolled her eyes and began tucking Connor into his carrier.

"Is Callie Italian, too?"

"My full name is Calandra, my grandmother's name. But no one calls me that."

"Calandra Pietra. Wow, I don't think I can be blamed for forgetting that."

"My name is Callie Kincaid. You think you can remember that, cowboy?"

Seth decided that if he couldn't, he'd keep it to himself.

Julia and Audra were bundling Maggie and Lily. So Julia must have won her argument with Rafe. Seth really needed to ask Julia how she did that.

The day warmed as they rode to the Gilliland cabin. The first thing Seth noticed was that the roof had collapsed on one corner. Seth shuddered to think what would have become of Julia and Audra if the Kincaids hadn't found them.

"Heath." Rafe jabbed a finger at the woods surrounding the ramshackle cabin. "Can you chop down a tree?"

Heath's eyes narrowed and he jerked his chin down once. "Better'n you, I reckon."

"Good. You and Ethan start chopping. Seth and I will get this cabin knocked down and see if there's anything we can reuse. Most of it looks fit for kindling."

"I'd be glad to help you tear this place down." Julia swung off her horse. The weather had warmed with the rising sun, although it was still a chilly day to have the children outside. Julia stalked up to the front door of the tumbled-down cabin, lifted her foot, and slammed it hard against the door. The leather hinges snapped and the door fell inward with a crack of splintered wood. A puff of dirt billowed up from it and blew into Julia's face.

Seth had a moment of sympathy for Wendell Gilliland. He'd been dead only a few months, yet it was pretty obvious that his daughter wasn't grieving.

"You can take over now, Rafe." Julia turned, dusting her hands off, as if the rest of her wasn't coated in dirt. "It's cold enough, the children shouldn't stay out. Audra, let's take them to my cabin and leave this shack to the men. Callie, you come along with us."

"I'm going to stay here and keep an eye on my husband, Julia."

"Well, hand over Connor, then. We should get him out of the wind."

Julia and Audra rode off with all the children in tow.

Ethan slung an axe over his shoulder, and Heath followed him into the woods, leading two horses to drag the logs.

Beyond the back of the house was a wall of rock that rose up and then dropped away to a rushing stream that formed the western border of the Kincaid Ranch. Julia and Audra had inherited the cabin and the land under it and brought it into the fold when they married into the family.

Just past the stream was a pit that led to the cavern where Seth had nearly died when he was a child. Seth had run wild in that cavern all his life after the accident. His desperate love for the cavern bothered his family, yet Seth felt more alive down there than he did aboveground.

He slid his hand into a pocket and pulled out his little flat tin of matches. Rafe had foisted the tin on him when he'd come home from the war and told him to never go anywhere without it.

Even now, Seth itched to go explore the cavern. He'd learned it well. He'd left part of himself behind down there after the accident. The thought haunted him that he'd sold his soul to the devil to save his life.

"What are you staring at, cowboy?" Callie drew his attention, and he realized he was staring at the rise behind the Gilliland cabin, as if he could see through it and across the stream and down into the cave entrance, into the belly of the earth.

"You've never seen the cavern, have you?" His heart lifted to think of showing it to her.

"What cavern?"

That startled Seth. "You mean I never talked about it?"

"I reckon not."

"You said I had nightmares, right?"

"Terrible dreams. I could hardly wake you up." The ring of an axe broke the silence. A second axe began hewing at a tree.

"And did I yell for my brothers?"

Callie nodded. "That's when I first learned their names. When you woke up, I asked you who Rafe and Ethan were. And you were always yelling that you were burning. Well, not always. You talked about the gunshots, too. And other things—explosions, battles. It was all the war."

"No, not all. Didn't I tell you about that cavern at all?"

"No."

Seth spent time every day thinking about that cavern. If he'd never told Callie about it, then he really was out of his head, and she didn't know him well enough to marry him. "When I was a kid, I had an accident in that cavern. I got burned."

Callie slid her hand to his neck just under his collar, touching his scars. "These are left from that? What happened?"

He loved her touching him. He had a flash of a memory of her rubbing his back. Or no, maybe bandaging his back. He was lying on his stomach, and he looked back to see her touching him, leaning over him. He felt her soft hair spilling onto his back. Loose. Surely a nurse kept her hair tied back. And she'd smiled down at him. He knew the moment was a true memory and not some dream. And the way she touched him, the way she smiled, this had to be after they were married. It sure better have been, considering where the memory took his thoughts. Oh, he could well imagine wanting to marry her bad.

"There was a fire." A blaze seemed to leap higher than his head and he stepped back.

"What's the matter?"

Callie's voice pulled him back from the waking nightmare. He fought down the memory.

"Nothing, just don't want to talk about the fire is all. Did I tell you the scars came from the war?"

"No, but . . . well, the doc said they were old, fully healed. But the war had been going on awhile. I thought it was an injury from an earlier battle. You never said."

Seth saw her looking at his neck. He touched her chin, and she lifted her gaze away from the ugly injury. It covered his back, his left arm. He had scars on his neck and even up in his hair. "Did you see all of them?"

Nodding, she said, "We had to take your shirt off to tend your bullet wounds."

Flinching at the thought, Seth asked, "And you still agreed to marry me? Even after you saw how ugly I am."

"You're not ugly." Callie caressed his scarred neck.

Seth leaned closer, enjoying her kindness.

"You're loco as a snakebit hoot owl, but not ugly."

Deflated, Seth turned to work. "I might as well get to tearing down that cabin."

She patted him on the back as if he were ten years old and she was sending him off to his chores.

Seth stalked over to the cabin, grabbed a likely piece of timber, and began ripping the log walls apart with his bare hands. Rafe had tools and they might need his heavy hammer and the saw, but for now the cabin was falling apart without a lot of effort.

They had most of the walls down, and Ethan and Heath had dragged in some good-sized logs and were back to their chopping when Rafe called for a break. He got the canteen and pulled off his gloves to take a long drink, then passed it on.

"Remember, Wendell Gilliland is supposed to have a fortune hidden somewhere," Rafe said. "Be on the lookout for it."

"A fortune?" Callie crossed her arms to stare at the cabin. "He had a fortune and he lived here?"

"Yep," Rafe said, staring at what was left of the shack. "He stole it back in Houston and ran for the West under a false name."

"So he stole money and no one can find it?" Callie looked at the derelict cabin.

"We've hunted but found no sign of it. So whether he gambled it away or hid it where we can't find it, we just don't know. But the man he stole it from sent outlaws after us twice to get his money back."

"Will he send more men?" Callie asked.

"We're on the lookout." Rafe studied the shack. "But it's been three months. And the men who came after us told the sheriff who'd sent them, so he's a wanted man now. On the run, most likely. Too busy to cause us trouble."

"Who was he?"

"His name's Jasper Henry, from Houston," Seth said.

"He's shaming my state." Callie's jaw clenched.

"I broke my leg when we were attacked the last time," Seth said. "Your letter came the day that happened. Rafe and Ethan took turns riding out to search for you. But there're a whole lotta trails from Denver, and we weren't sure where to look. I'd just gotten well enough to do the hunting when I found you." Seth was real glad he'd been the one to find her, to see how she'd fought for her life in the stagecoach robbery.

"So we're watching close," Rafe said. "A man needs to be ready for trouble in the Rockies, anyway."

A loud crack in the woods and the crash and snap of a falling tree told them Ethan was doing his part of the work. Before the crashing stopped, another tree fell. Heath was keeping up.

"We need to get busy." Rafe pulled on his leather gloves. "Ethan'll be done with the logs before we're close to ready to start building."

The cabin had come down fast. Seth grabbed another log. It was so narrow it had no business being part of a wall.

CHAPTER 17

"Callie, how much do you know about Seth's cavern?"

Julia had shown up at noon with food for them all. They wolfed down the meal and went straight back to work. Julia stopped Callie before she could join them.

"He told me about it today for the first time. Is it around here?" Callie had to admit she was curious about what had gone on with Seth to leave him so scarred. "Plenty of caves in a mountain range."

Julia looked left and right and whispered, "Follow me. I'll show you the entrance."

Callie would've preferred to keep tearing at the cabin, but she still ached from her shootout, and a little break wouldn't be the worst idea in the world.

Seth and Rafe were busy. Ethan and Heath had gone back to cutting down trees. Callie let Julia drag her along behind what was left of the cabin. They reached a steep trail that led down to a stream.

"We don't have time to ford that," Callie said. "Let's get back to work."

"It won't take long, I promise." Julia headed down into a dark gully that sent a chill up Callie's spine. What if there was a rainstorm? The steep walls edging this stream would fill up fast.

Julia went on fearlessly, so Callie tagged along, moving quickly.

When they'd climbed the other side, Julia went straight for a black hole in the ground and dropped to her knees beside it.

Following her, Callie peered down into a bottomless pit and took two quick steps back. "What is that?"

"It's a cavern."

Callie went to her knees, feeling a little less likely to go plunging in, and stretched out to look down into the pitch-black. "Seth likes it down there?"

Julia reared back to sit on her heels. "I do, too. It's the most beautiful place."

Callie looked skeptical. "How can you tell? It's pretty dark."

"I don't suppose you can draw a picture, can you?"

Strange question. "I've always had a knack for drawing."

With a thrilled gasp, Julia grabbed Callie by the wrist. "Can you really? Are you telling the truth?"

"Are you calling me a liar?" Callie asked with a scowl.

Instead of a shootout, Julia threw her arms around Callie and gave her about the biggest hug of her life.

Then Julia let go and began clawing in one of her pockets. She brought out a folded-up piece of paper and a pencil.

"Take this and listen to me. Draw what I tell you."

"What? We need to get back to the cabin."

"Just do it."

Callie jumped and took the paper.

"This is really important."

Callie suspected her idea of what was important was real different from Julia's. But right now, it seemed sketching out a quick picture would get Callie back to work faster than trying to escape from her overly excited sister-in-law.

"At the bottom of this cavern entrance is a room about twenty feet tall and about the same distance around."

Callie shook her head. "And you think that's more important than building a cabin?"

Julia tapped impatiently on the paper. "Draw it. And make it small; there's a lot more."

With a defeated sigh Callie began following orders, adding tunnels and rooms here and there. Julia oversaw it all, and before they were done, they had about five sheets of paper covered front and back.

"There's really a cave this big down there?" Callie had her doubts, but she couldn't figure out why Julia would make it up.

"Yes, and this is just the general outline. It doesn't begin to show the stalactites and stalagmites and the fossils." Julia seemed to be getting breathless.

Callie looked between Julia and the hole to make sure that if Julia fainted from excitement, she wouldn't fall to her death.

A steady pounding of axes and falling trees set the work the family was doing to a rugged kind of music.

"We need to get back," Callie said.

Julia's jaw looked rigid enough to crack. "I want Seth to see this. He knows that cavern better than anyone. He says he'll show me around, and he has a few times, but not nearly enough. He always has something to do that keeps him away. Herding cattle or building a fence or damming up a stream, some stupid job."

"Sounds like he's trying to run a ranch, Julia." Callie folded the paper.

"Wait!" Julia grabbed the map.

Callie was running slap out of patience. "What now?"

Julia looked from the map to Callie to the cavern entrance. Finally she nodded, frowning. "Tonight we can show this to Seth."

"Why does Seth know the cavern better than anyone else?"

"We can talk about it tonight. You can stay at my cabin and we can work on this map some more." Julia smiled. She really was a fanatic about the cavern.

"Can we go back now?" Callie was tired of sitting around drawing when there was work to be done.

"Right, we'd better go."

"Julia, where'd you get to?" Rafe's voice came from all the way across the stream.

"We're coming. I was just showing Callie the cavern." Julia got up and hurried back to the shack.

"You didn't go down in it, did you?" Rafe's question seemed to contain a threat of some kind.

"Not without me." Seth sounded more like he was pouting.

Callie, shaking her head, tagged along. As they crested the top of the gully behind the cabin, Callie saw there was no cabin. Not anymore. "It's gone."

"Yep." Seth came up the trail to meet her. "All that's left is the floor."

"There are split logs. Some of 'em might be reusable." Rafe straightened with an armload of kindling, the last of the inside wall of the cabin, which had separated the main room from the two small bedrooms.

Seth fell in beside her, and Callie liked having him close, so much she could cry.

Seth liked slipping his arm around Callie's slender waist, so much he could've howled like a mountain wolf. "Should we just leave the floor there?"

"No." Rafe had an answer, of course. "About half of these split logs are rotten. Let's tear it up. We'll build the walls and worry about putting down a floor later. Might be that men stuck here in the line shack this winter could lay flooring when the winds are too fierce to go outside."

Seth knew his brother hated to see a man waste a single minute. Being buried in snow was no excuse for idleness.

Rafe and Seth jerked the half-buried logs out of the ground. Julia and Callie teamed up to carry them away. Seth noticed the women kept up a friendly chatter, and he was glad to see Julia welcoming Callie to the family.

Rafe and Seth had to scramble to keep up with the women. As they finished the front room of the cabin and turned to the back, all that remained was the floor of the two bedrooms. Ethan and Heath appeared from the woods dragging more logs behind them. They had a nice stack.

Seth pulled up a split log and a small metal cylinder rolled out from between the flooring. "What's this?" He bent to pick it up and saw a second cylinder.

Julia came up just as he asked the question. "Oh, throw those away," she said. "My father's cigars. He carried them with him everywhere. Awful, smelly things. I burned the rest of the cigars but forgot about the ones he had in those tubes. I guess they rolled into a crack in the floor when I took his shirt off."

"They'd make good match tins." Seth turned to Rafe. "You guys have your matches with you, right?"

Rafe and Ethan each pulled flat containers from their pockets.

"I have matches, too." Julia produced her little container.

"Those are a little long and round to go in a man's pocket," Rafe said.

Seth took one of the tubes. "Callie, you should use these to carry matches with you. And Heath needs matches. And Audra." Despite his love for that dark cavern, Seth felt his throat swell a bit to think of being stuck down there in the pitch-dark. "We'll use these two and get some more."

Seth extended one toward Callie, who stood closest to him.

She unscrewed the lid and wrinkled her nose. "It must still have a cigar in it."

Seth took it back and tipped it. A cigar fell onto the ground. With a little click it hit a log lying at Seth's feet, so dried out it cracked into several pieces. Seth opened the other container and tipped it to dispose of the cigar.

"It's stuck." Seth lifted it to his eyes. "They do stink." Seth stuck a finger into the cylinder and tugged at the black cigar. He inched it out. A bit of tobacco leaf broke off and came out. Seth went back to digging in the little tube. The cigar gave slowly, a fraction of an inch at a time. Finally it was sticking out enough that Seth could get a solid grip on the crumbling thing and drag it out. It dropped and something pattered like tiny hailstones on the log at Seth's feet.

He bent down. "What's this?"

"Looks like broken glass." Rafe came up beside Seth. "Lucky you didn't cut yourself."

"It's not sharp." Seth picked up a single one of the bits of clear glass and held it close to examine it.

Julia hunkered down beside him. Her gasp drew everyone else toward her.

"Not glass, Rafe." Julia picked one up and stood.

"What, then?" Rafe took the little sparkling bit from her.

"I think . . . I mean I've studied geology, you know. I think these . . . they're . . . they must be . . . diamonds."

"Diamonds?" Seth turned a startled glance to the pretty stones.

"It looks like," Julia said in a hushed voice, "we've found the fortune my father stole."

Jasper had heard enough from listening around Colorado City that he could ride straight to the Kincaid Ranch.

He was pleased to realize he could still read sign, and the tracks told him they were approaching a good-sized spread. "The ranch is up ahead."

Bea hadn't done much grumbling, and Jasper hoped he could get through this without it. He wanted to still have a wife when this was all over. A wife and his diamonds.

"Let's scout it out, Bea, honey." He slipped off the trail

and tied his horse, along with Bea's, out of sight. There was a good lookout spot, and he settled in to watch for any sign of Seth Kincaid.

"This has to be the original Kincaid Ranch. It has an established look about it. Ethan Kincaid lives here with Audra Gilliland. It's her husband who stole from me." Jasper's jaw tightened as he thought of his money gone to these ranchers while he lived in a hovel. They stayed hidden for a long time.

"I'm freezing, Jasper. Why don't you just go up and knock on the door and ask Ethan Kincaid for your money, if you're so determined to be an honest man?"

"Now, Bea, hiding up here, watching a house isn't dishonest. I haven't seen anyone come and go from the house and there's no smoke coming out of the chimney. It's too cold for them to not keep a fire going."

"It's cold for a fact." Bea shivered.

"I think Ethan's gone. And since Seth was coming home with his wife and baby, it's a good chance Ethan is at Seth's house. Let's ride on and see if anyone's there."

He found the second cabin cut out of the mountains and forests like a raw sore. Clearly it was newly built. There was a small barn, but no hired men were in evidence and no livestock. The house had an addition so new that Jasper could still smell the fresh-cut wood. He was bolder about going up to this place. It also stood empty. So where were all the Kincaids?

"Let's get out of the cold for a bit, Bea. There's no one here."

Bea might've protested entering a stranger's house, but she was shivering until she could barely speak.

The place didn't have a fire, but getting out of the wind

helped a lot. He searched the cabin thoroughly under the guise of hunting up a blanket for Bea. The barn as well, which he excused by saying he needed to check the horses. The sun was setting when he finally gave up.

"We need to move on, Bea."

"It's almost dark. I don't want to sleep on the trail."

Jasper didn't either. And the next home built by the Kincaids was something of a mystery. No one in town really knew where it was, and the talk had only made it more confusing. Though it wasn't wise, Jasper's years spent living in luxury overcame his qualms.

"If Seth Kincaid comes home, we'll tell him we were out in the cold and used his house to sleep in."

"Or you could just tell him the truth and ask him if he's got your money."

Jasper met Bea's eyes. She was a smart woman bent on going straight. It made her mighty hard to handle. "All right. Yes, we can do that. I hope he does show up."

"Why can't you let the money go, Jasper? We're getting by as we are."

It was a hard question and Jasper wasn't sure she'd like his answer. "I feel ashamed, Bea. I feel like I've lost my pride. I live off you. I'm a bum."

"You work hard every day. A bum doesn't do that."

"Maybe not." He brushed her hair back off her face. "You've got no right to be so pretty when your life has been so hard."

"Hush with your sweet talk."

"Everything we have is yours. And somewhere right around here is the money I spent my life earning. It gnaws at me day and night. I lay awake and twist myself up thinking about it being so close. Thinking about these Kincaids living high off the money I fought years to earn."

"It's ill-gotten and you know it."

"I earned it more than the Kincaids ever did."

She patted his arm.

"Once I get it back, I can hold my head up. I won't try to buy us a big house or make you live a rich life. I know you like where we're at. But knowing I can call it mine instead of yours . . . well, I don't think I'll ever know any peace if I can't say that."

Bea looked at him. "It's a fool's errand. You know that. Better to just go back to Colorado City, and if you want to feel like you're part owner, then get a job. Hire on to work at the bank or somewhere."

"Me, in a bank?"

"You can add and subtract, can't you?"

"I can indeed, and I want to add my money to yours. I'd have to work for years to add a fraction of what's already mine."

"But it would be enough, Jasper. More than enough, and honestly earned." She rested her head on his shoulder.

"I can't go back without at least trying, Bea. Tomorrow I'll get my money, and then be the most upright man you've ever known. You'll be proud to have me as your husband."

"I'm proud now, Jasper."

"I'm going."

"I'll not stand by if you hurt anyone."

A smile escaped as Jasper realized she was agreeing to let him try. "You have my word that I won't. Now, let me get this place warmed up."

Jasper didn't intend to hurt anyone. He'd find his diamonds, sneak in, grab them and run, with no one the wiser. And staying in the cabin didn't seem like too big a risk. He felt confident no one was coming home anytime soon. It was too late at night.

The Kincaids must be staying the night at the third house, the one no one knew much about. In the dark he'd have the devil's own time following a trail. He'd heard twisted stories about Rafe Kincaid's house being in a hard-to-find canyon.

Jasper expected he'd hunt it down with no trouble, but not in the dark.

He built up the fire. It crackled in the silent room. The wind whined down the chimney and made the flames dance and sparkle like diamonds.

Bea had refused to use the beds, so they'd settled on the floor, wrapped together in a blanket. Tomorrow he'd find his diamonds and get back to his real life.

The warm room pulled Jasper into sleep, and just as he dozed off, the snapping flames and whipping wind changed until he heard what sounded like the devil laughing.

CHAPTER 18

"What's a little stack of diamonds worth?" Seth looked at his brothers. Who shrugged.

"A lot." Julia held the cigar cylinder packed with diamonds in her hands. She reached into the cylinder and pulled out one stone about the size of a baby's thumbnail. "I know the bigger they are, the more valuable. And as diamonds go, these seem big. All together, they're worth probably tens of thousands of dollars."

Callie couldn't help but gasp. "In that little tube?"

Julia held the diamonds just a bit farther away from her body, as if the tube had turned into a Texas sidewinder. As if holding it made her skin crawl, but she was afraid to let go and get bit. "I reckon you oughta take 'em somewhere. Sell 'em and buy something important like land and cattle and horses."

Julia shook her head, frowning. "We can't sell them. My father stole them and I refuse to get rich on his dishonesty."

"The man he stole 'em from sent low-down hombres after you to take the diamonds back, by force." Callie didn't hold with keeping stolen goods, yet was it right to return those goods to a thief? "An honest man would've contacted the sheriff and reported that he'd been robbed."

"True enough." Seth looked at the cleared area where the line shack needed to go. "Can we stop talking about diamonds and get this cabin built? I don't want to be all day about it."

It suited Callie to get back to work. She preferred ignoring something as stupid as stones that looked like broken glass. "Take 'em to the sheriff, then. The lawman in Rawhide can sort it all out. If the man who says those diamonds are his shows up, just tell him to talk to the sheriff. Bet he'll hit the trail fast enough."

"I don't want to take them to the sheriff in Rawhide. Working alone like he does, this might be a big temptation to the man, and I don't want him to go bad because of us. We need to take them to Colorado City."

"We can't get there before spring most likely," Seth said.

"If we can't get out before spring, then it stands to reason an outlaw can't get in." Rafe took the diamonds from Julia. "In the meantime, we need to tuck these away somewhere safe. These diamonds, once turned in to the sheriff, will buy us some peace."

"I could try the run to Colorado City, Rafe." Seth reached for the diamonds and Rafe handed them over. "Now that the blizzard is over, it shouldn't be hard to make it."

Rafe looked from the cylinder to Seth. "It could be done. But you need to start early."

"How about tomorrow?"

"No, not tomorrow." Callie snagged the diamonds from Seth.

"Why not?" Seth asked.

"Because I have to go with you, and I'm not in the mood for another long ride up and down a cold mountainous trail. And if I go, Connor has to go."

"Seth can make the ride into town and back in a long hard day alone, Callie," Rafe said. "You don't need to go."

"I'm not leaving his side until I'm sure he's not gonna run off again."

"Hey! I'd come back. I'm not running off. Why would I do a thing like that?"

"Why indeed?" Callie exchanged a long look with Rafe.

Rafe opened his mouth, then looked at Seth and scowled. "He'd almost for sure come back."

"I've got a wife and son out here. Besides, I want to show Connor the cavern." Seth's eyes flashed with wild enthusiasm.

"Okay," Rafe said. "You can rest up a few more days before you head to town. And if the cold weather shuts down hard on our heads, we can hope the varmint after those diamonds is locked away from us for the winter. Now let's get back to work." Rafe, always taking charge. "Ethan and Heath, we're gonna need a lot more logs."

Ethan looked at Heath. They both shrugged and led their horses back toward the forest.

They kept at their building until full dark. The cabin was close to done when the day ended. "I'll hang the door and shutters myself." Rafe pulled off his gloves and wiped his brow. The evening was turning colder, though Callie hadn't noticed until she'd stopped working.

"We'll ride for home now." Seth began saddling his horse.

"No, we have to get Connor." Callie got to work strapping leather on her own mount.

She saw Seth freeze, take a nervous look at her, then go back to tending his horse.

"Forget you had a son, cowboy?"

Seth's eyes got wide and his hands moved faster. Callie only kept from slugging him because she was exhausted and had a long ride ahead of her.

"Stay at our house tonight," Julia said. "It'll be the middle of the night before you get back to your place."

"It feels like the middle of the night now." Rafe swung up on his horse.

Ethan and Seth followed suit. Whatever their quirks, and they seemed legion, Callie had to admit the Kincaid men knew horses and they knew building. The line shack had gone up fast and sturdy.

Soon they were riding down another mountain by moonlight. Callie would get used to the whole world standing on end someday, but for now she missed the rolling hills and flatlands of her father's ranch.

They rode up the side of another mountain and swung down to lead the horses into a cave. "You live in this cave?" she asked Julia.

"No, this is a vent into a caldera."

Callie felt free to roll her eyes at the nonsense because they'd entered the cave and it was pitch-dark.

"The cave goes all the way through into a mountain valley," Rafe said. He was in the lead and his voice echoed back past the row of Kincaids, each leading their horse. Rafe first, then Julia. Heath, Seth, Callie, with Ethan bringing up the rear.

When they came out, Callie saw a vast stretch of meadow bathed in moonlight. It was too dark for her to see it clearly, but she liked the feel of it, the openness. Trees weren't trying to swallow up every bit of space.

When they reached the cabin, light gleamed in the window. Smoke curled out of the chimney, and Callie smelled something hot and meaty.

They saw to their horses. Inside, Audra was the only one there. She'd heard them coming and was mostly done dishing up plates from a huge pot of stew simmering on a rectangular cast-iron cookstove. The cabin was lit by several lanterns. There were doors to the right and left of the main room, both closed. And two more doors to the back. The main room held a big table near the stove on the right side, and two rocking chairs in front of the fireplace on the left.

Callie and Julia washed up and pitched in to prepare the meal while the men finished cleaning up. Rafe said the blessing, and Callie thought he sounded particularly sincere when he prayed for their safety and wisdom in dealing with the diamonds. Soon they were all eating the savory meal.

They fell on the food like starving lumberjacks and made short work of finishing it.

"Thanks, Audra, honey." Ethan took his plate to the sink. "A hot meal puts heart into a man."

With the meal cleared away, exhaustion weighed down

Callie's eyelids and she felt every ache left from her run-in with stagecoach robbers.

"I put the children all in the south bedroom." Audra looked them over. "Two more bedrooms. One for the women, one for the men?"

"I'll sleep out here in front of the fire," Seth said.

"Me, too." Heath rose from the table. His chair scraped on the floor, and he looked about ready to fall asleep where he stood.

Callie was relieved the boy had spoken up because she didn't want to be tempted to sleep with her husband.

"Callie, you stay out here with me," Seth said. "Let Julia and Rafe, and Audra and Ethan have the bedrooms."

Though she didn't like it, Callie felt churlish refusing to give the married couples some privacy. Then she realized she was included in that group—married couples. She hadn't said much in front of the others about not wanting to be with Seth, and now wasn't the time to bring it up. Nothing married would happen while she was sleeping on the floor in the same room as a half-grown boy.

They were soon settled with a generous pile of blankets that took some of the hard out of their hardwood mattress. Callie was too tired to worry much about Seth lying down next to her and covering them both with the same blanket. And she was barely awake when she realized that somehow her head was pillowed on his broad shoulder.

CHAPTER 19

A scream jerked Callie awake. Something hit her in the face. She clawed for her gun as she rolled aside.

She didn't have it.

"I'm on fire! Rafe! Ethan!" The cry for help dragged her out of her unthinking reaction as, with a whoosh of relief, she recognized Seth's voice.

She was kneeling, facing him, well out of striking distance by the time it all sorted through her brain. And she had a throbbing spot on her cheek where she was pretty sure her husband had just punched her.

Her poor tormented husband needed his arm broken.

"I'm burning!" Seth slapped at his arms and face.

She saw movement in the dark room, lit only by glowing embers from the dying fire.

"What's going on? Where's the trouble?" Heath was on his feet. He sounded like a boy ready to fight for his life.

A wise way to conduct yourself on the frontier.

"Seth has nightmares."

Two doors crashed open. And Rafe and Ethan came out of their bedrooms in their nightshirts.

"I'll get the cold water." Ethan turned to the kitchen side of Rafe's house.

Callie crawled toward her husband. "Heath, light a lantern please."

Rafe knelt beside Seth, opposite Callie.

"Forget the water, Ethan." Callie wanted to slap her insensitive brother-in-law. "I can wake him up."

Ethan came to her side just as Audra and Julia emerged from their bedrooms.

"Help! Rafe, help me."

"Seth, wake up." She rested one hand firmly on his shoulder, and he thrashed around, knocking her hand aside, and she barely ducked in time to miss getting a black eye.

"Let me hold him down while you try and wake him up." Ethan looked across Seth's flailing arms at Rafe. "Grab his arms."

"No, that's not necessary."

Ethan and Rafe moved before they could listen to her. Seth's cries rose.

"You might think the water is cruel, but it's fast." Ethan lost his grip on Seth and nearly fell across him. He caught himself and got a better hold.

"I suppose." Callie wondered if Seth would respond to her with his brothers holding him down. He screamed louder, fought their hands.

Callie had to bend around Ethan, who knelt near Seth's head. She leaned down and kissed him.

He bucked against her and cracked her in the face with his hard skull. She dove in again, wrapping her arms around his neck. Maybe to hug him, or more in the way of being a human straitjacket. She kissed him, long and deep. His head tossed and she found his lips again, and suddenly he quit fighting and kissed her back.

"Callie, is that you?"

From experience she knew he was still asleep, but his dreams had just changed.

"My back hurts. Callie, help me."

Something he'd said a lot in the hospital.

"I'm out of Andersonville, Callie. It's over, isn't it? The war is over." He struggled to free his arms and she knew exactly why.

"Let him go." Then his arms were around her and he went back to kissing her. The nightmares driven back. The war over—except in his dreams.

He'd always responded to her like this. Including the first time she'd tried it. The third night in the hospital—the night his fever broke—she'd found him deep in the grip of a nightmare, but he was soaked in sweat and his fever down. He'd live. Her relief was so strong, she wanted to wake him and celebrate with him. She believed that waking him one more time, to find himself on the mend, would be the end of the nightmares that he'd had repeatedly since he'd been brought in.

She'd been a cockeyed optimist for sure back then. She'd struggled to pull him out of the dream, and she'd remembered a fairy tale. Awakening a sleeping prince with a kiss. Or maybe the story had been about turning a frog into a prince. The frog part, that was a better description of her husband.

So she'd kissed him.

He'd awakened and kissed her back like a house afire.

And he'd held her tight. They'd celebrated his improved health for quite some time. After that, she'd stayed with Seth at night. Waking him, sometimes several times a night, with a kiss. The intimacy, though it hadn't gone too far, was definitely improper. One night a doctor interrupted them, very unhappy to catch his nurse kissing a patient. Seth was awake enough to propose.

Like an idiot she hadn't hesitated to say yes. They were married the next day.

He'd been released from the overcrowded hospital to stay with her that night. And though he was still weak and taking small doses of laudanum for the pain, he hadn't had the nightmares. Of course their sleep had been interrupted with delightful regularity by the joy of being newlyweds. Then when they'd been married just a few days, his first nightmare came. She'd awakened him with a kiss—and more. The next morning, Seth went for a walk and foolishly Callie hadn't gone along.

He'd never come back.

Since they had about a dozen witnesses here in Rafe's house, she needed to get away from her lunatic husband and his heated kisses.

She had her hands full pulling away. It was made worse by how wonderful it felt to be in his arms.

"Callie, no. Come back." He reached for her.

"Wake up, Seth." Callie coaxed him rather than ordering

him. He responded very well to coaxing once the dreams had been driven back.

"Callie."

"He remembers you in his dreams. He must." Audra came up and rested her hands on Callie's shoulders.

"Yes, if he's dreaming and he knows my name, he might be remembering." To her own ears, Callie sounded hopeful and eager and stupid as a chunk of rotten timber. So what if he remembered her when he was dreaming? He remembered horrible things even more.

"You're in there." Audra spoke as if she read Callie's thoughts. "He's just been really hurting for a long time. It sounds like he was sick when he left you. He got to Rawhide somehow, but before he could get home, a man got hold of him and gave him laudanum for a while. A lot of the confusion he's gone through can be blamed on the drug."

"Laudanum? Seth reacted badly to that. I let him have a little bit because the wounds in his back were so painful, but I never gave him strong doses." Callie had dispensed a great deal of it in the hospital, including to Seth, but the drug had always hit him harder than most. "A doctor was treating him?"

"No," Audra said quietly. "A man who was after those diamonds. He found Seth and realized Seth knew this area. The man wanted help finding where my husband had us living. At that old cabin we tore down today. When they got close, Seth remembered the cavern and showed the man. Then the man drugged Seth to keep him calm and confused while Seth showed him around in the cavern, because it was a good hiding place, close to where the man thought the diamonds were hidden."

"That stupid cavern again." Callie hadn't known about the cavern when she was back East, but now she knew exactly what to blame for Seth's nightmares and scars and general madness.

"Callie?" Seth sounded confused but awake. He reached for her. Callie knew he was still befuddled enough that she didn't dare let him get his hands on her.

She'd find out more about the laudanum later. Right now she needed to pull Seth all the way out of his tormenting sleep. "Seth, we're at Rafe's house."

"Rafe?"

"It's Callie."

"Callie, I've missed you so much." He sat up and dragged her against him and pulled her onto his lap. His lips rained kisses across her face and sunk one hand deeply into her hair. He'd always liked to touch her hair.

She wondered if they might not need the cold water after all.

"Another nightmare, brother." Rafe slapped Seth on the shoulder hard enough that his head bumped into Callie's lips. Callie figured Rafe knew exactly where Seth's mind was headed, and he wanted to make very sure it didn't get where it was going.

"Rafe? Is that you?" Seth sounded more awake by the moment.

"Yep, and Ethan and Julia and Audra and Heath." A howl came from the bedroom Ethan and Audra had emerged from. "And Lily."

Another cry sounded. Connor was awake.

"Yep, the whole family's right here watching you kiss Callie." Rafe slapped Seth again. "You oughta knock it off."

"Callie, you came back." His eyes went to her hair, which

he'd managed to get out of its braid. He combed through it, his strong fingers smoothing at the dark length.

As if Callie was the one who'd gone somewhere.

"Is that Maggie?" Seth looked past Callie just as Julia appeared with Connor.

Callie said, "Give me the boy, please."

Julia set him down, and the baby crawled with startling speed straight for Seth. He kept going until he used Seth to pull himself up. He stood, his knees bending to bounce himself.

"Papa!" Connor slapped Seth in the face.

Which Callie enjoyed.

"Connor." Seth pulled the little boy close and hugged him. That's when Callie knew the poor idiot was finally fully awake.

"I have a son." He pulled Connor up so he sat on Callie's lap, with Callie on Seth's lap. Callie's family formed one small pile.

Rafe buried his face in one palm, then scrubbed for a while. "Yep, you've got a son."

She tried to get off her husband's lap. He hung on, but he had her and Connor both and it was too much for him when he was still muddled from the nightmare, so she got away. "You can all go back to sleep now. The excitement is over." Callie wondered how long that'd last.

"I wonder how long that'll last," Ethan asked.

"Let's go." Rafe rested his hand on his wife's back. "Morning comes soon and I've still gotta finish that cabin."

"Since Seth is here, can we go down into the cavern again, Rafe?"

"Not now, Julia." Rafe sounded more exhausted than could be accounted for by interrupted sleep.

"What's the big deal about this cavern?" Heath asked.

"I think we ought to hide those diamonds we found," Seth said. "We need to put them somewhere safe until we can ride to town and hand them over to the sheriff."

"Somewhere safe like the cavern?" Julia sounded far too enthused about that idea. Callie wasn't sure why the woman was so excited about a cavern that had hurt Seth so badly.

"Yeah, great idea." Seth bounced Connor, and the two wild men smiled at each other. "You want to see the cavern, don't you, big guy?"

Connor squealed with excitement.

"We need to get him back to sleep." Callie tried to sound gentle instead of stern. Neither of her men were much good at settling down at the best of times. She slid her arm across Seth's shoulders, feeling the rough, scarred skin through his shirt. Hating the pain that still haunted his dreams after all these years. "Let me have him. We can talk about how to deal with the stupid diamonds tomorrow."

"Those diamonds have brought us nothing but trouble." Audra sounded worried. "We need to get rid of them. Whether or not they're ill-gotten gains on the part of the man who owned them, they were definitely stolen by my husband."

"You stole diamonds?" Heath scowled at Ethan, his blue eyes glittering in the lantern light.

"No, her first husband." Ethan tried to steer Audra back to bed. "Maggie and Lily's pa. He's dead."

"Ethan's your second husband?" Heath asked, sounding real doubtful. "How old are you, anyway?"

"Can we talk about this tomorrow?" Callie knew Connor was waking up more by the second. "At this rate we'll be gathered in here yammering when the sun comes up and we've got a long day ahead of us."

"We certainly do, hiding treasure." Julia didn't sound a bit sleepy.

Rafe urged her into their room and closed the door with a firm snap.

Ethan and Audra were gone next.

That left Heath and Seth and Connor to get to sleep. Callie was tempted to rock her husband to sleep—with a real rock—to the skull.

"Give me Connor." Callie found herself in a tug-of-war with her husband over the baby. Since Callie didn't know for sure how hard Seth would pull, she let go.

"I'll take care of him." Seth went to the rocking chair that had been pushed aside to make room on the floor for sleeping.

Bouncing Connor on his lap, Seth made silly noises and Connor started giggling.

Callie groaned and went to Maggie and Lily's room and got the drawer Connor was sleeping in. Callie put it a safe distance from the fire, then looked at her husband waking her son up more every second. She sat down, her aching back resting on the warm stones of the hearth. Her husband had no idea how to put a baby to sleep. And this wasn't the time for yelling, or a tug-of-war, or a rock to the skull.

She settled in to wait for the sun to rise. It was going to be a long night.

CHAPTER 20

"Rafe, Ethan and Heath can finish the shack. Seth, Callie, and I will explore the cavern and hide the diamonds. Audra can watch the babies here at the cabin." Julia gave Seth a pat on the back.

"I'd love to show Callie the cavern." Seth's heart sped up. The cavern always had that effect on him. He hadn't liked Julia all that much at first. She was a fierce kind of woman. But then he'd found out she loved the cavern and he'd been her loyal friend ever since.

Julia slid a skillet filled with a small mountain of fried potatoes onto the table while Audra brought over a platter of crisp side pork. Callie added biscuits and a pitcher of milk.

"We've got enough eggs for everyone to have a bite. Connor and Maggie get theirs first." Julia came from the stove with the last part of the meal. Everyone was busy eating, so no one started yelling about Julia's plan—yet.

Seth wolfed his food so he'd have his mouth free to support Julia. He swallowed and decided not to wait until the food was gone. Who knew if he'd be able to get a word in then?

"You really only have the roof left to shingle and the doors and shutters to hang, Rafe." Seth looked at his big brother. "Three of you can do that in half a day. I'll be back from the cavern by then. Callie and Connor and I can ride home with Ethan and Audra."

"And Heath, too," Callie reminded him with a sweet smile that did not match the glint of anger in her black eyes.

Seth remembered for the first time in quite a while that Callie had taken a shot at him when he'd come upon the stagecoach holdup.

But she'd had a real bad day. It's not like she'd shot at him lately.

A smile lifted his lips as he thought of some real nice things Callie had done lately. "So, Heath, are you sure you don't want to go on home with Ethan, get to know the old homeplace where our pa lived all those years?"

Heath scowled. "Pa didn't live there, he visited. He lived with me and my ma."

"Was Pa nice to you then? Because he was a grouch most of the time with us." Seth decided just a little bit of honesty right now might make a difference. "I always figured he hated me." He looked down at his plate so the hurt didn't show for the whole room to see. "I almost killed myself and my brothers in that cavern."

"It was because of me." Ethan eased back in his chair and

crossed his arms. "I hurt you, bullied you. I pushed you over the edge. All those nightmares were my fault. I confessed to Ma and Pa and they . . . Ma just started crying. She seemed to give up on all of us. After that, Pa was gone more than he was home. I'm the one who destroyed our family."

"It wasn't because of either of you." Rafe shoved his plate aside. "He told me to take care of you and I didn't. I lost control of the situation. Seth wouldn't have had nightmares. Ethan wouldn't have blamed himself. Ma wouldn't have taken to her rocking chair. And Pa—I reckon Pa wouldn't have decided he needed a better family."

"All that means is, it was my fault." Seth hated admitting it, but it was worse thinking his brothers blamed themselves. "And I was always a little crazy, Eth, even before the accident."

Ethan shook his head. "No, you weren't—"

"Seth, it wasn't your fault," Rafe interrupted.

"And I think," Callie said, her voice cracking like a bull-whip in a way that shut all three of them up, "a grown man with two wives and two sets of children is a worthless heap of buffalo chips, and the fact that you can all sit here feeling guilty, long after he's dead, is proof of just how worthless he was. It's a parent's job to take care of his children, not run off when times get hard. I don't know your ma, Heath, but she sounds like she took good care of you for as long as she lived."

Heath nodded. "She did. And Ma could hunt, so we always had food. She tended our milk cows. She had chickens and a big garden. Pa was . . . well, he was gone from us a lot. He chased after gold some during the rush, but never found any I could see. And he was a fur trapper. That took him away a lot, too."

"Then I'd say of the three parents in these families, she's the only one who's worth a lick of salt. Sittin' around cryin' like your ma did, Seth, or running off like your pa did to all of you is just plain worthless." Callie's eyes flashed, and then the flash changed and she clamped her mouth shut.

But Seth knew she had more to say. "What is it?" he asked.

"Nothing. I've said my piece. Let's get finished eating and—"

"Callie!" He realized it was the first time he'd snapped at her. For some reason it felt good. He pictured another time, a memory of being married. He'd been wrestling with her and her temper flared, then it flipped into passion. Oh, he had a nice vivid memory of that. At last.

Her eyes narrowed in a way that should have been threatening, but instead he wanted to grab her and drag her into his arms and calm her all the way down.

"I'm . . . I'm just wondering." Callie's eyes slid around the room. "How many other wives and children he had."

All Gavin Kincaid's children fell silent. And since they'd been doing most of the talking, it left a big, old quiet room.

Finally Seth pushed his chair back. "I'm going with Julia to hide those diamonds. And I want to show Callie the cave. We'll ride over to the new shack around midday."

He turned and looked at Julia and then Callie. Julia smiled and began pulling on her coat. She moved quick enough that Seth was sure she wanted to get away before Rafe found something else to fuss about.

Callie went to Connor and picked him up. "I'll change his diapers first."

"No, you go on," Audra said, reaching for the boy. "Changing diapers is something I've had a lot of practice at."

"I don't like you going down there without me." Rafe glared at Julia and tapped his fingers impatiently on the table. But he didn't demand that she stay out of the cave. He turned to Callie, still tapping. "Seth's obsessed with that cavern. Every time he goes in it, I'm afraid he won't ever come back out."

"I'm coming back, Rafe. I've got a son now to take care of." It was a good reason, but it struck Seth as strange that he actually needed a reason. Like coming back out wasn't real obvious.

"So long as you don't forget you've got him," Ethan said.

Seth turned to Connor and stared at him. It wouldn't hurt to spend some time memorizing that he existed.

Connor grinned at him and waved his arms wildly. The tyke's blue eyes flashed mischief and recklessness. Seth had a stab of fear to realize the boy might be just like him. He wondered how old Connor had to be before Callie'd let Seth and Connor go down in the cavern exploring.

"And Julia finds the place so interesting," Rafe went on as if no one had interrupted him, "that I swear she doesn't use much sense when she's in there."

"That is such a lie, Rafe Kincaid." For the crankiness of her words, she didn't sound that upset. "I am very careful in that cavern and you know it."

"So," Rafe said, his eyes on Callie, "since you seem like a sensible young woman—and marrying Seth gives me some doubts about that—"

"Hey!" Seth scowled.

"Hush, Rafe has a point." Callie patted Seth on the shoulder.

"—I'm counting on you to stay calm in there." Rafe held her gaze. "Pay attention to the passing time. Come back to the surface and bring both of them with you."

"We'll come back." Callie sounded so sure that Seth was sure, too. He watched his wife strap her six-shooter onto her neat little hip.

Julia thrust Callie's coat impatiently into her hands. "Let's get going. We have to make a short day of it."

While Callie put on her coat, Julia said, "So you like to draw, then?"

Callie whipped her Colt out so fast, Seth blinked and Julia backed up a step.

Ethan and Rafe sprang up from the table, their chairs scraping loudly on the floor.

"Uh . . . ahem." Julia cleared her throat and stepped forward again. Callie was aiming at the ceiling after all. "I meant you . . . you like to draw pictures."

His wife surely knew how to handle a gun. Seth felt a smile replace the fear, and his chest puffed right up with pride. Neither Julia nor Audra were even close to gunslingers.

"You said you liked my maps yesterday. Surely that's enough pictures for one hole in the ground." Callie holstered her weapon with ease.

Watching her, Seth was impressed all over again. He then realized what she'd said. "Pictures? You can draw?"

"Oh, yes, she's quite good. And we enjoyed ourselves creating those pictures, didn't we, Callie?" A smile spread across Julia's face.

"You seemed to be having a good time." Callie flipped the thong on her pistol so it wouldn't fall out of its holster.

Rafe sank back into his chair. "So she can draw pictures. Well, say goodbye to your wife, Seth."

"What difference does it make if I can make a horse look like a horse?" Callie said. She glanced between Julia and Rafe.

"I need someone who can draw."

"I already finished your map."

"But there's so much more. I want pictures of the fossils in the cavern." Julia already had a lantern, a canteen, and a sack with biscuits in hand. She dropped a chunk of charcoal in her pocket.

"You said that word yesterday. What'd you say a fossil is again?"

"I told you yesterday."

Callie shrugged. "Truth is, you're kinda boring when you start talking about that cavern, Julia. I missed a good chunk of what you said."

"Near to put a man to sleep with that cavern talk," Ethan muttered.

"I've often lost track of what you're saying," Audra admitted.

"I know what that's like." Seth picked up two more lanterns.

Rafe shook his head. "Happens to me all the time."

"Then I'll just have to try harder to get you all to understand," Julia said.

Most everyone in the room groaned, though it didn't slow Julia down one bit. "Fossils are the bones of long-dead animals. Extinct animals."

"You want me to draw fish bones like that've been left after someone ate lunch?"

Rafe snickered.

Seth couldn't help but really like his surprise wife.

"I can teach you so much." Julia swung open the door. It was a crisp fall morning, a good day for building. "And I don't mind if you ignore me some. I'm happy to repeat myself when I'm talking about the cavern."

"That is the pure and honest truth," Audra said.

"I already know how to catch, clean, and cook a fish. I suppose I know how to draw one, too. What more is there?"

Beaming at Callie, Julia said, "Have you ever wanted to see something of your very own, printed in a book?" Julia rested her hand on Callie's back and gently but firmly shoved her outside.

"No. Never." Callie looked over her shoulder to give Seth a worried look.

"Well, that's all right. We don't have to put your name on it, then."

Seth didn't have time to think on Julia's alarming ambition because he had to hurry to keep up with the womenfolk. "How much time are you going to want her to spend drawing, Julia? She's got a baby to raise and our cabin is a long ride from here."

Julia was busy talking to Callie and they ignored him like he was a buzzing gnat. Good thing he was far enough back to not be swatted.

For the first time ever, Seth was afraid he might have to spend a little too much time in that cavern.

"Wait!" Rafe hollered from behind them.

Rafe had a voice that commanded obedience and they all turned around.

"What?" Seth knew Rafe didn't like them going without him.

"At least pretend like you've got some brains in your heads." Rafe sounded exhausted. "You're supposed to go down there and hide the diamonds."

"Don't worry, we will." Seth thought of the cavern entrance, suddenly eager to get going.

"Then don't you think you oughta take them with you?"

Ethan came up behind Rafe, the little cylinder of diamonds in his hand. He held it up, and Seth went back and grabbed it.

"Try and hide it somewhere we can have a hope of finding it again, please," Rafe said.

It struck Seth that he was being treated like he was somewhat trustworthy—or maybe Callie was just too far ahead for Rafe to talk with her. It wasn't a common feeling when he was dealing with his brother.

It suited him right down to the ground.

He turned and ran after the women, who were now about halfway across the meadow, heading toward the cavern he adored.

CHAPTER 21

Callie followed Julia into the cavern and itched to get out. The cavern was interesting enough, but she wanted to get on with important things like settling into her own cabin, checking over the cattle herd, figuring out how to get some chickens, taking care of her baby, and reminding her husband she existed.

As she traipsed along in a big old useless hole in the ground, she wondered if Ethan had enough chickens to share. Or if there was time to ride to Colorado City to buy a few. Chickens were mighty handy to have in the West. Eggs were a good, steady source of food.

Julia pointed at some bones stuck in the rock wall. "I want a drawing of that."

"Now?" Callie was pulled out of her thoughts of building a hen house. She wondered how long this was going to take.

"Well, maybe not now. But soon. I want to show you something else first." Julia proceeded farther into the tunnel.

Callie recognized a mistake when she made it. She should have acted eager to draw. Maybe that would keep Julia from going in deeper.

Seth caught up behind Callie and handed her a lantern, so now they each carried one. She took it. He didn't let go. They had a brief tug-of-war until Callie looked at him and he kissed her.

Her heart warmed and her stomach tingled, and she wished she could trust him, wished it bad, because she had a feeling her insistence that they not risk making any more babies was going to be hard to live with.

"And this is . . ." Julia blathered on about something while she left them behind. Callie hurried after her brand-new sister. She couldn't quite understand what Julia was saying due to the echoing and Julia leading and talking while facing forward, and Seth being a powerful distraction and Julia not making much sense even when Callie could hear the words.

Callie didn't figure it mattered much what the woman was saying. Julia loved caves. Strange preference, but harmless. No doubt that love of caves was the bulk of what the woman was yammering about.

The tunnel had such a steep cant, Callie was afraid she'd end up sliding down this tunnel on her backside, but she managed to stay upright.

They'd been walking for quite some time when Julia said, "Careful, here's the hole." Julia's voice echoed back to Callie, who stopped dead in her tracks. Seth came up beside her. The tunnel widened out a bit, and Julia went to the side of the hole and stepped out on a ledge, then pulled back.

She took out a sheaf of papers. "I grabbed this stack of papers with the map already drawn." She turned to Seth, her eyes gleaming with frustration. "I forgot to bring blank paper for sketching." She looked between Callie and Seth. "I've got to run back and get it. Can you wait for me here?"

"No," Seth said. "Catch up with us in the big room with the towers."

"Towers? Down here?" Callie looked around the tunnel with the hole in the floor. Not much chance of any towers.

"Wait for me. I don't want us to get separated." Julia hesitated and gave Callie one of the most worried looks she'd ever gotten. Which made no sense. What was there to worry about?

"Fine then, go on." Seth slid his arm around Callie. "But make it quick. I want to get to showing Callie around."

Callie had the strangest feeling that she shouldn't be alone with him. Alone with her husband. What could possibly be wrong with that?

"You're okay?" Julia rested her hand on Seth's arm. "You could come back with me."

"I'm fine down here; you know that, Jules." Seth shrugged her hand off as if she was hanging on too tight.

"I do know, but maybe not right here." Julia looked past them to the hole in the ground. "Maybe you should come back partway."

Seth gave an impatient huff. "Get on with fetching your paper. We're fine."

"You'd better wait to hide the diamonds, too. I think several of us should know where they are. Just in case."

"Just in case what?" Callie asked.

"I'll wait." Seth spoke over the top of Callie. "Hurry up and get your drawing paper. We don't have that long."

With one last uncertain look, Julia hurried away, her lantern fading in the distance. Seth set his on the rocky floor, took Callie's and put it beside his, then pulled her into his arms.

Seth had been dying for a moment alone with his wife since he'd figured out he had one. He hadn't managed to get too many such moments. He kissed her so thoroughly, and she responded so willingly that he wished maybe Julia would linger back at the cabin. But this was Julia; she'd be right back.

So Seth got on with holding his beautiful black-eyed wife with no hope he could do more than kiss her. He planned on enjoying it fully.

"Seth." Callie slid her arms around his neck. He kissed her eyes and along her jaw. He slid his hands deep into her radiant black hair and felt the braid give way. He loved setting her riotous curls free. He remembered that. Her hair smelled faintly of the soap he had at his cabin, and it made her seem like she was truly his. The dank air of the tunnel cut with the acrid smell of burning kerosene faded as he concentrated on Callie.

"Did you remember me last night, when you were dreaming?"

Seth wished he'd kept her mouth fully occupied. He heard the hurt and confusion in her voice. "For a woman who can hold off four stage robbers, you sure do worry a lot."

He covered her lips, but she turned her head aside. "That's not an answer."

Instead of kissing her, he held her close, hugging her, feeling how alive and warm she was. And he thought of his nightmares. They'd been driven back by memories of . . . "I did."

He lifted his head to look down at her. She wasn't a little woman. She had strength and curves. Her eyes were at the level of his mouth, and she was looking right at his lips. "If you want me to talk, you need to quit looking like you wish I was using my mouth to kiss you."

A tiny smile curved her lips and her eyes closed. With a deep breath she opened them again and looked up into his eyes.

"That's not helping."

"What did you remember?"

Most of his dream was wiped away as soon as he was awake. But he still had a glimmer of it and he thought, he hoped, that was because it was a real memory, not a dream with all its twisted-upness.

"I remember . . . you taking something away from me. You snatched something out of my hands and I grabbed for it and we ended up sort of tangled up, falling down, and you got real mad at me."

"It was a diary I kept." Her voice gentled and he could see it pleased her that he remembered. He'd have to tell her every single time he had the least flash of remembering. "I wrote about my trip back East and how sick my brother was and it had a few things in it about you."

Seth shook his head, wishing it'd rattle loose more buried memories and they'd float to the surface. "I can't remember about the diary. I just remember you got mad and I sort of dragged you down onto the floor."

"You wouldn't stop and you still had stitches in your back. You could have broken them open."

"I didn't, though. I was fine." More than fine. He'd felt great. Seth swallowed hard. "This was after we were married, right?" It'd sure better be.

"Yes, we were married."

"And all that fire. Your eyes were blazing, and I wouldn't quit my teasing. I threw the book and wouldn't let you go get it. You took a swing at me." Seth smiled to think of the way he'd caught that little flying fist and hung on. Everything about that wrestling match had gone wild.

"You were tickling me. You wouldn't let up."

"I remember that. You're ticklish." Seth dragged her back into his arms. "I can't believe I managed to wait two weeks to marry you."

"You spent most of that time out of your head with fever."

"I reckon that slowed me down some." When the next kiss ended, Seth knew he had to stop or . . . not stop. And with Julia coming back soon, he had to stop.

He relaxed his grip.

She ran one finger down his cheek in a way so sweet it hurt. "You need to behave yourself."

"I sure enough do." Seth stole another kiss.

"We need to talk about something else." Her finger continued on down to his neck and traced a path under his collar to caress his scars. "Tell me what we're looking for down here. This is the cavern where you got those terrible burns, right?"

Her hands caressed his shoulders. Seth fought down the

urge to apologize for how ugly he was. "Right here. Right at this spot."

"Here?" Callie's eyes widened, and she quit looking at him and looked around. "How'd you get burned down here?"

"I fell right there." Seth tipped his head toward the hole in the tunnel floor.

"But what catches fire in a place made of pure stone?" Then Callie's eyes went to the flickering light of the lantern.

"I fell in. When Rafe and Ethan came to pull me out, they almost fell. They almost died because of me. I'd run off, left them behind, then, look . . ." Seth put a hand on her arm, picked up his lantern, and guided her to the edge of the hole. He knelt beside it and she came along.

"See how the ground is broken away?" Seth lit up the jagged edges of the thin sheet of rock. It was easy to see where the old cave floor had been. "It wasn't then. Rafe and Ethan and I had been down this tunnel lots of times. The ground was solid. But this time, it broke under my feet."

"How does rock form a thin layer like that? I've never seen anything like this before." She ran her hand along the edge of the hole.

Seth heard the quiet scratch of her hand on stone. "Neither have I, not in this cave, nor anywhere else. Julia studies things like that and she could probably explain it. I've got a picture in my head of boiling rock."

"Rock doesn't boil."

"In a volcano it does. Julia says lava is molten rock."

"Molten?" Callie asked.

"Yes, rock that's so hot it boils. I can imagine it bubbling up just as it finally cools off enough to stop being liquid. And this is the top of a bubble. When I stepped on it, it cracked. First just one leg went through."

"Oh, Seth, you must have been scared to death."

"It was pitch-dark and I didn't really know what had happened, but I'd been down this tunnel plenty of times and I knew there weren't any drop-offs. I screamed to beat all for help, because my leg was in a hole. Then the whole floor just shattered and I fell down to the bottom."

Seth looked at it with the most rational mind he'd ever used in this particular spot, and the hole didn't look all that deep, except for one dark corner. It wasn't the first time, though, that he'd thought if he just hadn't screamed and brought Eth and Rafe coming at a run, he'd've been fine. It was all stupid panic that had made things turn from a simple fall that left him a little bruised into life-and-death danger that had destroyed his family.

"Eth and Rafe came running and they almost fell. The hole was still small, and the ground broke under Ethan. Rafe caught him before he fell, but Eth dropped his lantern and the kerosene splattered all over, including on me."

"Oh, Seth." Callie slid her arm around his waist.

He extended his lantern so it lit up the depths.

"That looks deep. How did you survive it? How did you ever get out?" Callie pointed to one side of the hole that dropped off into the pitch-dark.

"I didn't fall there. I'd have died if I'd gone over that lower ledge. I only fell . . . look at that piece of lantern. That's the lantern Ethan dropped. That's close to where I landed." Seth pointed to the rusted lantern base about twenty feet down. He was tempted to go and get it. The glass chimney was broken and long gone, but maybe the lantern would still work if they brushed it up, got the rust off.

But he didn't go down. For all his exploring, he'd never gone down there.

"Thank God for that."

A broken laugh bubbled from him like lava in a pit. "Thank God?" He set his lantern aside and turned to look at her. "Never for one second have I considered thanking God for what happened to me that day."

"But it could have been so much worse."

"Worse than burns all over my back that kept me in bed, feverish, for a month? Worse than the nightmares I've had ever since? Worst than making life so miserable for my family that Ma died and Pa ran off?"

"You could have died. That would have been worse."

"It wouldn't have been much of a loss."

"Well, Connor would have missed you, seeing as how he'd've never been born."

"True." Seth managed a brief smile. "And he's a fine boy."

"You must hate this place."

"Oh, no. I love it. I spent most of my growin'-up years exploring it. I don't know if anyone will ever get it all the way explored, but I reckon I know it better than anyone."

"But how can you stand it when you were hurt so badly down here?"

Seth looked at the lantern, then at Callie. He wanted to say more. How driven he was to search and search until he found—

"I'm so glad you didn't die, Seth." She threw her arms around him and kissed him.

Kneeling there, facing her, holding her, he forgot what he was going to say. Forgot everything but how nice it was to have a wife. "You're really sweet, you know that?"

Callie snorted in a completely not-sweet way. "Ask the stagecoach robbers if I'm sweet."

Seth rubbed the silk of her hair between his callused hands. "Your hair is out of its braid."

She reached for her hair tie. "I need to fix it before Julia comes back. She'll probably think that we are—are—"

"We are." He kissed her again. "You're so beautiful, Callie. I do remember you."

She let the kissing go on a long time before turning her head aside. "Tell me more about that day, Seth. How did you ever get out of there? How sick were you from those burns? How long did the nightmares—?"

He kissed her quiet. "No more questions." He wanted to kiss her, but more than that, he did not want to talk about that day. Bring the nightmares into the daytime.

"But, Seth . . ." She turned her head aside. "How did you—?"

He kissed her throat. She shuddered, and he rested a hand on her cheek and turned her mouth back to his.

There was no more talk of burns and floors that broke like glass. There was only Callie in his arms in the lamplight. Then Seth heard hurrying footsteps.

"Julia's back." He eased away from her, stood, and helped her up. Longing for more time alone with her. Really alone, back at his cabin. Then he thought of taking his energetic little son and his hostile new brother home with him and knew he was never going to be truly alone with his wife, not for the rest of his life. He turned, his arm around Callie. Her knees seemed a little wobbly, and he couldn't help but enjoy that. He'd get her alone somehow for sure.

"I'm back." Julia came into sight just as Seth picked up his lantern, then Callie's, and handed it to her.

"Good. Let's get going."

"I'll cross first." Julia took one look at Callie's unbound hair, quirked a knowing smile, and went straight for the hole.

Callie gasped. "Be careful."

Seth took Callie's hand. "It's plenty wide enough."

Julia walked along the ledge running the length of the broken floor.

"I know the path we're traveling really well." Seth guided her onto the ledge. "As long as you're with me, nothing down here can hurt you."

CHAPTER 22

"I want your solemn vow that you won't hurt anybody, Jasper." Bea swung up on her horse before Jasper could help her.

"You have it. I'm just going to do what I need to do to get the diamonds back." He chafed at her being here. "You can't steal something that belongs to you already."

"So we're going to ride up to the first Kincaid we see and ask nicely if they've seen our diamonds and please give them back?"

Jasper hadn't really noticed how sarcastic Bea was before he'd married her. "They won't give them back."

"They might."

"If I have to I'll . . . I'll make some demands." Jasper was disgusted at his hesitance. In Houston he'd been ruthless. But now, it wasn't just his softening the words for Bea's benefit; he also felt his own hesitation toward cruelty.

"You mean you'll threaten them, maybe shoot or kill someone if you have to?"

"No, I just want what's mine. No one needs to get hurt."

Bea sighed and shook her head.

"You're with me, Bea. You'll make sure nothing bad happens." The thought that she'd be drawn into, for want of a better word, sin, when she'd cleaned up her life made Jasper feel worse than if he'd just planned a few little sins of his own.

"I married you for better or for worse, honey. I just hope it doesn't get much worse than this."

They rode on in silence, and every time Jasper thought about going home with Bea, forgetting his money, he'd picture those flashing diamonds. A lifetime spent gathering wealth, then condensing it into a pile of rocks no bigger than a deck of cards.

He just needed those diamonds and then he'd straighten up, live an honorable life with a man's pride. Maybe if things went well today, he could start being honest tomorrow.

"This is what you want me to draw a picture of?" Callie couldn't believe what she was seeing. "How did a fish get up here on top of a mountain?"

Even though they'd climbed down into a hole, when the hole was in the top of a mountain, a body was still up real high.

Julia turned, and even in the dim lantern light her eyes glittered with excitement. "I think this fish is proof of the Great Flood."

"There was a flood up this high?" Callie wanted to ask if madness might be catching in these parts. First Seth, now Julia.

Maybe the cavern caused it somehow. Maybe the air wasn't that good down here. Callie wondered if she ought to leave.

And yet, there was that fish.

"I've studied geology, Callie," Julia said.

"Geology?"

"Yes, the study of nature. Rocks, rivers, caves, soil. I've done a lot of exploring in caves in the different places I've lived, and I've seen fossils before. Though fossils aren't really geology. They're paleontology. Paleontology is—"

"Don't go to the next ology," Callie cut her off, "before I understand the first one."

Julia thrust a paper and pencil at Callie. "Draw while I talk. I want that fish, and I'd like a rough map of this place, too. I want to start naming the rooms, and I want to study the types of stone."

"Types of stone? Aren't all stones just stone?"

"Draw!"

Callie would have taken issue with Julia's bossiness if she hadn't planned to live quite a distance from the woman. "Let's hide the diamonds first. That's the main reason we came down here, right? Is there some crevice in here that we can all find again but that no one would stumble on?"

"This is the first good fish fossil." Julia pointed to a small ledge just above the fish. "Seth, put the diamonds up there. Push them all the way against the wall and see if they'll stay."

Seth reached up and slipped the little cylinder onto the ledge. "It slopes down just enough so it won't roll. It's only about three inches deep. See if you can reach it, Callie. Julia's not tall enough, but you might be."

Callie reached it easily. "Good spot for it."

Callie looked at Julia. "Can you remember this place for sure? I'd never be able to get back in here."

"Absolutely. And Rafe could find it too with a few simple directions. I've shown him this fossil before and he knows the cavern well enough to find it." Julia looked at Seth. "You'll remember it, too?"

"Yep."

"Now I'll draw that picture and we can get out of here." Callie took the paper and, looking between the fish on the wall and the pad, did a quick sketch of the fish. "It really is strange to see it up there. It's like it was swimming and just suddenly froze."

"You think it got trapped in lava, Julia?" Seth asked. "Why wouldn't it burn up?"

"Well, that's the thing. If it had been lava from a volcano, it would be burned up. That's what makes me think of Noah's Flood. If water had burst out of the deep—"

"Wait a minute. The flood was rain," Callie said. She quit her drawing and frowned at Julia.

She saw Seth making a shushing gesture, waving her off.

Julia smiled. "I'd be glad to tell you my theory. First I should tell you how a fossil is formed. Several things have to be just right for the animal that dies to become a fossil. My explanation will take a while but—"

Callie figured out Seth's gestures. Looked like once Julia started talking about fossils, she could go on talking about nonsense for a long, long time.

"Let her draw, Jules," Seth interrupted, "and look around for other fossils you want pictures of." Seth swung his arms wide to direct Julia's attention at the wall, and maybe to shoo her away.

"Yes, you're right, of course. I'd better look around and make some notes." Julia pulled out yet more paper, picked up her lantern, and walked off. Speaking over her shoulder, she said, "We'll talk about the fossils some other time. I've got so much to teach you."

Callie smiled until Julia looked away, then turned to glare at Seth. Who grinned and pointed to the fish on the wall.

With a shake of her head, Callie got back to her drawing. Seth came up behind her and looked over her shoulder. It should have bothered her, for normally she didn't like anyone watching her draw. But she liked him being close, and she hoped he was just the littlest bit impressed.

"You're good at that." Seth's warm breath fluttered a few hairs on her neck. She'd forgotten her hair was down. But now that he reminded her, she also remembered just why it had come out of its braid.

"Thank you." She made quick, confident lines with her pencil. "A fossil is really just lines. It's going to be easy to draw. It's not like a person's face or a tree or an animal."

Seth's voice dropped to a murmur. "Are you looking forward to being home with me? Are you starting to believe I won't abandon you?"

"I'm trying to draw." Her knees were getting wobbly, and it was mighty hard to concentrate on that stupid bony fish.

Seth's breath was replaced by his lips. She gasped loudly enough it echoed. A quick glance at Julia showed that she'd gone behind a tall rock that reached to the ceiling. A tower, just like Julia and Seth had said.

Seth's arm came around her waist. "Get to work, woman."

"Seth, stop."

"Ignore me and draw." His hand caressed her belly, and it was so intimate and reminded her so powerfully of being in his arms after they'd gotten married that she wanted to cry from the loneliness.

"I was so sure you were dead, Seth. I had hope, but . . ."

Seth turned her in his arms and kissed her. Just as well. She wasn't saying anything new anyway.

Between kisses he whispered, "I remember you, Callie, and I'm not going anywhere."

His strong hands settled on her waist and pulled her against him. "Say you trust me. Say you'll be married to me again."

Callie knew what he meant by married. She wanted that so badly. "Do you remember when we said our vows, Seth?"

Their eyes locked, and Callie could tell he wasn't going to just say he did without meaning it. She appreciated it at the same time she wanted to slug him for having to think of it.

"The parson was . . . did he have a Confederate uniform on? A really ragged one?"

A smile she could not control bloomed on her face. "Yes, he did. And his name—"

"Parson Pearson. I remember because we laughed about it later. Parson Pearson."

Feeling the tears burning in her eyes, Callie nodded. "You remember when we laughed about it? Because it was after we were back at my boardinghouse."

Seth laughed. "It wasn't easy getting your landlady to let me stay. She was a true daughter of the South and she didn't like a Yankee in her house."

"Then you almost collapsed and she took pity on me."

"Probably because you'd married a sickly man, a sickly Yankee."

"I'd told her I was from Texas, come to fetch my brother home, and she assumed he fought for the South. And my pa was a rebel tried and true, so she took to him right off and he didn't clear up her thinking."

"And you got me upstairs and . . . and she brought us a meal. Chicken noodle soup with almost no chicken in it and precious few noodles."

"You're remembering, Seth." Callie threw her arms around his neck and he kissed her hard.

"Will you two knock it off?" Julia's voice was a bucket of cold water.

Callie jumped back from him and whirled around to face the fish.

"For heaven's sake, Seth, leave the woman alone and let her draw. You're the one who just said we don't have long."

Julia marched up to him while Callie studiously ignored them both. Riveted on a fish she didn't give two hoots about.

With a single jab in the ribs with her pencil, Julia gave him a saucy grin. She knew exactly what she'd interrupted and had no remorse.

"Done." Callie turned from her drawing. "Next fish."

Julia took the sketch pad and lifted her lantern to study Callie's work carefully. "This is perfect."

Her eyes went to the fossil on the wall to compare the two. Then with excitement flashing in her eyes, she said, "Callie, you are going to be such a big help to me."

"I've got a ranch to run, Julia." Callie said it, but held

out no hope that Julia would give up. "Let's get these pictures drawn and get out of here."

Julia led Callie to the next fish. "I can keep you busy for years."

"Years? What?"

"There are thousands of fossils down here."

"Thousands?" Callie arched a brow.

"She isn't drawing a thousand pictures, Jules." Seth followed along, grumbling.

"Some of them are species that have never been written about."

"What's a species?" Callie asked, then regretted it when Julia answered at length.

"How can you know these are new species? You can't have read every word ever written about bones."

"But there are lists, books being published with details of every dinosaur."

"Dining on sour what?" Callie wished they could break for lunch, but she didn't want anything sour to eat.

Julia didn't answer. She just went on talking. "We can get our own book published. Make some money."

"Money from fish bones?" Callie had never heard such nonsense. She looked at Seth, who stood on one side of her, with Julia on the other. She was trapped between two people without a lick of sense.

She really hoped she remembered that the next time Seth went to kissing her on the neck.

CHAPTER 23

"Finished up here?" Seth rode up to Rafe's line shack with all the womenfolk and children. He saw Rafe, Ethan, and Heath packing up the tools. It struck him for the first time that the men had left him behind with the women. When had exploring that cavern gotten to be women's work?

Rafe talked with Seth briefly and then rode off toward his place. Ethan and Audra planned to cross the gulley and ride home that way, using horses the Kincaids kept corralled for just this reason. Ethan had Maggie on his back and Lily in his arms. Audra smiled at him like he was a knight in shining armor. Seth wondered what it would take to get Callie to look at him that way. He glanced over his shoulder to see Connor—in a pack on Seth's back—waving wildly. Seth decided he'd done his best to carry the load today.

"You'll drive some of the herd over here in the morning, then? We might as well use my meadows before that belly-high grass gets buried under ten feet of snow."

Ethan jerked his chin in agreement. "And I'll bring enough to drive some on to Rafe's. He's ready for a few more head now."

They made some quick plans for the drive, then Ethan hiked off with his wife and two children. Seth had a sudden urge to call them back. It hit him real hard that he'd be staying in his cabin with a bunch of people he didn't know all that well. A family that had appeared in force from out of nowhere.

What if Pa really did have more families? What if they all came to live with Seth? He could end up with his own town. He shouldn't have to take care of them all.

Why did he have to keep all the surprise Kincaids?

Because Callie said so, that's why.

Seth headed home with Callie, Connor, and Heath.

"Can you and Heath put the horses up while I get a meal on?" Callie arched a brow at Seth that looked like she had her doubts.

Her look stung his pride as if she doubted he knew how to unsaddle a horse. His jaw firmed and he didn't speak.

She didn't appear to notice his restraint. Instead she said, "Give me Connor."

He let her unhook their son from his back and took her reins while Heath led his own horse. Seth headed for the barn with his little brother. Between the two of them, maybe they could do the man's work around here.

"Seth!" Callie's sharp voice had Seth whirling around, his gun in hand, without making a conscious decision to draw.

Callie stepped out of the house holding her Winchester in both hands, its muzzle aimed at the sky. Her eyes were alert, studying the woods around their cabin. "Someone's been in the house."

"Any sign of someone in there now?" Seth headed toward the house as Callie backed away from it.

"I don't know. I grabbed my rifle and got outside. I didn't want to hunt alone with Connor on my back."

Knowing Callie expected him to protect her and Connor gave Seth a thrill so deep he couldn't breathe for a second. He started running toward the house, getting in front of his tough little wife, who'd turned to him for help.

He saw Callie pass her six-shooter over to Heath. The kid was too young, but he'd talked about trapping and hunting. Seth was a hand at hunting by Heath's age. But hunting a meal and hunting a man were a lot different.

"Come in behind me, Heath." Seth glanced back and saw that heavy Colt held steady, pointed up where a misfire couldn't hurt anyone. The gun seemed to fit comfortably in Heath's hand.

Seth swung the door open, standing off to the side. The thick logs would block a shot.

"The fireplace was cold and cleaned up. That stack of blankets isn't folded the same as I left them." Callie spoke low, a few paces back. A careful kind of woman. "Looks like two people. Probably left at first light."

"Yep, probably." Seth slid inside. The house felt empty. He reckoned Callie had read it exactly right.

He made quick work of checking all the rooms. "Now let's go see if anyone bothered our animals." Seth led the way outside.

Seth turned in a circle, looking overhead. He'd gotten into that habit in the war. "Let's check the barn first."

They walked past their mounts, ground-hitched, standing in the middle of the ranch yard.

Seth went up to the barn door and pressed his back to the wall beside it. Callie stayed off to the side, watching.

Heath said, "I'll swing the door open real easy."

Hesitating, feeling like it oughta be a grown-up's job, Seth finally, after a glance at Callie, nodded. "Stay low."

Crouching, Heath reached for the heavy wooden bar they used to latch the door. He lifted it and eased open the door, which swung in on smooth metal hinges.

There was no sound, no moving around. Heath looked at Seth, who said, "I go first."

Dragging air into his lungs to steady himself, Seth pivoted and charged in. The thrill of it making him think of how he hated being bored. How he craved risk and adventure and danger.

No shot rang out. Seth studied the dark corners of the barn and listened and smelled.

"The stalls are clean, just like we left them." He glanced at Heath and the boy's eyes were a sharp, startling blue. "But it wasn't as deep with straw. Someone cleaned out two stalls and re-bedded them."

Heath came up beside him. "Yep. They moved some of the leather, and I left that oats bucket in the oats bin, not standing beside it."

Sharing a long look, Seth turned back to Callie with a frown. "It's not unheard of for a man to lay up in an empty cabin when he's riding the country. Probably nothing to it."

"'Ceptin' he tried too hard to cover his tracks." Heath still had Callie's gun handy.

Callie kept her back to Seth's so they had eyes aiming in all directions. "Why do that if you mean no harm?"

Seth was impressed. His little brother noticed a lot for one so young. His wife was just plain savvy, maybe more than Seth, and Seth liked to think he was mighty good. Seth looked at Callie and saw Connor grinning from where he hung on her back. It burned like fire to think there might be someone around here endangering his wife and son.

"Let's check the corral." Seth led the way. They studied tracks and saw no sign of someone lingering in the woods.

"Whoever it was is gone," Seth said. "You okay to go back in the house alone, Callie?"

"Yep. But we'd best keep our eyes open." She headed in, leaving the menfolk to see to the still-saddled horses.

Seth and Heath worked side by side, and Seth noticed—and not for the first time—how well Heath handled a horse. He'd been good to have around when they were looking for trouble, too. Could the boy tell that he wasn't all that welcome? There were some guilt pangs, but Seth sure would've liked to be alone with his wife.

Seth looked across the back of the black mustang they were brushing just as Heath met his gaze.

"You got Pa's blue eyes. Like me and Connor." Seth didn't know if it meant all that much; it was just true.

"So you believe I'm your brother, huh?" Heath sounded his usual sullen self.

"Do you get crazy sometimes?" Seth asked. Did the eyes go with the reckless streak? "Do you ever want to go out and face down a grizzly? Or climb a mountain? Or explore dark caves?" Seth dropped his voice. "Do you ever think wild wolves are calling you?"

Heath gave him a hard glare. "I've been pretty much the man of the house from the first minute I was old enough to pick up a bucket of feed or lead a horse to water. No, I don't do reckless things. I don't hear wild animals calling to me. My family counts on me."

The kid was just tall enough to see over the back of the horse.

"They'd have been in big trouble without me. Why? Are you reckless? Or no, you're trying to warn me that I'll soon be the man of this family, too, when you go off into that cavern and don't come back. Great."

"I'm not going anywhere."

Heath's expression didn't change, but Seth thought maybe his chin was a little higher and his shoulders more square, like maybe he carried a heavy load and Seth had just eased it a bit.

Seth took a long moment to impress it in his spotty memory that he'd better not go anywhere. "C'mon. Let's help get supper on the table."

They walked inside, not talking but not growling at each other, either. When Seth swung the door open, it was to the smell of hot food. Callie was at the fireplace lifting a Dutch oven off the hook with one hand while holding Connor on her hip, on the side away from the fire. With towels to protect her hands, she set the pan on the table and lifted the lid to the smell of meat, sizzling and delicious.

"Ham." Seth couldn't remember a time when he'd felt so welcome. Oh, Julia and Audra had fed him and made him feel welcome. But this was his house and his wife.

It struck him then that having a wife was a wonderful thing in more ways than just having a pretty woman close to hand—a pretty woman who was blue blazes with her pistol. There were all sorts of good things about having a wife.

"I looked closer. Someone definitely spent the night." Callie gave him a level look—not worried, but just letting him know.

Seth couldn't help thinking of all the trouble that had plagued the Kincaids over the last months. "Anything missing?"

"Nope, not even food."

"Probably just passing through." Seth shrugged, but he'd keep his eyes open. Not a bad idea anyhow.

Callie nodded and began dishing up food.

There were plates and forks around the table. Seth wasn't even sure he'd seen all these things before. He'd been gone from this cabin as much as possible, staying with his brothers. He knew his cupboards had been stocked with food and dishes, yet he hadn't paid much attention to the details.

"Seth, can you take Connor?"

With Callie's request the night changed from a moment to savor, to chaos. Seth washed up quick and took Connor, who seemed happier dangling too close to the fire than being torn out of his ma's hands. Callie hustled around, getting food on the table.

Heath threw in helping Callie. Despite the kid's surly nature, Seth couldn't help but see he was a decent sort. He'd been raised right. Probably his ma's doing.

Things didn't settle down much through the meal, mostly thanks to Connor. And Seth didn't really have much chance to do more than eat and pass dishes and wrestle his son before they were all done and cleaning up.

"This is new, Jasper."

Jasper gave Bea a sharp look. "I can see that."

"It can't be the place Gilliland and his wife lived; it's not old enough."

"It's the place all right, just not the old cabin." Jasper stared at the cabin, figuring, then directed his eyes to the ground. "Just as I thought. Look at the footprints. There's been someone here just today, probably just finished building it. And that pile of kindling over there is what's left of the old cabin."

He dismounted, lashed his horse's reins to a scrub oak, and stalked toward the remains of the structure. "If Gill had anything hidden in the cabin, it would've come to light when they tore it down. We've got to assume the Kincaids have my diamonds."

He stopped at the front door beside a forgotten slab of flooring and glared. How was he going to get back those diamonds? Gilliland had a saloon in Rawhide. His men had written that they'd searched it thoroughly. Disgusted, he kicked the flooring hard, knocking it into the sturdy door. It bounced back and rapped his shin so hard he stumbled.

Mad clean through, he bent down to grab the wood and give it a hard toss. And saw something sparkle in the dirt.

Dropping to his knees, he scratched at the dirt that nearly covered it.

"What's wrong, Jasper? Are you hurt?" Bea came to his side just as he reared back, lifting the diamond to eye level.

"They found the diamonds for sure."

Bea gasped. "It's beautiful."

Jasper clutched it in his fist, then leaned down again. "Help me search. Maybe they lost more of them."

Bea was on her knees hunting just like a good little crook. She'd done her best to leave the sordid life behind that she'd lived in Houston, but Bea had a taste for pretty things. And she'd worked hard all her life and come away wearing cotton instead of silk.

With a twist of satisfaction, Jasper knew that sparkling stone was winning her over to his side.

"Nothing. Do we need to dig? Maybe Gilliland buried them right here. Maybe they almost unearthed them while they were building, but they never found the gems." Bea used her fingernails to claw at the hard dirt.

"It's solid rock down only a few inches. Nothing was buried here; it was dropped. That means they took the diamonds somewhere." Jasper lifted his head from the futile search and studied the surrounding area.

"Two riders went that way." Jasper pointed toward a mountain to the west. "And we saw three riders heading back to the cabin where we slept last night."

"We'd be better off going after two." Bea didn't say a word to discourage Jasper. That's when he knew he had her.

"But from the talk I heard in town, the two who went that way are probably Rafe and his wife. Rafe Kincaid is a tough man, and I don't know where Rafe's cabin is exactly, but they said something in town about a hidden canyon that was well defended. Something about a mountain gap with a tight entrance. Almost impossible to get into."

"But there were more of them going back north."

"I wish we'd've seen who was with that party. I didn't even hear them go past while we were eating. We should have just trailed after them when their tracks showed up on the road, but I wanted to see where Gilliland lived."

"Seth Kincaid owns the cabin we stayed in last night. He's the one I saw in town. He's the one they say isn't right in the head. He'll be there alone with his wife and child. That's a man I could make talk."

The day was wearing down as Jasper looked back at the trail to Seth Kincaid's spread. Then he looked at the new cabin, standing empty.

"One more night on the trail, Bea. Tomorrow we'll go have a little talk with Seth Kincaid. We'll end this and go on back to Colorado City." He turned and looked her in the eye. He saw the shadows of greed and temptation, and it fed those very things in himself.

"We might as well use another Kincaid cabin tonight." Bea gestured toward the tidy house. "They don't even know we've been living off them for two days now." A hard laugh escaped from Bea.

Hearing her laugh left Jasper with a strange feeling he couldn't quite identify. Unpleasant, like guilt. Like maybe . . . sin. He himself was no stranger to sin, but causing Bea to sin when she was trying so hard to change—that was a different kind of sin altogether. Jasper couldn't tell if God was poking at his long-sleeping conscience, or the devil was poking him straight into the flames of Hades.

CHAPTER 24

The long day was over and they settled around the fireplace.

Just like a family.

Which they were, Seth admitted—even though all three of them had been sprung on him in the last week.

Seth owned a single rocking chair and he waved Callie into it and placed Connor on her lap. Heath took a spot near the hearth, his back resting against the warm stones. Connor squirmed to get down, and Heath moved just enough so as to block the boy when he crawled toward the fire.

Seth grabbed a chair from the table, dragged it to Callie's side, and sat down. The crackling and flickering of the fire, the warm scent, eased his tired muscles.

"Can you turn the lantern light up, Seth?" The crinkling of paper drew Seth's attention to what Callie held in her hands.

"What've you got there?"

"Those maps Julia had me draw." Callie thumbed through them, then frowned. "I'm missing a page."

"What page?" Seth rose from his chair and dragged it closer.

"The one that shows what's right below that pit by Julia's old house. I drew it that first day along with several others."

"Maybe you left it at Rafe's?"

With a jerk of her shoulder, she said, "Maybe." She was silent a few seconds. "No, I had them out when we were at the line shack; when we stopped for Ethan today I remember studying them with Audra while we waited for the others to pack up. I must have dropped it. I never went down through the pit entrance. So I don't really know what it looks like down there."

"I know it really well. I can tell you what that part of the cavern is like."

Callie gave him a worried look, then turned back to her papers. "Okay, let's draw another one."

"Can I see what you've done already?"

Seth looked at Heath, who was concentrating on Connor. Yet there was a sadness about the boy that made Seth feel guilty for wishing the youngster would go away. "You want to look at the maps of the cave?"

"I don't care about that stupid cave."

"I'm sorry things aren't how you'd hoped, Heath. I'm still trying to get the notion that Pa had two families settled in my head."

The boy met his eyes, his brow furrowed. "I don't like living off you. I want what's mine."

Looking at him, Seth wondered if the kid weighed a hundred pounds soaking wet. He was mighty small to think he was up to being on his own.

"I know you do, Heath. I . . ." Seth glanced at Callie, the brains of this family.

Callie had stopped studying her papers. "There isn't anything much to give you right now," she said. "For the winter at least, you need food and a roof over your head."

Heath sighed until Seth worried the boy's body might deflate.

Callie extended the maps to Seth, and he took the stack of papers and studied them. "You really are good at this. These are all rooms I recognize. Like this one." He pointed to the tunnel with the hole. "You really show what it's like there." He shuffled some more pages until he found her fish fossil. "And you did a great job with the fish bones."

"Let's figure out the one that's lost."

Seth talked quietly in the warm room, pointing and describing the cavern. Callie asked good questions, and soon a clear map took shape on the page. Going back over details, Seth helped her make it realistic looking. Then a yawn broke off his description of the tower room.

It drew her attention and their eyes met. The crackling fire was the only sound in the room.

Which shouldn't be true. Connor was never quiet. Just as Seth thought that, Callie looked away while at the same time nudged him. A smile bloomed beautifully on her face and he almost couldn't look away.

But he did, and saw Heath and Connor sound asleep. "Guess we wore 'em out. Let's get them into bed."

Callie set the drawing aside and picked up Connor. Seth shook Heath awake, gently, remembering the times he'd run so hard all day with his brothers, he'd fallen asleep the second he quit moving.

Before long the house was settled for the night, Heath in a bedroom by himself, and Connor in a drawer in Seth's room, which was padded with a thick blanket. Seth was eager to build a cradle for the boy. Put a cradle in the room he shared with his wife—he liked the sound of that.

Seth and Callie went back to the main room and sat together by the fireplace.

"I'll work on this picture more tomorrow." Callie picked up the sheets of paper she'd left on her chair.

"Just give it a few more minutes." Seth was thinking fast. Trying to come up with an excuse to keep her with him. "Tell me what happened to your pa. I never met him, right?"

Callie's eyes narrowed, and Seth wished he'd've picked something to talk about that didn't remind her of the missing chunks of his memory. Hurrying on, he said, "I'm sorry he died. What happened?"

The anger then went out of Callie's expression. "Things didn't go like they should've when Pa got Luke home."

Seth had no idea if he'd heard of Luke before or not, but he didn't admit as much. Instead, to keep her talking he said, "What do you mean?"

"Luke always loved the ranch when growing up. There was never any question that he'd stay on the ranch with Pa. But then Luke went off to war and fought for the North against Pa's wishes. Pa was firmly for the South."

"Texas was with the Confederacy, wasn't it?"

"Yep, but we had neighbors, free black men, two brothers, who owned a nice ranch. Luke grew up being best friends with one of their sons. Pa got on with them, too. And one of them had a real nice wife who came over and helped a lot after Ma died and I loved her, we all did. They were good folks."

"So Luke couldn't see backing slavery?"

Nodding, Callie went on, "It's hard to put it into words because there was so much ugliness with the war, but our whole family just knew those folks were regular human beings. They weren't a color; they were people. It never made sense to any of us that there was slavery."

"So why did your pa get upset about Luke?"

"To Pa that war wasn't about slavery. I heard him explain it to Luke, and Pa never flinched from admitting it to our neighbors, either. It wasn't about slavery. It was about government thinking it ruled over the people instead of serving the people. And he didn't think the president in far-off Washington, D.C., had the right to make decisions for the states. He thought the South was being true to the Constitution more than the North."

"And he wouldn't forgive Luke after the North won?"

"Pa welcomed Luke home and there was no talk of anyone needing forgiveness. Pa knew Luke had done what he thought was right. It was Luke who couldn't get over Pa picking the South over the North. Luke was in Andersonville same as you. And it changed him. He didn't have nightmares like you do, but he was mixed up in his head, angry all the time—even in the hospital. We thought we'd lose him for a long time, which is why I ended up working in that hospital, because Luke was too sick to take home. He was starved near to death and he'd had a job at the prison camp working in the infirmary because there was trouble in the camp and the warden knew Luke would be killed if he didn't get out of the prison yard. Luke had seen so many awful things. Watched so many men die. He was like a stranger to us.

"As soon as he was able to travel, Pa took him home, just to get him away from all the ugly memories. Pa didn't even think it was a good idea for me to travel with them because Luke was unpredictable and sometimes violent. Since the doctors asked me to stay at the hospital, we agreed Pa and Luke would go and I'd come home later. It wasn't a hard choice to stay; the need was so great.

"When I got back home, Luke had already left. Pa had no idea where he'd gone, and it took the heart out of him. Then there was a lot of trouble with renegade soldiers and carpetbaggers. Just a new kind of trouble every time we turned around. Pa was killed in a shootout. There were witnesses who called it a fair fight. I know Pa was goaded into that shootout, but the sheriff wouldn't act. And the gunman vanished and had no known connection to the land-grabber."

"When you needed a husband, I wasn't there. I could have backed your pa and held the ranch, maybe saved his life. Maybe kept Luke on the ranch." Instead he'd run off and left Callie on her own.

Callie said nothing that would ease Seth's guilt. "Within hours of Pa dying, a man who wanted to buy our land came out to the ranch and told me he'd bought up the mortgage at the bank and owned every acre, every cow, every building free and clear. I couldn't fight him. I knew if I did, I'd end up dead and leave Connor alone in the world. All I could think of was you talking about Rawhide, Colorado. I hoped maybe you'd gone home. And if you weren't there, I hoped Rafe and Ethan would take in their brother's widow and his child."

"How long ago did your pa die?" Seth asked.

"Been about four months now. I knew I had to get away. I couldn't hold the ranch or protect Connor, so I wrote those letters to you and Rafe. I took what little cash money we had in the house and set out on horseback. When I got to a town with a train, I sold my horse and bought a train ticket. I walked away from everything because I knew I wouldn't live to turn it into cash."

"I'm sorry, Callie. I'm so sorry." Seth stood from his chair and pulled her into his arms. Wishing he could take away all her pain. She held him so close it hurt. When she finally let go, it seemed like her eyes were a little brighter and her chin a bit higher.

"We've talked enough for one night. Let's get some sleep."

Callie gave him a sweet, tired smile. He saw the scratch on her forehead and knew she still had some stitches to cut out. But she was beautiful. Perfect.

He hoped he wasn't seconds away from finding out he was sleeping out here in front of the fire.

"Go on in and get ready for bed," she said. Her cheeks might've been red from the fire, but Seth thought she was blushing. "I'll wait here while you change."

Her blush made him hope he wasn't the only one thinking on marital happenstances. It was past time to see just how hard his wife was going to make him work to earn her trust.

With a nod he stepped past her into their room, then stripped off his clothes and quickly pulled on a set of clean long underwear. He went to the door, opened it and said, "Ready."

Though she was much slower going about it, Callie was soon ready for bed, too. Connor remained asleep in the drawer. Seth went over, lifted the baby, drawer and all, and carried him out of the room.

"What are you doing?" Callie asked.

After setting Connor down just outside the bedroom door, he turned back. "I want to talk to you and I don't want to disturb the baby." Yep, this was all about not disturbing the baby.

"Oh . . . well, all right. But we need to bring him in here when we're done talking. He can crawl out of that drawer. He could get into the fireplace and get burned. We have to get him a better crib."

"I'll build one tomorrow." Seth wondered if they didn't need another bedroom, as well. Or maybe he could move Connor into Heath's room.

Seth went to Callie and took both of her hands in his.

"Now, Seth, I told you . . ."

He didn't want to hear what Callie had to say, so he kissed her.

Seemed likely that she didn't have much interest in what she had to say either, because she kissed him right back.

Sliding both arms around her waist, he pulled her closer, enjoying the touch of her lips against his. He angled his head to deepen the kiss just as her arms slid up to encircle his neck. A shudder of relief went through him. She wasn't going to push him away. The tug of attraction between them was so powerful that Seth knew it was why they'd ended up married so quick. It ignited with such force that he hooked an arm behind her knees, swept her into his arms, and carried her over to the bed. He lowered her and followed her down.

Pressing both hands flat on his chest, she said, "Seth, I don't think—"

"Thinking can wait." Somewhere Seth realized he'd lost his shirt. Now if he could just get Callie to do the same.

"No, Seth." Callie ducked her head when he came in to kiss her again. "We passed over thinking before, and I ended up with a baby to raise alone."

"You're not alone anymore, Callie." Seth caught her by the waist and pulled her back. "Surely you're noticing that I'm here."

"Stop!" She slapped him on the chest, hard. "Stop or I'm throwing you out of this room."

He fought with his self-control, which awakened in him the memory of fighting for survival during the Civil War. The thought helped him to relax his grip and step away from her. "I'm sorry. You're right."

She was so wrong.

"I don't want you sleeping on the floor, Seth." She moved closer to him then. Under the circumstances he'd've preferred she stay far away. "But if you don't behave, that's exactly where you're going to end up."

The woman had a bossy way with words. Seth pondered for a moment the notion that he'd married someone like his big brother. He looked at her black hair, escaped again from its braid. Her lips swollen from his kisses. Her slender figure swathed in white cotton. Her black eyes flashing in the lantern light.

Well, not a lot like his big brother.

"Now turn down the lantern and go to sleep before I decide to throw you out of here."

It was an order Seth was glad to obey. The bed was set so a window was behind Seth's back when he faced her. The moon shone blue on her raven-black hair. She lay on her side, her head propped up on her right fist, her left hand resting on him. Her black eyes studied him.

"Go to sleep, husband." She lifted her hand from his chest and caressed his chin with her fingertips. "We've found each other again. You clearly like the notion of being married. So do I. But give me some time. We got married too fast. I realized after you left I knew almost nothing about you. I didn't know you weren't thinking right. I didn't understand how upset you were by the war, or how sick you still were. I barely knew enough to begin hunting for you. Now we are going to take some time and get to know each other. I don't think I can honestly trust a man I don't even know. So let's go about this marriage business in the right way."

Seth nodded, but mainly because he was afraid of what might come out of his mouth if he unclenched his teeth. He had his own ideas about what was right. And nothing felt so right as holding Callie, his wife, in his arms.

She pulled up the blanket to cover his chest, as if she were tucking in a child, then went and fetched Connor and his drawer, rebraided her hair—which Seth regretted fiercely—climbed back into bed, rolled onto her side so she faced away from him, and fell asleep.

Seth was mighty slow following her lead.

CHAPTER 25

Callie ripped out of a deep sleep.

She grabbed for her rifle. It wasn't there.

Before she'd finished fumbling for it or figured out what the danger was, she was on her feet, escaping.

"Fire! Rafe, help. Ethan."

Her muddled thoughts cleared enough to know her husband was having one of his stupid nightmares.

"I'm burning!"

The poor tormented lunatic.

Help came in a rush and she hurried to the door and opened it before it could be knocked down. Heath stood outside. Connor was fussing in his makeshift crib, sitting up, rubbing his eyes while Seth screamed.

Callie picked Connor up. "I can wake him up."

"Rafe, help." The screams from Seth were bloodcurdling. "Ethan!"

"He's been in the war." Callie knew just how shocking it was to be awakened by screaming. Oh, did she ever know. "A lot of men who went through war are bothered by it."

"Hasn't the war been over for a long time?" Heath tried to give Callie his usual sullen look, but Seth's shouting was too upsetting.

"Ethan! I'm burning!"

"Not long enough, I reckon." She watched Seth slap at his horribly scarred arm and the back of his head. The full moonlight pouring in lit up the room nearly as bright as day. "I can wake him."

"You need help?" Heath had seen her wake Seth before.

Callie hesitated. Then she had a real bright idea. "Can you take Connor and get him back to sleep?"

Heath reached for the baby, then looked at Seth and flinched. "The war did that to him? Is that where his scars came from?"

"The worst of the scars are older than the war, though he got some new ones during the fighting. But what happened to give him the old scars is part of his nightmare."

Seth's cries got louder and wilder. Connor broke into a full-throated howl. He sounded a little too much like his pa, confound it.

"Go now," Callie said.

"If you need help, just holler." Heath looked past Callie as Seth screamed for his brothers.

Shaking his head, Heath took the baby and left. Callie swung the door shut and turned to her husband, her heart breaking for him.

She'd been strong in denying him earlier, but this tore at her and weakened her good intentions. She knew how it always ended when she woke him.

Thrashing, casting the covers aside, he shouted as if he were in agony.

Callie approached him with caution. "Seth, wake up!" She said it over and over again. One of these days maybe he'd hear her.

Then she thought of his brothers throwing water on him. They claimed it was fast and there was truth in that. A lot of truth. But it was downright mean.

Seth threw himself onto his stomach, and in the moonlit night Callie saw the terrible scars and couldn't stand to be unkind. She really had to insist he wear a nightshirt to bed so she could be stern with him.

Flinging himself over again, she knew she had to stop the shouting for the sake of the rest of the household, as well as to bring the nightmares to an end.

With a careful eye she ducked inside his flying fists and landed flat on top of him, locking her arms around his neck. "Seth, Seth, wake up."

She kissed him.

The shouting cut off instantly.

Clinging to his thrashing body, it was more a wrestling match than an embrace. Suddenly Seth's arms came around her so hard it was almost a blow. But it felt wonderful.

He held her tight and returned the kiss. The fight went out of him and he whispered against her lips, "Callie, Callie, I found you."

The affection she heard in his voice was impossible to

resist. He rolled with her and tucked her beneath him just as his eyes opened fully.

He was with her again, awake and rational. Though his face was shadowed by the night, she felt the wildness in his burning blue gaze, the rigidity in his muscles as he realized he wasn't fully sure how he'd come to be lying in her arms.

"I didn't hurt you, did I?" His voice broke. He rested his forehead against hers. He always asked her that.

And she always answered, "No, you didn't hurt me at all. You were having a bad dream. I woke you up."

His strong hands slid into her hair, caressing as if the touch gave him intense pleasure. And there went her braid again.

"I've missed you so much." He went to kiss her again.

"No, Seth." Her last ounce of common sense stepped forward and she slapped both hands flat on his chest.

Common sense, which she had in good supply, had told her even back in the hospital that she shouldn't put much stock in a man so riddled with nightmares, not even if everything about him spoke to the deepest, most vulnerable place in her heart. She hadn't listened then, and she'd paid a high price for it.

He froze. She could feel him gather himself, and nearly a minute passed when finally, slowly, he moved away. Lying on his back beside her, he said, "Well, at least come here and let me hold you." He pulled her against him, and she couldn't resist resting her head on his shoulder.

"I'm glad you're here, Callie Kincaid. And I'm going to prove to you that I'm a man to be trusted."

Callie didn't say it out loud, but inside she was fervently hoping it didn't take him too long.

She rested her head on her husband's chest, listening to

his heart pound. She wanted to cling to him. She wanted to show him how much she loved him. But she couldn't risk another baby until she was sure of him. She hadn't begun to let him know how harsh her father had been when she'd turned out to be with child. Or how many nights she'd cried from the loneliness. She was terrified of going through that again.

After their marriage, the nightmares hadn't appeared at first. Callie remembered her foolish belief that her love had healed him. Then he'd had another terrible nightmare. There'd been passion after she awakened him. But when the morning came, she found herself alone.

She thought of that now as they lay together in each other's arms. "Seth?"

"What, honey?" Seth caressed her arm as she rested against him.

"When we were in the hospital, I thought your nightmares were about the war. And they were, at least partly. You talked about cannons and battles, but you also talked about fire and called out for your brothers."

Seth rubbed his face with his free hand. "I had bad dreams right after the accident in the cavern for a long time, but they faded—mostly. The war started them up again."

"I think you need to tell me what happened in that cavern, Seth."

"I told you when we were down there."

"But there's more, isn't there?"

Seth tightened his arm around her. "How am I supposed to get it out of my head if I talk about it?"

Callie shrugged. "Not talking about it hasn't done any good."

"It did, back then. They finally stopped. Almost. They will again."

"After how long?"

Silence stretched between them, and she decided he wasn't going to answer. Maybe his brothers would tell her, but getting Seth to talk was the whole point.

"I had nightmares," he said, "for about three years."

Callie gasped.

"I tormented my family for three years. I destroyed my family with my nightmares."

"No, you didn't, Seth. A sick child can't destroy a family."

"It wasn't just being burned. It wasn't even just the nightmares. It was the cavern, too. After the burns healed, I went back down there. I couldn't help myself. That cavern . . ." There was a long silence before he added, "I couldn't stay away. That made everything worse. Rafe drove himself into the ground trying to protect me. And Ethan didn't seem to be part of the family anymore. He wouldn't come out and run the hills with me like he'd done before, hunting and practicing our tracking. And he never once came to the cave. He was the first to leave . . . well, not counting Ma dying and Pa running off. Before that accident the three of us were together all the time, working and playing. I ruined all that."

Callie whispered, "Can you tell me more?"

He kissed her forehead, her hair, her eyes, and for a moment she thought he meant to distract her from her question. She suspected she'd let him.

"We were just kids. Just dumb kids. I look at Heath and see a little boy but with grown-up ways. Rafe was like that. I can't say I thought of him as a father; we were too close in age. But more like—like the leader. He and Ethan and I were always pretending. War or Indian raid or stagecoach holdup or hunting grizzlies, always some crazy pretend game. And whatever the game, Rafe was the leader. Eth made it fun. I made it reckless."

"Sounds like normal play for a boy." Callie prayed silently that he would go on talking.

"We ran wild all over our property. I can't remember a time we didn't just take off from the house and go wherever we wanted. Ma and Pa didn't seem to care. And then we discovered that cavern. We went down every chance we got. I loved it. I was always looking for a chance to spook Rafe and Ethan. Of course they were too tough to ever show it, but I got 'em good a few times." Seth chuckled at the thought. "Rafe was always so careful. I told him he ruined our adventures." His smile faded. "Until I almost killed us all and did end up killing our family."

CHAPTER 26

"I'm Cochise." Seth picked a man known to be wild and dangerous. He rushed for the black hole in the ground that led to the best place in the world. He caught the free end of the rope and lowered it.

"I'm Kit Carson today." Rafe grabbed at the rope, always wanting to check it over, but Seth was too fast for him.

"I'll be Daniel Boone." Ethan smiled and let Rafe and Seth race to go first.

They made a good team. Rafe had the caution, boring but not so bad as long as Seth didn't have to do any worrying. Ethan made them laugh. Seth pushed them to take chances. All together it added up to being an adventure. The cavern was the perfect way to spend a day away from the sadness of home, with Pa gone trapping and Ma moping.

Seth flashed a smile that as good as dared Rafe to stop him from going down that uninspected rope, but Rafe just waved him on. Seth knew the rope was well made because Rafe had made it himself.

Seth skidded down. There were toeholds in the rope, and Seth could slide past them quick. He knew exactly where he wanted to go. And how he planned on spooking his brothers.

His feet hit the stone ledge, and then he hurried along it to the side with the best toeholds and climbed down to the cavern floor.

"Wait for the lantern, Seth." Rafe's voice echoed from above.

Snickering, Seth sprinted into the dark and paused at the first tunnel, covering his mouth to squelch a giggle as Rafe beat Ethan to go next, lowering himself down with a lantern hanging from his neck. Eth would come last. He never hurried. Seth knew Ethan wasn't that thrilled with the cave, though he never admitted it.

His brothers were coming fast. With knotted loops for their hands and feet, they could scamper down and back up in a flash. Seth turned and rushed away from the dim light, toward the best tunnel. When he went in, he left all light behind. His hand ran along the wall guiding him through the pitch-dark. He passed two openings, then ducked down the third. This one went on for a long time. They usually went straight instead of turning off, because they all liked a big room down that way. Seth had never gotten to the end of this tunnel. But he would. Someday. Today maybe. For right now he was just picking a spot to lie in wait.

Footsteps echoed as Rafe and Ethan came toward him.

"Seth, get back here. We have to stay together." Rafe, always bossy. But he couldn't control Seth down here and Rafe knew it.

The smell of the lantern was nice in the cool cavern. Seth didn't mind the light. There were beautiful things to see. Even so, he moved farther down the tunnel until he knew Rafe's and Ethan's lanterns wouldn't reach him when they walked past. As Seth moved he bided his time. He'd make a sound that would lure Rafe and Ethan his way, then jump at them.

Liking the feel of the coarse stone on his fingertips, Seth enjoyed the solitude. He wanted to be a guide and lead people around in here when he was grown up. Maybe he could earn money being a guide like Kit Carson.

Next time he'd pick Kit Carson instead of Cochise.

Ethan's voice echoed, "C'mon back, Seth. I wanna get to the room with all those huge pillars. We can eat lunch there."

"I wish we had more lanterns so we could see the whole room," Rafe said, his voice sounding closer.

"Where'd Seth get to?" Ethan asked.

"Seth, come back." That was Rafe. Giving orders again. "We're gonna eat without you and we won't leave you nuthin'."

Seth saw the light as Rafe and Ethan neared the tunnel he'd turned down.

"Seth, you little skunk, get back here!" Ethan's holler echoed dozens of times.

There were torches all along the tunnel. Seth heard Rafe and Ethan pause to light them. He smelled the kerosene as each one of them ignited. Knowing they were close, Seth laughed, doing his best to sound like a ghost with a shimmery, wavering laugh.

"We need to teach that kid a lesson," Ethan whispered, but Seth heard every word and loved listening in.

"We oughta go back, leave him in here in the dark. That'd teach him." The sound of Rafe's footsteps told Seth he was still moving forward. He'd missed the turn. "Maybe we can make him believe we left him."

Ethan laughed.

"I wish we had more light. I'd sure like to see the whole place at once." Now Rafe's voice was fading just a bit with each word.

"Oh, I don't know." Ethan had moved past the entrance to the tunnel Seth was hiding in. "Not being able to see to the end is kind of fun. Using your imagination, wondering where all the side tunnels go." Seth knew exactly what Ethan meant. Ethan added, "I'll bet that little varmint's gettin' ready to jump at us."

"Sounds like Seth."

Even though they knew, Seth bet he'd still manage to make them leap out of their skins.

"Do you ever think that maybe monsters live down here?" Ethan knew spooking each other was part of the fun, so he was helping.

"Or maybe outlaws hid a buried treasure in here. We could find it and get rich."

"Maybe the outlaws are still here, watching us."

"Or maybe we could strike gold."

"Or maybe one of these tunnels goes clear and away to the center of the earth where the devil lives."

A chill of pure ice raced up Seth's spine.

There was a scuffling sound, Rafe tussling with Ethan.

Seth wished he was out there with his brothers, wrestling and talking about danger and treasure. Ethan laughed.

"Let's get on with letting Seth scare us." Rafe led the way. "We can light the rest of the torches later."

The torches were just sticks wrapped with oil-soaked rags, but there were many of them and they cast a much better light than the one lantern. Rafe had made them all. He'd wrap them real tight so they'd burn a long time. Rafe was always planning ahead.

Seth moved down the tunnel away from his brothers, planning to laugh again, draw them this way.

A cracking sound was his only warning.

Seth's foot broke through what he'd thought was solid rock. He shouted in surprise. Then the rock seemed to bite into his leg. All the spooky things they'd talked about seemed to be coming true. He was being swallowed up, sinking right down to where the devil lived.

"Seth!" Rafe and Ethan both had heard him.

He fought to drag his foot loose, but it was like there were teeth sunk into his ankle. "Rafe, help!"

Grabbing his leg, he pulled up. The stone under his other foot snapped. He fell through to his backside.

"Ethan!" Clawing at stone for something to hold on to, Seth lay flat on his belly and tried to escape whatever was eating him alive.

Two sets of running feet pounded down the tunnel.

The rock gave again and he dropped through to his chest. Now only his arms held him up. Seth cried out. The ground kept crumbling around him as he fought to escape the jaws of death.

"We're coming, Seth!" Rafe would save him.

"Rafe! Ethan!" Then with a loud crack he went straight through, falling into a dark pit.

Screaming, he landed with a sickening thud. He hadn't fallen forever. He was on solid ground again. Gasping, the breath knocked out of him, Seth looked up, and a faint light caught his attention from overhead.

"Be careful!" he shouted. "There's a hole!" Trying to warn his brothers.

Seth's warning came just he saw Ethan skid right to the brink of the hole. With a short cry of fear Ethan stopped, teetered on the edge for a second, then got his balance and dropped to his knees. "Seth!"

"Back up!" Seth looked at the lantern Ethan carried as if it held the answer to life and death. As if God himself had come to light Seth's way to safety. "The ground won't hold."

"Won't hold . . . ?" Ethan reached out his lantern. The light trembled and Seth knew it was going to be okay. He hadn't fallen forever. His brothers were here.

Rafe leaned forward while Ethan lowered the lantern past the edge of the pit. Seth scrambled to his feet, and from below he saw Rafe and Ethan kneeling on stone as thin as an eggshell. "The ground won't hold," he repeated.

"Back up, Ethan," Rafe ordered as he quickly scuttled backward. Then he shouted, "Hang on, Seth! We'll get you out."

Ethan started back just as the stone under his hand cracked and his whole arm fell through the floor. Seth watched in horror as Ethan landed hard on his face and belly. An ugly crack sounded when his chest hit. Ethan yelled in fear. He scooted back farther, lying flat now.

"Get your weight off this layer of rock!" Rafe said from behind Ethan.

Ethan shoved himself backward and the stone broke again and again, showering stones down into the pit. Seth flung his arms over his face to protect his eyes, but he couldn't look away. The collapsing ground followed Ethan. Was hungry for him. Then it all shattered and Ethan plunged forward—and stopped.

Rafe clung to Ethan's waistband.

Ethan's collision jerked his lantern loose. It fell and cracked. Flames shot up as the kerosene splashed and ignited, rushing straight for Seth. Seth whirled away as the kerosene splattered his back and burst into flames.

"Rafe, help me! Ethan! I'm burning!" Frantically Seth tried to slap at his back and arms, twisting and fighting the fire. Coughing, choking on the smell of his flesh burning.

"Get your shirt off, Seth!" Rafe yelled. "Get it off, throw it away!"

Seth caught the front of his shirt with both hands and tore it off his body, throwing it aside. He felt his head burning and slapped at his hair. The high-pitched shrieking was a sound he'd never heard come from his own throat. "Rafe! Ethan! It hurts!"

His voice broke as hot tears filled his eyes. He blinked them back and saw the fire that separated him from his brothers. This is what it would be like, a lake of fire, if he didn't get into heaven. In horror he thought he'd already failed.

"Seth, the fire's off your body now." Rafe's voice, steady and strong. "We're here. We'll get you."

But the pain was unbearable. Seth couldn't think beyond

it—beyond pain and being in a lake of fire. "I'm all burnt. It hurts bad, and . . . and you can't get me."

Of course it would be like that. There was no way out. Seth fought the tears, but they escaped anyway. He'd never felt pain like this. He watched stones burn, haunted by the sight.

"Hang on, we're going to be down there in a minute!" Rafe said it, but Seth didn't believe him. The fire never went out in Hades. Seth knew it; he knew where he was. He hadn't been a good boy. He deserved this.

"It's pitch-dark. I've got to get another lantern." Rafe making decisions, taking charge. It almost penetrated the pain of his back and arm, the terror of knowing he'd spend eternity trapped down here.

"Eth, talk to Seth, make sure he knows we haven't left him."

Seth realized he was crying. It hurt too bad, and the certain knowledge that he'd died and gone to hell was too terrifying. He couldn't quit his sobbing.

"Talk to him!" Rafe said again. "I'll be right back."

"No, don't leave us!" Ethan shouted.

Rafe was leaving them? "Rafe, help!" Seth screamed.

Seth heard pounding feet. He was alone.

"Rafe'll be right back." Ethan hadn't left! "We're going to get you out of here."

"How . . . ?" Seth couldn't lift his eyes from the demonic flames cutting him off from Ethan.

"You're going to be all right, Seth." Seth forced his head up until he could make out Ethan's shape. On the other side.

Just then Rafe came running back with a burning torch, handing it to Ethan. "I'll be back! You just hang on, ya hear?"

"No, Rafe, wait!" But Seth's cry was for nothing. Rafe was already gone.

Ethan held the torch up so Seth could better see him. "Hey, little brother, I'm right here. Can you stop crying and talk to me?" Ethan being his usual self.

The pain made it impossible for Seth to think. He wanted out. Every move hurt so bad. He tried to force himself to ignore the burns. How long would Rafe be gone? Had Rafe gone for help or just run away? Seth wouldn't blame him. Ethan should run, too.

"You know what'd be great?"

Seth didn't want Ethan to leave, so he forced himself to answer, "Wh-what?"

"You oughta try and climb out of there. I mean you haven't really tried, have you? The fire isn't burning everywhere, so go around it. Then find some handholds. I'll bet you could do it, if you weren't so busy crying."

The taunt reminded Seth of how reckless he always was. How fearless. Suddenly the fear faded. Not the pain, but in the twinkling of an eye he no longer feared hell. He no longer feared the devil. He gritted his teeth and saw a way around the fire. One step and the skin on his back seemed to split apart. He took another step, looking between the jagged stones underfoot, the fire, and Ethan. He felt the wildness that was always in his blood turn into something worse, something devilish.

"Maybe I oughta come down there and help the little crying baby."

That brought Seth's eyes up and gave him a backbone.

"'Course if I fell, then we'd both be stuck in the hole. Then Rafe'd have to pull us both out."

"No, I-I'll try and climb up!" Seth felt the cavern flow into him, become part of him, or maybe he became part of it. He felt . . . something, some part of himself, which longed to stay in the pit.

"Go around the fire this time, baby brother. Not through it."

In the light of the fire Seth saw handholds. He reached for one with his right hand and pain tore at every muscle in his back. Then he reached with his left and saw blackened skin on his arm, bleeding red in the flickering fire.

It didn't stop him. He left behind the weakest part of himself and now he only had strength. The pain was almost welcome because it matched his rising sense of power, his complete fearlessness. Seth climbed, one step at a time, out of the pit until he stood beside Ethan. Two inches shorter than his brother, but inside Seth felt like a giant. Dangerous. Crazed.

He looked straight into Ethan's eyes, and Ethan stepped back. Afraid now of his little brother.

Seth smiled and took one look back down into the pit. The fire was dying although Seth knew he'd be carrying it on his back, and in his soul, forever.

Something down there called to him. The part of himself he'd left behind. He wondered if it was his soul, if he'd sold it in exchange for survival. "I'll come back and look."

"What?" Ethan asked.

Seth turned to his brother. "Nothing. Let's go find where Rafe ran off to."

Seth remembered it all. How he'd thought he was in Hades. How he thought Rafe had run away from eternal fire.

How Ethan had taken that one small step back in fear. How Seth had felt that crazed bond with the cavern, as if he'd left part of himself behind.

"We went after Rafe and found him coming back for us. He'd strung together the lassoes from our horses, hoping he had enough to reach me."

"Why didn't he just stay and help you climb out?" Callie asked.

"With it all on fire, he said he couldn't see a way down. So he went for a rope and a lantern instead. He's a man of action, my big brother."

"And you just rode home, with no trouble?"

"It was like I didn't even hurt for a while. I remember leaving that cave. They made me go first, afraid they'd need to catch me. But I just climbed right out, mounted up onto my horse, and headed out. Rafe told me later that I passed out and fell off my horse a little ways from home. Ethan ran for help because they were afraid to touch me, all burned up like I was. Pa had come home. He carried me into the house. I don't remember much after that. I got a real bad fever. Then the nightmares started coming. I tossed and turned in bed, which made it hard for my burns to heal." Seth turned to look at his wife. "I didn't have the nightmares so much after a while. But by the time I was out of bed, Ma had started sleeping most of the day."

"That's not your fault. You needed her and she failed you."

Seth kissed her quiet. "And Pa was gone off trapping more than ever. He didn't really live with us anymore. I guess we know now where he went, huh?"

"Your pa failed you, too. You were just a boy. You couldn't

help the nightmares. At least Rafe and Ethan were tough enough to stick with you."

"They didn't, though. Not really. Rafe was so watchful, and he blamed himself. He seemed to grow up overnight. I didn't have a big brother anymore. I had a very young father. And Ethan . . ." Seth shook his head. "Ethan saved me. He goaded me into showing some backbone and climbing up that rock wall. But he said he'd been too hard on me when I'd been hurt so bad. It was like something broke inside him. No matter how bad things got with Ma sick and Pa gone and me climbing down in that cavern every chance I got, he never did nuthin' but smile."

"You went back down?" Callie stretched her arm around his shoulders and rubbed his back, her fingers caressing the ugly scars as if they didn't repulse her.

"I swear I could hear the cavern calling to me. I still hear it sometimes. I'd lay awake and hear it whisper, speak to me. On the nights that happened, I'd have the worst nightmares. I always thought if I could just go down in the cavern, I'd sleep all right. But Rafe watched too close for me to sneak out in the night."

"Is that what happened the night you left me?" Callie lifted herself away from him and he suddenly felt cold. But she didn't leave the bed. Instead, she propped herself up with one elbow, and Seth could see her ink-black hair in the first light of dawn.

Dear God, thank you for this woman.

An ache in his chest grew and spread as he thought of his good fortune. He had the most beautiful woman in the world for his very own wife. He had a strapping son who seemed to love him, even when he'd abandoned the little guy.

He remembered being on fire, thinking he'd gone to where the devil lives, and thinking he deserved it for his reckless ways. And now God had blessed him by giving him Callie. By giving him a family. He was blessed in so many ways.

Seth closed the distance between them, and this time he was thinking clearly and didn't ask for more than a simple kiss.

She came willingly into his arms.

And he did his best to let her know just how wonderful she was.

CHAPTER 27

Callie woke up alone.

The panic struck before she was fully awake. She was dressed and running out of the bedroom before she gave her actions a rational thought.

It was full daylight. The cabin was empty. A quick glance in the other bedrooms told her Connor and Heath were gone.

Her whole family had abandoned her!

She flung open the door and rushed outside in her bare feet to hear an axe sing in the woods, not that far away. She could have heard it inside if she'd taken a second to think.

Heath came from the chopping block with an armload of kindling, carrying Connor on his back.

"Reckon you were tired after Seth's nightmares." Heath

slipped past Callie into the house. As he passed, Connor flashed a huge smile at Callie and waved wildly as they went in. Heath added over his shoulder, "Feet cold?"

Callie looked down and flexed her toes. "They most certainly are."

Trying her best to be calm, Callie followed Heath inside. "Where's Seth?"

Heath shrugged. "He rode off this morning early. I just caught sight of him through the window. Didn't talk to him."

Fighting down the urge to sprint for the barn and saddle up a horse to hunt her husband down, Callie stiffened her backbone as she watched Heath dump kindling into the woodbox.

"Have you eaten?"

"I had some jerky." Heath acted like it wasn't important, but Callie thought she saw a flash of hunger in his eyes. After all, he was a growing boy. "Connor ate, too."

She spent a few minutes dressing properly and getting a dry diaper on Connor, then let him crawl on the floor while she started breakfast. Heath helped get a hearty meal on. Hunger made a child cooperative, Callie decided.

She put a lot of energy into the cooking to keep from jumping out of her skin and was just washing up when she heard the hoofbeats.

A lot of hoofbeats.

She rushed to the window as a longhorn steer came into sight, from the direction of Ethan and Audra's house.

Heath came up beside her to watch, and by the time a dozen cattle had begun to mill in the yard, Ethan rode in.

He shooed the cattle forward, through the clearing around the house and on down the trail until they were swallowed up by the woods. A grizzled cowhand with a steel-gray mustache came along from where Ethan had first emerged, then a few more men riding herd, then finally Seth.

A shocking desire to cry swelled in her throat and burned her eyes. Seth hadn't abandoned her.

They'd brought part of the cattle here to graze on the open meadows. Seth had mentioned Ethan bringing them, but Callie hadn't heard any plans about Seth going off to help herd them.

She hurried to the door. Swung it open, mindful of how easily cattle spooked, and caught Seth's eye. He had a coil of rope in his hand to haze the cattle down the trail. He lifted it in a lazy salute and his wild blue eyes flashed. Too much passed between them to be possible with a single look. He hadn't run off.

Riding drag, Seth took the time to stop. "We'll leave half the herd to graze on a pasture near this place, and take half on to Rafe's. We're planning to do it in one day. Ethan wants to get there and get home so he can sleep in his own bed tonight. We'll be a half hour or so cutting the herd. Is there anything we can have for a meal before we head on?"

For a minute she thought she might break right down and cry. It was such an embarrassing inclination that it brought her to her senses. She nodded.

"We can manage without a meal if it's too much trouble, but something warm would sure be good. Then afterwards I want you to saddle up and come along. I'll be all day about this and I don't like leaving you alone here. It's high time I started turning you both into cowhands, anyway."

"I can outride you any day of the week, cowboy." Callie

leaned on the doorframe, so relieved her knees were a little wobbly.

"I'll just bet that's right, Mrs. Kincaid. I'm counting on it." He smiled, the teasing clear in his eyes.

Heath slipped past her. "I'll saddle up for us both." He headed for the barn.

They were all fed and on the trail for Rafe's within the hour.

"Look at this." Jasper grabbed a piece of paper that scudded across his path in the sharp wind.

"What've you got?" Bea asked.

They were ready to saddle up and start tracking. Jasper was in the midst of thinking about his warm house back in Colorado City when he'd spotted the paper. An unusual sight, out in these remote mountains. He pressed it flat and listened to the paper crackling. It hadn't been out here long. His eyes caught on a detail that couldn't be mistaken for anything else.

"This is a diamond." He jabbed his finger at a little angular shape. The whole page was covered with drawing, most of it just squiggly lines.

"Could be, Jasper." Bea studied the picture. "And that's the cabin."

Nodding, Jasper looked between the paper and the little building where they'd spent the night. "There looks to be a trail up behind it. It might lead us to the diamonds."

With an eager nod, Bea said, "Let's go."

They followed the map across a deep gully and found a hole in the ground right where the map said it'd be. "What do you think it means?" Jasper looked in the black pit. "Should we go down there?"

"According to the map, there's a ladder around here somewhere." Bea looked and Jasper threw in. Scratched-up dirt led them straight to a boulder, where they dragged out the ladder.

A few minutes of working up the nerve and Jasper climbed down into the belly of the earth. When he reached the bottom he knew immediately he was in for trouble. It was too dark. Bea almost knocked him off the ledge when she reached his side.

"Be careful, this is narrow." Jasper produced the map, barely visible with the light from overhead. "Look at all these twists and turns. If we had a lantern, maybe we could find the diamonds hidden somewhere."

"I don't think so. Look at the way the diamond is drawn. It's off to the side, almost like someone was just fiddling with the pencil. If it was a treasure map, then the diamond oughta be stuck inside the lines, marking the spot."

Jasper scowled at the map. "Well, we know that whoever drew this most likely has the diamonds."

Taking another look at the drawing, Bea said, "Appears this cave runs deep, with tunnels going off in different directions. But they don't show the ends of 'em. The page is filled; I'll bet whoever drew it made a second page."

"It'd make pretty good sense to hide the diamonds down here. It's about as safe a place as you can find. And drawing a map to it makes sense, too. All we need is to get our hands on one of those Kincaids and make him tell us where they hid my gems."

"We could scare 'em good and not have to hurt anyone. We could . . . hold one of them for ransom." Bea's eyes gleamed in the dark cave. "If the one we grab can take us to the diamonds, then we'll get them and scram. Leave whoever we grab behind and pull up the ladder. Then we'll leave a note in that shack for the rest of the Kincaids. No one'll get hurt."

"There was a lantern in the cabin and we've got enough supplies that we could hide down here quite a while."

They laid out a plan Jasper liked real well and headed back up the ladder. They were a while getting everything in place. Then they set out to find one of the Kincaids and make him talk.

They went down the same trail they'd taken up there until they came to the place it divided. One direction headed back toward the cabin where Jasper and Bea had spent the night before. The other direction might lead them to Rafe Kincaid's spread.

Jasper hadn't yet decided which way to go when he heard approaching hooves. He jerked his head toward the woods and quickly dismounted. Bea followed suit.

They led their horses off the trail, then slipped back to where they could watch. Seconds later a longhorn came up the trail, then another and another. Jasper crouched in the trees and watched silently as a herd of cattle moved slowly through, pushed along by Seth Kincaid, a couple of cowhands, and a half-grown boy with a baby strapped on his back. A woman trailed along riding drag.

When the woman passed, Jasper rose to study the direction they were headed.

Bea came to his side. "What are you thinking?"

"Did you see how the woman brought up the rear?"

"What about it?"

"Let's grab her."

Bea's expression looked doubtful. "You heard the parson talk about what happened to that one Kincaid woman. He mentioned dark hair and that she had a baby. I'll bet that's her. She held off a band of outlaws single-handedly when they tried to rob the stage. Sounds to me like she's mighty tough, Jasper."

"What it sounded like to me was she was cut to ribbons and almost died before help got there. The parson was impressed all right, but he's from back East. She'd be easy to kidnap. Maybe she can tell us where the diamonds are, and if she can't, we'll have our ace in the hole to make the Kincaids talk."

He pulled out the one diamond and looked at it, then took a step toward his horse. Bea grabbed his arm.

"What?"

"You've got to promise me you won't hurt anyone, Jasper. Swear it. I'll stick with you while you hunt down your gems, but we come away from this with what's yours and no harm done."

"I swear it." Jasper wondered whether she was fool enough to believe a word he said. He looked at Bea for a long time. "I'm going to cover my face, but how'll we disguise you?"

"If she can identify us, we'll have to leave Colorado City."

Jasper heard in her voice how much she hated giving up her little home. "Let me get hold of her, gag and blindfold her. You stay back until I've got her, then don't talk. She doesn't even have to know a woman is along."

Bea hesitated.

Jasper watched her as she mulled over what he'd said. Up to now they hadn't done a thing wrong. No crime had been committed. That was about to end when they laid hands on that woman.

"I'm going," he said. "If you want to ride away, I'll understand." He was careful about it, but he lifted the diamond just a bit higher, rolled it between his fingers to catch the light.

Jasper waited for her to trust him—or want the diamonds bad enough to accept his lies without question. When she broke eye contact and stared at the diamond, he knew he had her.

She beat him to the horses.

Usually drag was a dirty job, but on these barely broken forest trails, more rock than dirt, there hadn't been much dust kicked up.

Callie knew the way to Rafe and Julia's, and the cattle were docile after walking miles this morning. So all she had to do was shout a little encouragement when one of the critters started dogging it. It gave her plenty of time to think with pleasure that her husband hadn't abandoned her.

Things really were going to be just fine.

A hand clamped over her mouth. An arm wrapped like an iron band around her midsection. Thrashing, she yelled as she was dragged off her horse. But no sound escaped her lips. She clawed for her gun yet couldn't reach it.

Her head was pulled against a hard chest.

"Get her gun." A voice hissed in her ear as the last straggler cow curved around the trail and vanished. Leaving her alone with her assailant. Then her eyes were covered and she couldn't see anything.

A second set of hands tightened the blindfold and then slipped her gun from its holster. Increasing her efforts, Callie elbowed whoever had her. There was a grunt of pain, but his grip didn't loosen.

"Get her tied up. Fast. We need to get off this trail." A rope lashed around her, securing her arms to her sides. Screaming behind the hand, still no sound escaped. She tried to bite the man, and his grip tightened, holding her jaw closed.

"Don't fight me. I'm not going to hurt you."

She had no reason to trust such words. The kerchief over her eyes was so tight it hurt. The ropes cut into her arms and stomach until it was hard to breathe.

"Bring her horse." The man issued terse orders under his breath.

As she drew in a breath to scream again, suddenly a wad of cloth was shoved into her mouth.

Choking, fighting to breathe, she was thrown on a horse. Her hands weren't tied and she grabbed for the reins, but couldn't find them. The man lashed her wrists to the pommel.

Breathing was a battle. It took all her attention to draw in each bit of air, and before she could think how to fight back next, her horse began walking, then trotting fast.

Think! She had to think. Why would anyone bother her?

Those outlaws she'd fought when they'd robbed the stagecoach. Had they broken jail? Were they out for revenge?

"You hide the horses where we planned. And leave the note. I'll get her across the stream. Bring the map."

Map? The only maps Callie knew of around here were in her saddlebag. Except that one she'd lost.

But who would want a map of the cavern?

"Your family will be hunting you soon. I want some space between me and them. So I'm not letting you make a sound."

Rough hands dragged Callie off her mount. The second her feet hit the ground, she kicked the man hard.

"Ouch!" The man grabbed her by the front of her blouse and shoved her to the ground. "You little wild cat." Her captor knelt beside her. Something slammed into the side of her head, a fist or maybe a gun butt. He whispered, "I'm sick of you fighting me."

The stunning blow had knocked the fight out of her. The hoofbeats of three horses faded. Callie was alone with the man who'd grabbed her and bound her with such cold, ruthless skill.

The world upended and she was hanging, head down, over the man's shoulders.

"You go first with the end of the rope. That gully is steep. We'll need to pull her up."

Callie had a thin line of vision, and she tried to see who was coming up behind her. But for all her twisting around, she couldn't get a good look.

The partner who had taken the horses passed quickly to take the lead. These two worked well together.

Callie felt as if the ground had dropped from beneath her. The trail was so steep, her face scraped against the rock when she tried to lift her head. She glimpsed rushing water and realized what the man had said. If he wanted to raise her up with a rope, he'd have to let her go. She had a knife in her boot. She tested the bonds. Her arms were tight to her sides, but her hands weren't bound. She wiggled her fingers to see how much reach she had. If the man let go of her, she might have a chance to—

She was dropped to a rocky ledge at the bottom of the gully. Through her blindfold she saw the man, his face covered with a bandana.

But she knew who it was. Someone she'd seen on a Wanted poster.

Jasper Henry. Come to retrieve his diamonds.

A gasp behind the gag and her startled reaction drew his attention. He bent over her, tugged the blindfold down, and caught a handful of her hair painfully to tip her head back.

"I see you recognize me, Mrs. Kincaid. Too bad. I'd hoped to end this without you being harmed. You've got what's mine, and I aim to get it back. For now, the less you see, the better off you'll be." With painful jerks he tugged her hands together in front of her and pulled a leather strip off his belt. Her hands were secured until she couldn't move a finger. He pulled the blindfold back in place.

Shaking her head, she grunted at him through the gag, wanting to tell him this wasn't necessary. She'd let him have the stupid diamonds if he'd just take them and go. But the guttural noises didn't get her message across.

She felt a strangling tug on the rope at her waist, and then Jasper left her there. She fought with the leather strip to get enough movement to reach her boot. She hadn't gotten anywhere before the rope began dragging her up the gully. And she knew where they were going next. That stupid, dark, deadly cavern.

When or if she got out of here, she was going to make those idiot Kincaids find a home with the sense to lie flat. And they'd make sure there weren't any holes in it.

They all needed to move this ranch to a sensible state. Like Texas.

CHAPTER 28

"Where's Callie?" Seth checked Connor on Heath's back, and the little tyke chortled at him and waved his arms.

He'd've liked to spend more time playing with his son, but caution made him watch the trail where his wife had oughta be bringing up the rear. The last of the cattle has passed. Callie should have been along by now.

"She was right behind me." Heath took a long swig on his canteen. "She probably just needed a few minutes of privacy."

"How long has it been since you've seen her?"

Heath shrugged. "A long time, I reckon."

Seth thought of whoever had been in his cabin two nights ago and felt twitchy. "Ride up and tell 'em to rest the herd until we catch up. I don't like getting strung out this far."

Seth whirled his horse and headed down the trail at a sharp clip.

"Callie!" He knew he'd come too far about the time he rode past the turn to the new line shack.

"Callie!" If she'd stepped off the trail for personal reasons, he would've seen her horse by now. No reason to hide a horse on a cattle drive.

"Where are you?" He tried to tell himself he was fretting for no reason, but this was a hard land. There were plenty of ways to get swallowed up in the Rockies.

Seth studied the tracks and almost turned and rode back to the herd to get Ethan. His brother was the best tracker Seth knew. But surely Callie was just up at the cabin for some reason—though it went against what he knew of Callie. She wasn't a woman to turn aside from work. Seth had picked out Callie's horse, knowing she'd come along last, so the tracks weren't that hard to make out on the churned-up ground. There were more tracks overtop of the ones left by Callie. It looked like three horses had turned up the trail toward the line shack.

Seth pulled his gun and fired three times into the air. His horse tossed its head and wheeled as the gun blasted. Seth waited a few seconds, then did it again. That was all the help he had time to ask for.

He spurred his horse, racing up the trail toward the old Gilliland place.

The rope around her midsection was so tight that Callie had trouble getting a breath. The gag in her mouth made it worse. By the time they lowered her down the pit, she was barely conscious.

Hands crawled over her like insects. She shuddered and tried to fight off the muddled thinking left over from the blow to her head.

She felt the hands slip and suddenly she fell a long ways. She had a split second to think of Seth and floors that broke like glass before she slammed into the ground.

"Is she all right? The rope—" A woman's voice. One of these polecats was a woman.

"Quiet!" the man said, cutting her off.

Moaning behind the gag, Callie tried to figure out a way to get them to let her talk. She had no intention of dying rather than give up the secret as to where those diamonds were hidden. But neither did she trust these two to be kind-hearted and let her go on her way once they had what they wanted.

Maybe they would, but she'd heard the cruelty in the man's voice. And anyway, it wasn't going to be possible to bargain with a gag in her mouth.

They hauled her to her feet. "Bring the lantern but don't light it. For now, I think darkness is a good idea. No risk she'll see my face."

Which she already had. Which the man knew very well. Which meant the man didn't want the woman to know that. Why? He marched her forward. Even with the blindfold in place, she could tell they'd stepped into complete darkness.

"We want those diamonds." The man shoved her along in front of him. Callie thought of the hole Seth had fallen in and wondered where else there were deep holes in this place.

"We'll keep you down here until your family brings them to us."

"How . . . ?" She tried to talk, but it was so garbled it was impossible.

"You'll get your chance to talk once we're away from this entrance. And if you tell me where the diamonds are, all nice and polite, we'll let you go. If you don't, we'll wait until someone in your family reads the note we left in the shack. They'll miss you soon enough and get around to checking there. Then we wait for someone to bring the diamonds and trade them for you."

Callie growled at the man to the best of her ability as he forced her ahead of him. She had no idea how far they'd come when finally they stopped.

"I'm going to take the gag off now."

As soon as it jerked free, Callie yelled.

The man shoved her backward and she stumbled into a wall. "Yell all you want. No one's gonna hear you, Mrs. Kincaid."

She shouted again. He laughed.

Giving up on the futile effort, Callie opened her mouth to tell the idiot she'd be glad to lead him to the diamonds. But the words died unspoken. She had no idea where she was, so how could she guide them to the diamonds? She'd never come to this part of the cave with Seth and Julia.

Her shoulders slumped when she realized that unless she came up with a real good idea, she was going to have to do exactly what Jasper and his lady friend wanted. Wait for a Kincaid to come and rescue her.

"Ethan, Seth wants you to stop and rest the herd. Wait for him and Callie to catch up." Heath's shout turned Ethan around.

Ethan headed back toward Heath to see what the holdup was. Before he reached the youngster, three shots fired. He spun his horse in the direction of the sound. Three more shots.

"Steele!" The gunfire assured everyone was listening. "There's trouble. I'm going back."

"Seth's hunting for Callie!" Heath shouted.

With a jerk of his chin Ethan saw more of the Kincaid hands coming after him. "Steele, send the men to tell Rafe something's wrong. You and Heath come with me."

Steele barked out orders, then he, Ethan, and Heath took off riding in the direction they'd just come.

Seth pushed his horse hard up the narrow trail leading to the line shack. Iron-shod hooves clattered along the stony path. He crested the hill in front of the cabin and saw no horses in the corral. "Callie!"

No spitfire of a wife could be seen anywhere.

"Callie!" He was just yelling now. Scared to death. She'd have already answered him if she could.

He swung down off his horse and tied him to the hitching post in front of the shack. Pushing the door open, he saw immediately that the fireplace had been used. In one day? Who'd had time to find the place and build a fire?

He went back outside and studied the ground. It was heavily trodden from their days of building. The only place he could think of around here was the cavern.

But if someone had taken his wife down there, then they'd picked the wrong hiding place. No one knew that cavern better than Seth. No one could hide from him for long, not down there. With a flash of sense he thought to leave a message for Rafe or Ethan or one of the hired hands. But no paper, no pencil. He prayed desperately for inspiration and thought of Julia marking the cavern wall. He dashed back into the cabin, and as he went to get a piece of charred wood he saw the paper lying on the mantel. A note demanding that the diamonds be handed over. Threatening Callie if he didn't get them.

Jasper Henry.

Seth reread it, then grabbed charcoal out of the cold fireplace. He went back out, and on the clean-split wood of the front door he wrote Callie Kidnapped Cavern.

His brothers would know he needed help, but how long would it take for them to come?

He sure as certain wasn't going to wait for them.

Scrambling down and up the deep gully, Seth's fears were confirmed when he saw the ladder dropped over the side of the pit. He could see clear enough to know the first room was empty.

He swung over the edge of the hole and slid more than climbed down the ladder. Every second of the descent he was conscious of how clearly visible he was. He could feel the heat of a rifle trained on his back. He hit the ledge and was down to the cavern floor in a flash. He went straight to the tunnel and stopped. Light or no light?

The floors had a thin layer of dust in most places, so he might be able to pick up some tracks. But a light was like an open invitation for him to be seen. He knew there was no other direction for a dozen yards, so he went down the tunnel until he felt the first turnoff. Listening with every ounce of concentration he could muster, he did his best not to make a sound as he moved. When he got to the turnoff, he pulled a match from his pocket and crouched down. A light scratch seemed to echo and call to every outlaw in the Colorado Territory that he was there. The match flared to life. Seth used it to study the ground, but it was near impossible to make out any tracks. The light was just too dim.

Knowing he had to risk it, he grabbed a torch stuck into the wall. He lit it with a whoosh as the fire jumped to life and blinded him for a second.

It flowed, like a river of fire, straight toward him. Seth felt the fire splatter on his back.

He could smell the burning. It was his own flesh. He heard the thin cry of terror. He slapped at his burning hair.

The gunshots had sounded right by the trail to the line shack. Slowing only to make the turn, Ethan charged up to the cabin with Heath right on his heels, and Steele coming hard behind them.

"Where'd they get to?" Ethan swung his horse around, looking in all directions.

"He rode back to find Callie. She disappeared."

Steele's gray brows lowered to an angry line. "Well, Seth's almost loco enough to leave a cattle drive, but Callie'd never do it."

"You don't know her." Heath scowled at Steele. "You've barely met her."

"I heard about the stagecoach robbery and what she done. I know the type they breed in Texas. I'm from there myself. She's solid. She'd've never left when there was work to be done. So that means there's trouble."

Then Ethan rode close enough to see the front door of the cabin. In large letters scrawled with charcoal were the words *Callie Kidnapped Cavern.*

"Seth went down into that blasted cavern after her." Steele's eyes sharpened. Ethan knew his foreman was smart and savvy and could be dangerous if he needed to be.

Ethan wasn't ever going to like that cavern, but he'd made his peace with it. He'd go down after his brother if he had to, and it looked like he did.

"Heath, ride back to the herd and tell—"

"No, I'm going with you."

Ethan nodded. Better to send Steele to handle the cowpokes anyway. "Steele, get to Rafe. Leave the cattle; we can round them up later. Tell Rafe I went to the cave from here to find Seth and Callie. He should come a-runnin' from the cave entrance at his place. We'll cover more ground that way." Ethan didn't say more, knowing Rafe would give the orders the second the men were within the sound of his voice.

Steele jerked his chin in agreement.

"Hey, wait!"

Both men stopped and turned to Heath, who was taking Connor from off his back. "Steele, you take the baby."

Steele arched a brow until it disappeared under his Stetson.

"Well, we can't take him to a gunfight." Heath gently but firmly hooked the carrier holding the baby onto Steele's back.

"This is the strangest foreman job I've ever had for a fact." Steele turned and galloped away.

Ethan looked at Heath. "Let's go!"

CHAPTER 29

Callie's head cleared as she walked. The blindfold had sagged down, and with the lantern she could see where she was going now. But none of it was familiar to her.

Then they stepped into a good-sized room. Just above eye level she almost yelped with pleasure when she saw a real big fish on the wall. She knew exactly where she was. She'd made a fairly accurate map to this place. She wouldn't be a bit surprised if she could find her way back to Rafe's valley from here—even in the pitch-dark. And she knew exactly where she'd hide until these outlaws quit hunting for her.

Seeing a handy boulder, she stumbled over it and toppled to the stony floor, crying out in pain.

She did her best to make it look and sound natural, not that hard considering how tightly her hands were bound.

If they wanted her to move another inch, they could just carry her. She was tired of making this easy for them. And if she was going to make a break, this is the place she needed to start from.

A toe prodded her stomach and she did her best to sob. It didn't suit her to cry, waste of salt and water to her way of thinking. It came more natural to respond with her fist in this man's belly.

But for the purpose of acting helpless and slowing these varmints down, and considering her hands were bound, she just cried like a little orphan calf.

"Get up." Jasper's toe prodded harder, but Callie had been kicked by a mama longhorn a few times and this didn't even get her attention.

She did cry louder, though. "I c-can't. I hurt my . . ." She tried to think of something a weakling might complain about. Honestly she didn't know any weaklings. The West tended to kill them off or drive them back East. "I hurt my ankle. I think it's broken."

"Untie her." Bracing herself for the kick to come harder, she didn't expect the woman to speak. She'd only slipped and spoken once up until now.

"Quiet," Jasper said.

"No, I won't be quiet."

Callie wanted to get a look at the woman for the purpose of identifying her to the nearest lawman, but for now she lay facedown trying to act defeated.

"Untie her right now. There's no reason to have her hands bound down here. She can't find her way out if she runs away from the light. She's not going anywhere."

Much as Callie appreciated the compassion, the woman was dead wrong. The first chance she got, Callie was definitely going somewhere. She'd run off into the dark. Find a place to hide and wait until the coast was clear. Yet she wasn't about to overload the woman with all that truth.

"M-m-my hands are numb. I can't f-feel my fingers. And I can't w-walk." The crying was real annoying and a little humiliating. But Callie knew a softhearted criminal when she was in the presence of one—even though, truth be told, she'd never been in the presence of one before, nor believed such a critter existed—so she wept some more.

"She's not hurt. She fell against a stone and now she's acting like—"

"Untie her or I will."

Jasper grumbled as he crouched beside Callie and rolled her over. She felt the cold edge of a blade. With a couple of tugs her hands were free. He yanked the blindfold away, too. "No sense worrying about her identifying us, I guess."

Turned out her hands really were numb. She'd have grabbed the knife out of her boot if her fingers worked.

Before she could begin to make them obey her, Jasper hauled her to her feet. Her ankle really was sore. Not something that would slow her down much, but the cry of pain was easy enough to come by.

She collapsed and only his iron grip kept her upright. And that grip hurt, so she cried out again.

"Jasper, let her down." The woman was beautiful in a faded way. Kindness and strength shone from her eyes. "Get the lantern over here. I'll take a look at her ankle."

"Thank you." Callie sniffled as she sank to the floor and

offered the ankle that didn't hurt, since there wasn't a knife in that boot.

She pulled her knee up close to her chin. The man stood over her with the lantern. The woman knelt at her feet. Callie tried to think of something that'd distract them and at that instant she remembered something else really important. She knew exactly where the diamonds were.

She could just hand them over and hope these folks would leave. But Callie wasn't real trusting of kidnappers. Instead, she moved her hand closer to her knife.

Rafe loved it when Julia was happy, and right now she was ecstatic. She'd gotten her first contract for an article, and cash money had been included in the letter they'd fetched home from town. Rafe had agreed to ride in with her, knowing he had a few hours before his brothers showed up with the cattle.

He heard pounding hoofbeats, not what he expected. There was no herd, just one man riding alone.

Steele came charging down the slope from the entrance to the caldera with reckless speed. The foreman didn't push his horse like that without trouble on his heels.

"Seth left a note at the line shack saying Callie's been kidnapped and taken into the cavern!" shouted Steele as he rode up and swung down off his winded horse. Rafe noticed with shock that the man had Connor strapped on his back. "Ethan went after them, heading into the cavern from there. He wants you to go in through the entrance here."

Rafe was still on horseback and he turned to Julia. "We've gotta go."

Then Rafe had a vision of bad men getting past him in that cavern and threatening Julia. "Nope, not we. Just me. Steele, you stay here and stay on guard."

Julia was busy getting Connor into her own hands.

Rafe took off at a full gallop for the cavern entrance. Just minutes later he was running into the cave mouth with a lit torch in his hand, down into that awful hole that had tried to swallow Seth alive.

Swept back by the river of fire into the past, Seth beat at the flames and in doing so must've knocked some sense into his head. Getting a tenuous grip on reality, he saw his lit torch on the floor. That was the only fire. No river. No burning stone. Shaking, he thought of Callie. She needed him. He didn't have time for anything but her.

He separated himself from the madness. He breathed in and it was dank air, no fiery smoke. No burning flesh.

Once he corralled the madness that sometimes overtook him, he had Callie back in the front of his thoughts. A new beat of panic rushed along his spine—but being scared for her was reasonable when some desperado had kidnapped her.

"Find her. Think. Use your head. Stay in control," he told himself.

He picked up the torch and went to the spot where the tunnel split off. Hunkering down, he studied the floor. Close to the tunnel wall he found a footprint. Not a clear one, but someone had definitely been down this way very recently.

They'd gone straight rather than turn off toward the tunnel that led to Rafe's caldera. He marked the wall for Ethan and Rafe. Then, even knowing it was dangerous, he kept the torch burning. Speed outweighed caution. As he thought that, he realized it was the kind of reckless choice he'd made a thousand times in his life. The kind of reckless choice that had ended with him falling through a stone floor, burning himself. Upsetting his brothers until they couldn't love him anymore. Driving his father away. Killing his mother. His eyes went to the torch and it seemed to grow, flow, run like a river.

Fighting down the image, he tore his eyes away from it and hung on when he wanted to hurl it away from him.

"I'm not thinking right because I'm scared for Callie." Saying her name out loud helped. "I just need to find her." His words became a prayer. "Find her, and once I know she's all right, I'll be fine."

He clung to the light and hurried down the tunnel. Listening with every bit of strength for any sound, however faint, watching the floor carefully for tracks when a tunnel divided. Marking the walls to show which way he'd turned.

He was confident he was on the right track, but where was she? Who had her? Seth rushed on, his stomach twisting to think maybe that footprint was an old one and he was going the wrong way.

What if she wasn't even down here?

The fear for her grew.

The torch flared up. It seemed to billow smoke.

Who had her? The fire in his hand crackled so loud he couldn't hear anything else.

Was she still alive? Fire seemed to crawl toward his arm, and he shook the torch and watched it even as he kept walking.

Would she be lost down here, dragged even deeper than Seth had ever gone? The fear was so strong it was like a wall of fire in front of him that he had to push through. Each step was harder than the last.

He thought of the place he'd fallen through. There was a ledge at the bottom of that hole. He wondered how deep it was. For all his hunting around, he'd never explored what was over that ledge. Thinking of it pushed away the fear for Callie.

Why hadn't he ever tried to reach the bottom of that hole? Maybe he'd find beautiful things down there. Maybe he'd find the part of himself he'd left behind.

He heard someone call out.

Callie? Shaking his head to dislodge thoughts of that black hole and the wall of fire, he heard it again. It sounded like a child's voice. His own. But he hadn't called out and his voice was deep. It was as if the child from so long ago called to him. Or maybe not the child, maybe the part of himself he'd left behind. Maybe today he'd finally find his soul.

He stepped into a large room, lifted the torch high, and saw those stunning pillars of white. The steady quiet drip of water soothed him. The fear receded and the fire was more comfort than threat now. This was where he always wanted to be when things were bad. And now he was here. He found calm and serenity.

His shoulders squared and he breathed in the cool air and listened to the echo of his footsteps and the aloneness of his cavern.

He'd come here, in his head, during the war. He'd done so much scouting and it had taken him to lonely places where he had to lie silently for hours.

And when the tension was too much or the fear started to swallow him whole, and fires seemed to blaze all around him, he'd come—inside his head—down into his cavern. It was the only place in the world that was truly his own.

He'd been able to wait for anything in complete silence and utter stillness if he could just come here.

Seeing a favorite spot to view these towers, he pushed all his terrors away and let the peace of the cavern ease into his bones.

"I hate this stupid cavern." Ethan slid down the ladder so recklessly he felt like Seth for a second. Then he hit the ledge. Heath was right behind him.

"Be careful here. This ledge is about a foot wide. Follow me; we can't climb down here."

Heath came along quickly and was beside Ethan by the time he had a torch lit. He found a second one for Heath, and then Ethan charged for the tunnel, cutting time, trying to close the gap and catch Seth so he wouldn't have to face the kidnappers alone.

He rushed past the tunnel that led to Rafe's, but there was no sign of his big brother. Ethan had to be ahead of him, and there was no time to waste waiting. He knew Rafe would come, sure as the sunrise.

"Seth left a trail." Ethan, with the torch held high, pointed at Seth's marking, which he could tell was new. "Hurry! We can get to Seth before he catches up to trouble."

And this time Ethan promised himself, when he caught up with his little brother, they'd fight side by side. Ethan wouldn't taunt him. Instead he'd be the kind of big brother that helped a kid in danger.

Then a split in the cavern stopped Ethan. "Do you see a marking?"

Heath studied the wall, shaking his head. "Nuthin'."

Ethan knelt to check the ground. A thin layer of dirt on stone didn't make a great surface for tracking. If Ethan picked wrong, he'd leave his little brother on his own down in this pit. He'd be failing Seth one more time, only this time it might cost Seth his life.

She judged the man to be wily, his eyes sharp. She didn't move for the knife.

She needed a distraction. Until then, she didn't have a chance with one puny knife against the two kidnappers. She prayed for something, like a runaway rock to land on the man's head, or that fish to come to life and bite them both.

The woman knelt at Callie's feet and unlaced her boot. It didn't seem all that smart to let the woman take her shoe off. She'd need it to go running over rock. Callie let herself relax. She was ready, but not tense. No sense letting the couple know she was thinking of making trouble.

"It doesn't look swollen."

"Don't take her shoe off. Stop it. We don't have time for that." Jasper raised the lantern higher, and Callie thought of this place—of lanterns and Seth's scars. Since the lantern had been right in front of her eyes the whole time, she wondered how come that idea had popped into her head at the exact same moment she'd been praying.

The woman tugged off her boot, ignoring the man's orders.

"Where are you taking me, anyway? If you're going to keep me a prisoner, haven't we come far enough?" Callie looked between the two.

"We can stay right here." The woman held her foot in one hand and her calf in the other. She twisted the foot gently. "Does that hurt?"

"Ouch, yes!" There wasn't much Callie hated more than a whiner. She had no practice at it, but she was doing her best.

"We hunted around some." The woman inspected her ankle. "We've got a room farther down, but no need to go on right now."

"We had a plan."

"Part of that plan was not to hurt anyone," the woman said. "I saw you hit her. I'm not going to hurt her anymore."

"She's fine. She was just stunned for a few seconds and now she's faking the injured ankle." The lantern swung a bit as the man's temper rose.

The lantern . . . A lantern could do a lot of damage without much trouble at all. Lots of light, though, if a lantern broke and fire spread. And splashing kerosene could get on her as well as on them. Would that be the kind of idea God would give her anyway, setting someone on fire? That seemed mighty mean. Though God used fire a lot in the Bible. Why not here in Colorado Territory?

"It h-hurts. I can't walk." Callie did her best to sound defeated.

"I don't see why we need to hurry." The woman set Callie's foot on the ground as if it were made of glass.

"It's cold." More whining, which made Callie want to punch

someone just to prove she wasn't a weakling. "Can I put my boot back on? If it swells up, I might not be able to get it on later."

Kneeling there, the woman raised her eyes and looked straight at Callie. With Jasper standing behind, he couldn't see her face.

The woman's eyes said plainly that she very much doubted Callie's act. With a sad look, almost resigned, she didn't give away any doubts to the man but just drew the shoe on so carefully she might've been dressing a child.

"We want those diamonds because, well, because they belong to us." The woman spoke, studying the boot as she laced it. "It eats at my man that he's lost all that fortune. It's like there's no peace to be had as long as he knows it's beyond his grasp."

"Peace . . ." Callie watched the woman, who was kneeling as if in prayer. Her head was so low, Callie could see part of her hair, a faded red, with threads of gray that picked up glints from the lantern.

"Yes, I want peace," the woman said.

The man's hand came down on the woman's shoulder. "Get away from her. You've fussed over her long enough."

"You promised me you wouldn't hurt her and now here she is, hurt pretty bad."

"It's not my fault she tripped over that rock."

"Oh, yes it is." The woman's head came up just enough to look Callie in the eyes. She dropped her eyes very deliberately, down and to her right. Callie glanced at the spot where the woman had looked and saw her revolver stuck into the waistband of the woman's skirt. Looking away quickly so Jasper wouldn't notice, Callie saw the woman give her a tiny nod.

The strange calm that always came over Seth when he was in the cavern wouldn't settle.

He craved it. He'd come home from the war but ended up in this cavern, not on his family's ranch.

The cavern quieted the haunting cannons. The screams of dying men. The gunfire and blood and pain. The fire. Once he'd seen that mountain and knew how close he was to the cavern, he just had to go down. And once he was down there, the flames that burned inside his head died away, the noise faded. Then the man drugged him. Seth hadn't figured that out until later. Most of that time was hazy, nightmarish.

But since then he'd been down in his cavern several times and the old peace had been there, waiting for him. But not today. He couldn't be calm. He couldn't let go of the world as usual. His eyes blinked suddenly as he remembered Callie. Like a flash of fire, the worry for her jolted him out of any wish for peace. He didn't want peace. He wanted his wife.

Dear God, what am I doing?

Seth reached out for godly peace instead of seeking it in the cavern. Instantly he was washed with a serenity he'd never known. As if God himself had laid a hand on Seth's frenetic, reckless mind and brought calm.

He raised his torch. The fire wasn't an enemy; it was light and warmth. It gave him strength in a way Seth knew came straight from the Light of the World.

As if that Light illuminated his mind, suddenly he remembered everything. His memories of Callie were fully awakened. Callie caring for him after Andersonville. The almost crazed need he'd felt when she'd awakened him from a nightmare. How generously she stayed with him day and night. It seemed as if she never slept, never left his side. He remembered waking up one dark night with her in his arms, drawing him out of the nightmare and helping him to cling to sanity. A doctor had come into the room and found them in bed together. He'd demanded that Callie leave, dismissed her from the hospital for her improper behavior.

Seth had proposed on the spot, and she'd said yes immediately. They'd been married shortly after sunrise and then he'd left the hospital, leaning on her, although still on his own feet.

So many men were left behind without feet, without arms. He'd been lucky that way.

More came to him about the first nightmare after they were married, when he'd awakened and made love to his wife. He'd hated what he was putting her through, and so, thinking it would help him to sleep through the night, he'd reached for a bottle of laudanum.

He thought he could remember even more, yet he had to put that out of his mind for now. He needed to keep moving, keep searching for Callie.

His brothers would be coming. After a few frantic seconds of wondering how to let them know where he'd gone, he remembered the charcoal.

He'd used it, but carelessly. Now he'd leave a sign at every turn for his brothers. They were watchful men. They'd be along as fast as they could come and they'd notice the markings.

As he continued on, it seemed certain that Callie was headed straight for where they'd hidden the diamonds.

The kidnappers were forcing Callie to take them there.

Seth felt stronger with every step as he rushed forward now, racing to help his wife. His very tough wife. He picked up the pace, hoping she left something for him to do.

He wouldn't mind being a hero in her eyes after all the times she'd been a hero in his.

Rafe went down the slope so fast he almost ran right over the edge of the pit where Seth had fallen. He scooted quickly along the side of it, then hurried on. When he got to the next turn, he saw that Seth had left a charcoal mark on a wall and had written SK beside the mark. His initials.

"I should have protected Seth and Callie better," Rafe said. The thought hit Rafe so hard, he spoke it out loud. "Why did we have to move the cattle today? We knew those diamonds were trouble. We knew that varmint wouldn't quit looking for 'em."

Rafe swore an oath that once he rescued Callie and made sure Seth was out of this pit and Ethan was safe, he would be more vigilant. He'd hire more hands so no one ever went anywhere alone. He'd dynamite this cavern so no one would ever be threatened by it again. He'd get those diamonds, and no matter the weather, he'd make the ride to Colorado City and get the things out of his hair.

The more promises he made to himself, the more Rafe could hear just exactly how much he wanted to control the whole world. And he knew that wasn't possible. Which was a pure blasted shame. Because if he controlled the world, things would start shaping up.

He rushed on, his heart beating with the frantic knowledge

that he couldn't control this and he couldn't always protect his brothers. And he shouldn't want to. That was a job best left to God. They were grown men, after all.

Even though Rafe knew all that, it didn't slow his pace one bit.

CHAPTER 30

The woman had changed sides. At least Callie hoped she was reading the sign right. Honestly her head still hurt. It wasn't easy to have so much to think about.

The woman finished lacing Callie's boot and rose to her feet. She offered Callie an arm. Standing wasn't what Callie wanted; she liked having her hand closer to her knife. But since she could think of no good reason not to, she let herself be lifted. Jasper watched her stand with narrow, suspicious eyes.

Callie leaned on the wall, right under the fish . . . and the diamonds. There was a tunnel just a few feet to her right. She planned to dart down it if she got so much as a single chance.

Callie conjured some tears. "I . . . I'm new around here, you know. I don't know what's going on. Why did you take me?"

"You were bringing up the rear."

With a frown Callie had to fight not to curl a fist. To think she'd been put through all of this because she chose the hardest job on the drive. It was purely annoying. She didn't punch the man, though. It didn't fit with her delicate maiden act.

"Jasper—"

A footstep echoed in the tunnel just off to Callie's left. The instant she heard that, Callie moved. In one smooth motion she bent, grabbed her knife out of her boot, and threw it hard.

Jasper whirled toward the sound and that saved the polecat's life.

The knife sunk deep into the arm that held the lantern. He staggered, lost his grip on the lantern, which then shattered on the stone floor. Flames whooshed high. Kerosene splashed wildly and the fire followed, running like a river of fire.

Jasper pulled the trigger when he fell. His gun thundered as he fired and fired and fired. A volley of bullets smashed into the wall of the cavern, hitting and ricocheting.

Callie grabbed the woman's gun out of her skirt's waistband and dived behind a stone that grew up in a cone shape from the floor. Callie slammed to the floor, her grip on her gun solid. She crawled forward and peeked around the base of the stone, taking aim. But before she could pull the trigger, she saw a bullet strike Jasper.

Bullets whined around the cave, hitting the stone near Callie and stinging her face. She saw something bright drop to the cave floor and recognized the cylinder that held the diamonds. A glance upward told her the little shelf where they'd been stashed had broken off.

"Jasper! Stop!" The woman rushed over to Jasper, ignoring the gunfire. She blocked Callie's shot.

Then Seth emerged from the tunnel entrance, running to the side, away from Callie. She took one second to enjoy him coming to save her. Their eyes met through leaping flames. He nodded, smiled, then took aim at Jasper. Callie leveled her gun.

A crack of shattering stone echoed through the cave. Jasper dropped with a sharp scream. The rumble of stones made Callie look overhead for a cave-in, but the roof held. She rose to her knees and saw that Jasper had broken through the floor up to his hips.

His eyes went wide. "Bea! Help me!"

She was on the same side of the flames as Jasper and she reached for him. "Grab my hand!"

Their eyes met. More passed between them in an instant than seemed possible to Callie. Love. Heartbreak. Regret. Maybe the knowledge that even now it wasn't too late to decide where Jasper would spend eternity.

He reached for Bea, and the floor collapsed and he vanished. The little cylinder plunged into the pit after him. His scream went on and on until it faded away. They didn't hear him hit bottom.

The woman, Bea, collapsed with a cry of terror. Callie leaped from her hiding place and rushed toward her.

"Callie, no!" Seth shouted. The burning kerosene was an arch that curved around Bea, and left Callie on one side of it and Seth on the other.

Callie looked across the flames to see Bea hanging from her stomach on the edge of the hole. Her arms clung to the broken floor.

"Stay back, Callie! The whole floor can cave in any second."

"I have to help her." Callie whipped her coat off and dropped it on the fire, then started moving toward Bea.

"No!" Seth jumped the flames and threw himself at Callie, tackling her. As they landed, only feet from Bea, the floor broke again. Bea screamed and fell. Only her fingers still clung to the lip of the hole.

She screamed and cried out, "Help me! Please, God . . ."

"We have to help her, Seth. She took care of me. She kept him from hurting me."

Seth met her eyes. She saw sanity. Clear, bright sanity shining in his wild blue eyes. Callie's heart almost broke with love for him.

With a jerk of his chin he turned and, lying flat on his stomach, grabbed Bea's hands. "Get behind me, Callie. Hang on to my feet. We don't know how much more of this floor will break off. I need you to anchor me."

Quickly she wrapped her arms around his legs and held on tight.

"Climb up!" Seth shouted. "Here, grab my hand!"

"I can't . . ." Bea cried.

The floor cracked and Seth fell forward to his waist.

Bea's scream told Callie the woman was still hanging on.

"Don't let go, Callie!" Seth's shout gave Callie strength. Her desperate prayers helped even more.

Then an arm reached past her and grabbed the waistband of Seth's pants. "I'm here, Seth."

Callie recognized Ethan's voice.

"Hang on, Bea. We've got help." Callie knew the woman's

weight added to Seth's was too much. How much more of this floor might break off?

"It's still thin under my legs, Ethan. We've got to get off it."

The fire crackled within inches of where Ethan stood. He ignored it and pulled until inch by inch Seth started emerging from the hole.

"Heath, get the rope around Seth!" Rafe was there, giving orders.

A rope thrown with sharp precision settled over Seth. Yet one more break in this floor and Seth would be gone forever. If Seth hadn't been busy fighting for his life, he'd've smiled to hear his big brothers' voices.

"Get your arm through the rope." And Heath's, too.

Seth looked into Bea's terrified eyes. "Can you let go of my hand and grab the rope?"

The woman's eyes were wild with fear. She had her hand sunk into his sleeves. She couldn't let go to climb up his body or take the rope. Seth ripped one hand loose from her clawing grip. She screamed as he shot his left arm under the rope and quickly caught her again. As he was about to pry her other hand loose to get the rope around himself more securely, the floor snapped again. He plunged forward and jerked to a stop, dangling from one arm and his neck. Holding on to Bea's hand with the other arm.

The rope ripped at the skin on the right side of his throat. Bea's hand slipped.

"Hold on, Heath!" Rafe yelled. "Callie, get back."

"How far back is it thin, Seth?"

Seth glanced over his shoulder, and his stomach twisted as he looked along the bottom of the stone just above his head. "It'll break all the way to the tunnel you came down."

Seth gritted his teeth as the rope cut into his arm. He lifted his and Bea's weight enough so he could slide the rope to support them at his shoulder socket instead of just his arm.

The way he dangled now, he could get a better grip on Bea. If the rope would just hold their weight and the stupid floor would stop collapsing, they'd be fine.

"Get back into the tunnel, Callie. Help Heath hang on to the lasso. Eth, you next, get back. You got a firm hold now, Seth?"

Not really. "Yeah, I'm fine."

Seth's eyes shifted downward, thinking of the man who'd started all this. He couldn't see the bottom, even with the lights from the dancing flames overhead. Whatever this pit was, it was deep. To fall here meant certain death.

Bea looked half mad with fear, but she reached up with the hand he wasn't holding and caught hold. If Seth let her go, he'd be pulled up easily, and with far less risk to his brothers and Callie. Instead, he tightened his grip on her hand, this woman who was part of a scheme that almost cost Seth his wife and now risked his brothers.

The rope pulled him up an inch, then another. "Can you grab my belt, Bea?"

Much as he hated risking so many people he loved, he wouldn't have dropped her, even if he could've gotten her fingernails pried loose.

Another inch and the floor crumbled again. Seth dropped two feet with a jarring thud. Bea let loose one of her ear-piercing screams. Seth looked up and saw the rope sliding back and forth against the sharp edge of the rocks. But now, finally, it was against solid rock.

"I think it's done breaking, Rafe! I'm against a wall now."

"How many times have I told you all not to come down here?" Rafe said, now that the rope was being drawn up steadily.

With four hands lending strength, Seth popped up to the surface in seconds. Then Ethan's hands slid under Seth's arms, and he was dragged up onto the hard, blessed rock.

While Seth was being helped by Ethan, Rafe reached down and grabbed the back of the woman's dress. Yet even after Bea was pulled to safety, she still didn't let go of Seth.

Finally she was peeled off of him. Seth thought she took chunks of his skin with her, but then the woman was wise to hang on tight, so he didn't complain.

Seth scrambled well away from the ledge until his back was up against a thick wall. He'd taken one deep breath when Callie launched herself into his arms.

"Callie!" He wrapped his arms around her. "My beautiful wife." He held her almost as tight as Bea had held him. But without the fingernails.

"The first time I laid eyes on you, you were wearing a pink blouse scattered with white flowers and a black skirt."

She kissed the side of his neck and he almost forgot what he'd been talking about.

"You were a mess, your hair mostly out of its braid." He sank his fingers into her hair. "Just like it is now. And your sleeves were rolled up. You were soaking wet with sweat in that overheated hospital. I'd never dreamed there could be a woman so beautiful. And you were crying for me, trying to wake me up from a nightmare. The first thing I said when you woke me up was, 'You're not Rafe or Ethan.'"

Callie gasped and pulled back. "That is what you said. Seth, you remember!"

Happiness soaked all the way into his soul—his soul that wasn't left behind in some dank old cavern. It was firmly seated right in his own body and given over to the keeping of the Lord. "I surely do remember everything that passed between us. Every word." His voice dropped to a whisper. "Every kiss."

"Well, let's get going." A hard slap on his back stopped him from adding another kiss to his memories.

Rafe, always organized, said, "Julia's crazy with worry."

Seth turned and saw Bea, crying, staring at the hole.

"We have to try and save him . . ." Bea said, taking a step toward the hole.

Ethan moved forward and blocked her from getting any closer to the edge.

"It's too deep," Seth said gently. "I couldn't see the bottom. He didn't survive the fall."

"But we can't just leave him down there. It's like being buried in . . ."

Seth didn't say it, but he knew what Bea was thinking. Her man had made his choices, and he'd been swallowed into the belly of the earth. To help the poor woman accept the truth, he picked up a small stone.

"Listen," he said, his voice cutting through her crying. Seth then tossed the stone into the hole. Seconds passed. Two. Ten. Thirty. They never heard it hit bottom.

"Oh, Jasper . . ." Bea whispered. Tears began streaking down her cheeks.

Callie shook her head. "And all for diamonds."

"What about diamonds? Is that what this is about?" Rafe asked. "That was the Jasper who Wendell Gilliland stole the diamonds from?"

Seth suspected none of them knew the whole of what had happened. But the mention of diamonds lifted his eyes to the ledge above the fish on the wall. The fish was still frozen in stone, but the diamonds were gone—down in the bottomless pit with Jasper.

He finally had his diamonds back.

"Let's get out of here." Seth slid his arm around Callie's waist and turned her toward daylight and family and home.

As they walked out, Seth realized that the next time he came down here, he'd come for a better reason than to search for a part of himself. And he'd never be reckless in this place again. "You know, Rafe, you were right."

"About what?"

"This place is dangerous."

Rafe growled. Seth shifted Callie around in his arms to use her as a shield. Rafe's eyes narrowed, Ethan grinned, and Seth laughed as they all began making their way out of the cavern.

CHAPTER 31

When they reached the place in the cavern where Rafe would split off, not far from the hole that had been the source of so much pain, instead of keeping up his usual forward march, Rafe stopped and turned to his brothers.

"Let's go look at that hole. Together." He looked at Seth and Callie, then at Heath. "All of us."

A few moments later, the Kincaids stood beside that awful hole. Bea was there too, though she'd withdrawn into herself now, silent and grief-stricken.

Rafe raised his lantern and stared at the dark place.

"What are you thinking, big brother?" Seth asked.

"I'm going down there."

Seth gasped. Not real loud but they all heard it. His eyes went to Rafe's lantern. "I've never done that."

Rafe spun around from the hole to look at Seth. "In all these years, with all the exploring you've done, you've never climbed down there?"

"Nope, not since the accident."

Ethan pointed to a black corner of the hole. "Looks like it goes on forever there. No bottom to it."

"Like the hole that man Jasper fell into," Heath added.

Bea made a soft sound of pain, but silenced it almost immediately.

"Do you know how deep it goes?" Rafe asked Seth. "You're the one who knows this place better than anyone else."

"I told you—I've always avoided it." That suddenly struck Seth as very strange. "Let's go."

He stepped forward and started climbing down. "This is where I climbed up that day, when Ethan goaded me into it."

"I was cruel to you, Seth. I don't know where I found it in myself to be so heartless."

Seth glanced up at his brother. "It's all right, Eth. I understand now."

It wasn't an easy climb. Twenty feet or so, with slim handholds and toeholds—far enough apart that Seth was surprised he'd been able to reach them when he was only nine.

Below him there was no level spot. The hole, about twelve feet across, exposed a floor of broken stone that had shattered and fallen. The floor itself was jagged, sloping toward that black corner.

Seth dropped the last few feet and moved to make room for his brothers. His throat thickened as he thought of being down here before. He'd been so badly hurt. Trapped. Burning . . .

Clearing his throat, he looked up at Callie and waved.

She'd stayed up top—along with Bea—but was watching, ready to help if called on.

Seth backed up farther until he passed the rusted-out lantern. It had been lying down here all these years. Then it all came back to him in a rush. But not in a nightmare, not through the tormented eyes of a badly injured little boy.

He watched calmly with a man's clear thinking as Rafe and Ethan helped Heath reach the bottom. The three of them turned to Seth.

"You fell down here?" Heath looked around, wide-eyed. A little boy.

Picking up a stone, Rafe went to the hole in the corner and tossed it in. It hit bottom almost instantly. "It's not even deep." Rafe had brought his lantern down and he extended it over the hole. "Look. It's nothing—just a drop of about four or five feet. Doesn't go anywhere."

"I always figured it went all the way to hell." Ethan came up beside Rafe and looked down.

"You're right," Seth said. "It's nothing . . . I'm going down there."

Rafe caught Seth's arm. "No, that's reckless. We don't know if the floor's solid or not."

"I'm sure it's fine." Seth looked at Rafe, then at Ethan. It was a painful moment. A clear moment. Rafe being in control, Ethan feeling everything too deeply, Seth being reckless.

But they were doing it as men. Strong men with common sense. Seth laughed.

Before long, his brothers joined in.

Well, two of them anyway.

"Nothing funny about this," Heath said. The pint-sized

kid was the only one of them with any real sense—at least when it came to this pit. He wasn't scared. He wasn't obsessed with this hole in the ground. He was curious, though, like any young boy his age.

Seth's laughter died when he noticed Heath picking up the rusted-out lantern. "You know, I always figured that lantern shouldn't be moved."

Heath frowned. "Why would you leave it here?"

"I guess I always thought of it as a kind of tombstone. In a lot of ways we all died that day. And came back different. I wasn't innocent anymore. I knew the cost of my recklessness."

"My childhood died," Rafe said.

Ethan crossed his arms. "Our whole family died."

Heath shrugged. "No one died. From what I've heard, it sounds like you found yourselves in a tight spot and you were tough enough to get yourselves out. Seth's got some ugly scars, but he still managed to marry about the prettiest woman I've ever seen. She's way too good for him."

"I have to admit, that's the truth," Seth said.

"It is for a fact," Callie called out from the rim above.

"The nightmares are annoying, though. Can you stop that?" Heath asked.

"I'll try." Seth thought he really might be able to after today.

"And Julia and Audra are way nicer'n either of you deserve." Heath looked from Rafe to Ethan.

"No denying that," Ethan said.

Rafe shrugged. "I married well."

"And it sounds like your ma was on the crazy side."

Heath sounded real chipper about that. Seth suspected it was because the boy's own ma had been a real fine woman.

"And heaven knows our pa was worthless," Heath went on. "He didn't take care of us worth a lick. It's a wonder any of us grew up to amount to much with him as an example."

Funny but Seth had never really thought of his pa as worthless. Well, maybe he'd thought it a few times since he found out about Heath. But now he *was* thinking about it and the boy had a point.

"I think you got through that day in good shape," Heath said. "I mean, if Ethan hadn't dropped the lantern that burnt you, and if Rafe hadn't pulled so hard that he and Ethan both cracked their heads till they were both stupid, and if you'd have jumped into that black hole to hide from the fire . . . well, you'd've all been fine. But that would've been a loco thing to do without knowing how deep it was. Things like that happen when you're in a tight spot. Yep, I think you handled it pretty well."

Ethan rubbed the back of his head, while Rafe touched the scar on his temple. Seth didn't bother touching his scars. It was too hard to pick just one.

"You know what, Heath?" Seth said.

"What?" That sullen expression was back. Heath wasn't about to admit he wanted his brothers to like him.

Seth smiled at him. "I think having a little brother is going to be fun."

"Yeah, finally someone you're tough enough to beat up." Ethan added his charming grin.

"I can take you any day. I'd prove it too, if you were worth the bother." Seth slapped Ethan on the back just a little too hard.

Even bossy Rafe found a chuckle. "We'll whip 'em both into shape when we've got a few spare seconds, Heath."

Heath gave in to temptation and let the corners of his mouth turn up.

The Kincaid men stood there, in that pit that was the heart of all their worst fears, and laughed.

"Let's go home." Seth turned and scaled the pit like it was a stairway. Why hadn't he ever climbed down here in all these years? "I want to spend the rest of this day with my wife."

When they reached the top, Rafe said, "Heath, we're going that way." He pointed to the other side of the pit.

"You sure?" Heath sounded skeptical.

"I want you to come home with me for a time, and learn to obey your big brother. Let's go."

"Huh, never gonna happen," Heath muttered.

"The men will have the cattle settled in by now so you don't need to traipse over." Rafe nodded at Ethan and Seth. "I'll bring Connor home tomorrow. Julia's all worked up about a letter I fetched from town this morning from some magazine. It sounds like they're going to publish her writings. She's gonna want more pictures, Callie. She'll probably ride over with me in the morning to talk about it."

Seth groaned.

"We'll see about drawing when I've got some spare time," Callie said.

Ethan said, "I've got horses in the corral on this side of the gulley, so I'll head out from here. Bea can ride along." He turned to Bea. "I'll send some cowpokes to see you back to Colorado City. I'll give you a couple of good horses to replace yours; it'll cut hours off the trip to go this way. Seth, you take Bea's horses on back to your place along with mine."

Seth realized he was going to ride away from here with

his wife. His lawfully wedded wife, and no one else. "I'll get them home, Ethan. You can count on me."

It struck Seth hard that it was true. His brothers could count on him and so could his wife and son.

Heath followed Rafe along the ledge side of the pit. They were soon lost from sight with Rafe's lantern lighting the way.

Seth grabbed a torch, slid his other arm around Callie's waist, and they all left the cavern behind.

Seth was surprised to see it was still full daylight. He felt as if he'd been in that cavern forever. Maybe for his whole life. But he'd won the fight.

"I want you to know I expect to pay for the crimes I committed today," Bea said as they climbed the ladder.

"What crimes?" Callie asked. "Jasper's who hit me."

"Jasper hit you?" Seth turned to look Callie over.

"There's nothing to see." Callie patted Seth on the arm. "I've got a bump, but my hair covers it and I'll heal."

"I was party to it," Bea said. "I was right at his side."

"I heard you say he'd promised no one would get hurt," Callie said.

"Don't matter. I'm turning myself in. The law can decide, one way or another. Where'd Jasper's diamonds ever get to, anyway?"

Dead silence fell over the group. Seth wasn't sure the rest of them had thought of the diamonds up until now. But he sure had. He figured the rest of them were remembering exactly where those diamonds were. Ethan hadn't been along when they'd stashed them, but he knew well enough. No tool, or ladder, or rope Seth could imagine would ever be able to get the diamonds out of that deep, deep hole.

Suddenly it struck Seth as purely ridiculous that they'd had so much trouble over a tiny pile of shiny rocks.

"We hid the diamonds in the cave that collapsed," Seth replied. "They're unreachable now." He didn't see the sense of giving a thorough explanation. "Jasper can guard those diamonds for all eternity."

It might be better than the fate Jasper had before him, but who was to know how much time Jasper had to think as he fell to his death? Maybe enough time to make his peace with God.

"He wanted those diamonds more than he wanted a wife or love or God. I guess now he's got them," Bea said. After that, she didn't mention Jasper or the diamonds again.

"I'll be over tomorrow to round up those cattle." Ethan touched the brim of his hat, and then he and Bea headed for the Kincaid Ranch.

Seth and Callie crossed the gulley, saddled up, and set out for home.

CHAPTER 32

Seth had his wife all to himself. He wasn't sure how it happened, but he liked it. He had his hands full even missing little Connor, though he was glad the boy would be back home tomorrow.

"You really remember marrying me, Seth?" Callie asked.

Earlier they'd had a quiet dinner, and their time together was exactly what Seth needed.

"Every second of it," he said. Seth sat next to her by the fire, enjoying the crackling flames without hearing a word they said. Maybe fire didn't talk, after all. "More than anything else, I remember how much I love you."

She turned from watching the fire and smiled. Her hair had flashes of flame in the black silk. He rose and pulled her out of the rocking chair, and she didn't hesitate one second as he took her into his arms.

"And what about you, Callie? Can you ever love me after I abandoned you?"

Her strong, clever hands brushed across his shoulder. She slipped one hand in at his collar and touched his scars without flinching. "I don't know if I really did love you when we got married, Seth."

Those words hit hard. He felt his hopes fade as he considered what it would take to convince her to love a man like him.

"I was drawn to you, and I cared about you, and I was wildly attracted to you . . ."

That got his hopes up a little.

". . . but I don't know if a person can really love a stranger. And we didn't know each other one bit. I realize that now." After a short pause, she went on, "But, Seth, you're not a stranger anymore. And if I didn't love you enough before, then today I've fallen completely in love with you."

"Why today of all days? Because I remembered?"

"No, although your remembering has given me hope that the worst of your burdens have been lifted. I hope your mind is working better, clearer. I hope it all goes together with besting your nightmares."

"Then, what?"

"It was when you came running into that cave."

Seth grinned and stole a kiss—though it couldn't really be called stealing when she just handed the kiss right over. "Liked me being a hero, did you? Racing to the rescue."

"Sure, I liked that. But what I loved is the way I felt when I saw you. Not that you'd saved me, but just that you were there. There was no denying how much I loved my husband showing up. It was love, pure and simple." She stretched up and kissed him.

Seth wasn't sure if she'd ever kissed him first before. She'd cooperated a few times when he kissed her, but she'd never started it. He gave the kiss right back in full measure—and then some.

"I shouldn't say it before we go to sleep, but I don't think I'm going to have nightmares anymore." He tried to be subtle, yet he had no knack for subtlety. He did have a knack for sneaking around, though, and this was kind of the same thing. "Should we go on to bed? See if the nightmares come?"

"I reckon it's time." Callie smiled and kissed him again.

Time for what exactly, Seth couldn't say. He wondered, though. He wondered mighty hard.

"I hope you're right about the bad dreams," she said. "If they're gone for good, then we'll thank the good Lord. If not, we'll handle it."

Nodding, Seth said, "Today I faced some of the things that have been haunting me since the accident. I feel like a weight is gone from my mind. For the first time I could look back at what happened without all the childish terror and confusion. I can even be . . . well, sort of proud of myself and my brothers."

He thought of what Heath had said. The little pint-sized polecat might be the smartest Kincaid brother yet. "We were in a tight spot. I think we handled it pretty well."

He led her to their room, and she came along so easily that Seth's heart was pounding by the time they got there.

Once they'd settled in, Callie said, "You forgot to turn the lantern off, Seth."

"I want to be able to see for a while yet."

"Okay." Callie must have decided she could trust him, because she came into his arms.

As they held each other, Seth knew that today, in that cavern, he'd found his soul and made his peace with God.

He knew he'd found his heart too, held in the steady hands of his loving wife.

Now, as he kissed her and she returned his kisses without reservation, he found the safest, sanest place he'd ever been.

And he was here to stay.

ABOUT THE AUTHOR

Mary Connealy writes romantic comedy with cowboys. She is the author of the acclaimed LASSOED IN TEXAS, MONTANA MARRIAGES, and SOPHIE'S DAUGHTERS series. Mary has been nominated for a Christy Award, was a finalist for a RITA Award, and is a two-time winner of the Carol Award. She lives on a ranch in eastern Nebraska with her very own romantic cowboy hero, Ivan. They have four grown daughters—Joslyn, married to Matt; Wendy; Shelly, married to Aaron; and Katy—and two spectacular grandchildren, Elle and Isaac. Readers can learn more about Mary and her upcoming books at:

maryconnealy.com
mconnealy.blogspot.com
seekerville.blogspot.com
petticoatsandpistols.com

Don't Miss the First Two Kincaid Brides!

To learn more about Mary Connealy and her books visit maryconnealy.com.

Rafe Kincaid is a man used to being in charge. Julia Gilliland takes orders from no one. Tucked away on a remote Colorado ranch, can a controlling cowboy and a feisty free spirit overcome their differences before they lose each other—and their sanity?

Out of Control by Mary Connealy
THE KINCAID BRIDES #1

Two fearful hearts settle for a marriage of convenience—Audra Gilliland doesn't want to be a burden, Ethan Kincaid doesn't want to take a risk on love. As trust grows, can they let go and fall in love?

In Too Deep by Mary Connealy
THE KINCAID BRIDES #2

More Page-Turning History and Humor

When her attempt to repay a twelve-year debt goes awry, an act of sacrifice leaves Meredith Hayes injured, her reputation in shreds. And suddenly four brothers are drawing straws for her hand!

Short-Straw Bride by Karen Witemeyer
karenwitemeyer.com

When undercover Pinkerton agent Ellie Moore's assignment turns downright dangerous—for her safety *and* her heart—what's this damsel in disguise to do?

Love in Disguise by Carol Cox
authorcarolcox.com

BETHANYHOUSE

Stay up-to-date on your favorite books and authors with our *free* e-newsletters. Sign up today at bethanyhouse.com.

Find us on Facebook.

Free, exclusive resources for your book group! bethanyhouse.com/AnOpenBook